Apr 2016

SOLO ACT

AN ELDER DARROW MYSTERY

SOLO ACT

RICHARD CASS

FIVE STAR

A part of Gale, Cengage Learning

GALE
CENGAGE Learning·

Farmington Hills, Mich • San Francisco • New York • Waterville, Maine
Meriden, Conn • Mason, Ohio • Chicago

GALE
CENGAGE Learning®

LIBRARY OF CONGRESS CATALOGING-IN-PUBLICATION DATA

Cass, Richard.
  Solo act : an Elder Darrow mystery / Richard Cass. — First edition.
    pages cm
    ISBN 978-1-4328-3113-4 (hardcover) — ISBN 1-4328-3113-5 (hardcover) — ISBN 978-1-4328-3108-0 (ebook) — ISBN 1-4328-3108-9 (ebook)
    1. Murder—Investigation—Fiction. I. Title.
  PS3603.A86786S86 2015
  813'.6—dc23   2015013107

First Edition. First Printing: January 2016
Find us on Facebook– https://www.facebook.com/FiveStarCengage
Visit our website– http://www.gale.cengage.com/fivestar/
Contact Five Star™ Publishing at FiveStar@cengage.com

Printed in the United States of America
1 2 3 4 5 6 7 20 19 18 17 16

SOLO ACT

CHAPTER 1

"Red Norvo used to keep a jar full of bumblebees on top of his piano." Burton drained the foam from his whiskey sour and rapped the foot of the glass on the bar.

"That's the hairiest Norvo story there is." I leaned against the back bar, making the hanging glasses tinkle. "He denied it in a *Downbeat* interview, right before he died."

"Seriously." Burton grinned. He'd been trying to cheat.

I poured out the rest of the drink from the shaker for him anyway, bent down, and switched out the Michel Petrucciani CD for some Paquito Rivera. Maybe a little Latin would warm the place up.

My place, now. The Esposito, owned and operated by Elder Darrow, my last chance at straightening out. All forty-four by fifty feet of it, sixteen-foot tin ceilings and the twelve metal stairs, same number as to the gallows, with a steel-pipe railing up to the street door. I had that open for the air, though it was only March. A garbage truck stopped out on Mercy Street, drowning a high note from Paquito's sax.

Off to the left, a triangular stage set in the corner, big enough for a trio as long as none of them was fat. The concrete sub floor peeked up through the black-and-white checked linoleum in places, but only when the lights were up. A forest of chair legs pointed up, like fingers telling me where to go. That's how much fun owning the place had been so far.

I lit a Camel. It was eleven a.m. and Burton was my only

customer so far, but he wasn't likely to arrest me for violating the city's indoor smoking ban. His cop mind only engaged for murder—the mesh in his brain was too wide to hold anything smaller.

"Here's one I know you don't know shit about," he said.

He'd been trying to cut down on the drinking since the first of the year, but he hadn't outrun his thirst yet. And I'd skated out to the edge and back of Planet Drunk enough myself to know what it looked like in other people. If I hadn't been dry for a year and a half, we would have been drinking buddies. I buffed the counter in front of him.

"Fred Archambault. Norvo's so-called autobiography? Substantially plagiarized."

I stubbed out the cigarette, which had tasted like chewing a wooden match, and washed my hands in the bar sink.

"That's worth a beer, if you can prove it."

I grabbed a knife from the junk drawer and opened a red mesh bag of limes. Not only was Burton a fan of the music, he read books about it. My attention span hadn't recovered from those twenty years of serious drinking yet, and I was starting to wonder if it ever would. I used to read the Russian novelists for hours at a time: Mr. Tolstoy, Dostoevsky.

"Jack Roonstone. 'Bumblebee's Flight,' 1973." He tapped the heel of his glass on the bar top again.

"I'll take your word for it."

I popped out the Paquito, pushed in Bill Evans. Some days you just couldn't get the music right. A framed poster from the Newport Jazz Festival, signed by George Wein, shimmied on the wall as the garbage truck pulled away from the curb. I popped the cap on a Heineken and pushed it across.

"You having music tonight?" He didn't quite snatch the bottle.

I slid a single from his stack of change and stuffed it in the tip jar. I didn't mind buying him a drink now and then, but my cook Marina got paid out of the tips.

"Saturday. Piano player from the music school."

"Trad jazz? Fusion? Any good?"

"You stop beating your wife? I haven't actually heard him play. Cy recommended him."

Burton's pager beeped three times. He grimaced, as if he thought he'd turned it off, grabbed his cell phone, and walked off toward the empty stage.

I finished slicing the limes, rinsed off the cutting board and knife, and racked them in the dishwasher.

Moving faster now, Burton snapped the phone shut and swept the money off the bar into his pants pocket. I was glad I'd already tipped myself.

"I hate these," he said. "Sidewalk diver."

"I didn't know you covered suicides too."

He drained the bottle and belched quietly.

"Everything's a homicide until I say it isn't."

His shoes rang on the metal stairs going up.

I slid his empty into the carton, wiped down the place where he'd been sitting, and assumed my position against the back bar, ready for anything. Even a customer.

My first day at the Esposito, eighteen months ago, Burton had asked me what a drunk was doing running a bar. I wasn't wearing a badge that identified me as an alcoholic, but as I said, we tend to recognize each other.

"Greed," I said.

He looked around the bar, which still looked like a bucket of blood—I hadn't even repainted the walls—and laughed.

"Not going to make your pile here, unless you're dealing out the back. You're not, are you?"

I already knew Burton was a cop. I shook my head. It was

midafternoon and I was already bored. I hadn't developed the bartender's tolerance for random bullshit yet, either.

"The bank owns too much of the place for me to fuck around."

"Your father's bank," he said.

I wondered where he'd dug that up. It was actually my mother's family's bank. But when her generation turned out only one son, who preferred to paint flora and fauna of the American West, she'd done the next best thing to becoming a banker herself, from the family's point of view: she'd married one.

"Yep."

"You went to college to be a bartender?"

"Why the interest?" I said. "You want to go steady?"

Sarcasm, as I would learn, rolled off Dan Burton when he was after an answer. You needed pliers to pry him loose.

"I grew up in Charlestown," he said. "My old man paid for college. He would have kicked my ass if I wound up behind the stick."

At least he didn't know I'd gone to Harvard. Nor that it was my father's decision that put me here. Two years ago, I'd fallen in love with a singer named Alison Somers, who wouldn't go out with me unless I quit drinking. At almost the same time, the money my mother had left me ran out. Thomas, my father, wanted to bring me into the bank to succeed him, but the board wouldn't risk it without proof I could stay dry. Twenty-four-month trial, run the Esposito at a profit, and not drink myself, he could hire me then. It was the best deal he could negotiate.

"Think of it as self-abnegation," I said.

"Some kind of Zen thing?" He was smarter than I gave him credit for. "Think of it as bullshit, you mean. This is like putting a pedophile in charge of a nursery school."

His flattery rocked me.

"Thanks," I said. "Another whiskey sour for you?"

Now, a year and a half later, Thomas was dead and one of his vice presidents had been promoted to run the Adams Bank. Alison had moved on to New York City, launched a high-profile solo tour and a recording contract, and I hadn't heard from her since, which resigned me to counting her as another lost opportunity. On the upside, I'd been sober for a year and a half, and if I couldn't say I liked it, at least I was starting to get used to it. The big question starting to surface, though, was why I still bothered.

I didn't find out that Burton's sidewalk diver was Alison Somers until later that afternoon. Two of my postprandial drinkers were debating whether Kurt Cobain was still alive.

"I read it in *USA Today*," Del Woodley said. "He's a vegetable. In Seattle, they said."

"I have one word for you," his buddy said. "Shotgun. In the face."

"That's four words," Del said. "You seen his wife? No wonder he did it."

I was old enough to remember the rumors about John F. Kennedy being kept alive on a ventilator in a Dallas hospital, but that was long before cable, 24-hour news, and the Internet could keep something like that alive for years on end.

Del and his buddy weren't extending the genre any, but there's no one as obsessive as a drunk with half a notion, and I knew if I didn't find something else to do, I'd end up right in there debating the evidence with them. I turned on the TV at the end of the bar just as Del raised his glass and caught my eye.

The photo of Alison behind the commentator stopped me midpour. A blue banner scrolled across the bottom of the screen: Hub Singer in Suicide. I had one of those whip-strikes

11

of vertigo I remembered from nights when I'd been into the booze too deep. I wasn't quite sure where my feet stood.

The picture came from the cover of her first CD. She wore the wig that made her look like Dionne Warwick, not her best style. Her head was thrown back, eyes shut, the caramel column of her throat stretched out and her mouth wide open. The image only hinted at all the wild dark energy contained inside.

"Didn't you used to date her?" Marina, my new cook, spoke from the kitchen doorway. She was a short stringy woman with big forearms and hands, pale-skinned despite some Mediterranean blood. She wore a sleeveless lime-green top above her apron.

"A while ago," I said.

Alison and I had been utterly absorbed in each other for six months or so before things started to cool off. She turned out to be very young for her age, and needy. Just before the New York thing came up, I started to realize that spending my free time in bars listening to her sing was putting some pressure on my attempt to stay sober.

"She is beautiful." Like a lot of unattractive women, Marina imagined a pretty face would solve all her problems.

"She was indeed."

"I don't get it," she said. "Suicide, I mean."

I frowned at her. I knew she was Catholic, but I'd assumed she could think for herself.

"Not because of religion," she said. "She just had so much. She was talented, pretty."

In the live feed over the news-muffin's shoulder, Burton walked out of an apartment building, his plaid suit coat mercifully blurred.

Only someone who'd never laid down with the black dog could believe that talent or good looks was enough, or understand that always trying to live up to your gifts could cause the depression. Alison had taken antidepressants since she was a teenager, and tried suicide at least once.

I spent the rest of the night behind the bar vacillating between grief and guilt, wondering what had happened to make her give up. We'd made a pact early on—I wouldn't drink as long as she'd take her pills—but I had no idea if her side of the promise had survived her move to New York. We hadn't been checking in with each other, and now that seemed like a terrible mistake.

Finally, the night was over. The last drunk stumbled up the stairs, and I turned up the lights. The ache in my breastbone was equal parts pain and fear.

"You need me to call a taxi?" I said.

Marina walked out of the kitchen in a long black topcoat, carrying a plastic container of leftover ratatouille for her mother. She shook her head.

"Carlos's supposed to pick me up."

A diesel horn bleated outside. Her smile lost a little power.

"See you tomorrow," she said. "You're OK?"

I climbed the stairs and locked the door behind her, and once I was alone, the grief just swamped me. Tears in my eyes, I poured a rocks glass full of eighteen-year-old Macallan and set it on the bar. The deep peaty fruit sang in the air like a hymn as I double-locked the alley door, made sure the grill and fryer were off, and pulled the last tray of glasses out of the dishwasher to cool.

I locked the cash in the safe, then came out front and found the CD I'd burned with all the lady singers I'd ever loved: Sarah, Ella, Carmen McRae. Susannah McCorkle. Alison Somers.

I sat down and leaned over the Scotch, inhaling its omnipotent seduction, and let the ladies sing, and when Alison's voice started to come from the speakers, I raised the glass.

Isn't it strange? Aren't we a pair?

Dry heat pricked at my eyes. I breathed in, deeply enough to suck all the smell from the whiskey, put my lips to the rim, and stopped. If I drank it, I'd be denying the discipline I'd so painfully accumulated, an hour at a time, over the last year and a half. That would be bad enough.

But there was an even chance that if I gave in now, Marina would come in tomorrow and find me dead drunk on the floor, maybe even just plain dead. I couldn't do that to her.

I carried the brimming glass around the end of the bar, set it in a niche above the call shelf, shut off the music and the rest of the lights. At the top of the stairs, I keyed the alarm and locked the door.

Standing on the sidewalk on Mercy Street, my body throbbed in the cold March wind as if I were hollow. I started walking north toward my apartment where I could mourn for Alison without temptation. By the last block, the need was so urgent, I was almost running.

I didn't sleep more than an hour or two, and it was that sleep where your brain spins around the same way as when you're awake, so you can't swear you slept at all. We had a very slow lunch hour, too, so I was in no mood for any shit when Carlos Tinto descended into the midafternoon gloom, clanging his boots on the steel stairs like a kid stomping in mud puddles.

His black ponytail stubbed up on the back of his neck, and he wore baggy green wide-wale corduroys, a brown crewneck sweater, and a canvas barn coat. No one would mistake him for a college student, though. He had old acne pits all over his neck and a gold cross dangling from a chain in his left earlobe.

"I told you I didn't want to see you in here again," I said.

The Esposito was a bucket of blood when I took it over. Crack sales, twenty-dollar blow jobs and other minor transactions filled up the dark corners. The heavier stuff—guns, wholesale drugs—showcased in the alley. It took calling in the cops every Friday and Saturday night for a while, but eventually I convinced everyone that the Esposito was going respectable. Carlos was a street-level dealer, strictly retail, and one of the last of the old clientele to accept the change.

"Just came to see my girl," he said.

I would have banned him outright if it weren't for Marina. She'd been so happy when he started to pay her attention, I tried to make allowances.

"Five minutes," I said. "She's working, you know."

She stepped through the doorway from the kitchen, smiled, and said something crisp to him in Spanish. I was surprised she knew the language—her family was Italian, from somewhere up in the North End.

Carlos lit a cigarette.

"No smoking in here," I said.

He inhaled deeply, his shiny black eyes locked on me, then stubbed out the butt on the bar. I reached underneath for my Little Leaguer.

Marina put a hand on my arm.

"I'm sorry," she said. "Let me see what he wants."

I shrugged. Carlos blinked slowly, gave me a toothy smile.

She walked him toward a table. She was a good cook and as reliable as her mother, who'd once cooked for my family, but if keeping her on meant having Carlos around, I might have to fire her. I sifted through a stack of CDs, looking for something I wanted to listen to.

The fast chain of words she threw at him overran my kitchen Spanish. He hunched his shoulders so the leather collar of the jacket touched his earring, then snapped back a sentence, the only word of which I caught was *dinero*.

For a guy who dealt drugs, Carlos never seemed to have much money in his pocket.

She stood up. He said something low, sibilant. She came to the bar.

"He wants a drink."

I shook my head. "And I want him out."

"Please. I'll pay for it."

I hated him for making her beg.

"Someone has to," I said. "I just wish it wasn't you."

"Cuba libre," Carlos called.

I snorted, doubting the punk knew enough of his homeland's history to call a rum and Coke by that name.

Marina returned from the kitchen as I mixed the drink, and handed me a five. She put a dollar from the change into the tip jar.

"One drink," I said.

Carlos gave me the grin again and drank off half the glass. Marina handed him two bills, which he slipped into his coat. He finished the drink and pushed the empty back at her.

"Otra vez."

I shook my head. "I don't want to have to throw him out. But I will."

She looked hurt and confused. Carlos stalked over, his skinny chest shoved out.

"Fuck, man. This a bar or not?"

"Not for you," I said. "You've caused enough trouble in here."

He reached in his pocket, balled up Marina's money, and threw it back at her.

"Guess I don't need your fucking money, then, do I?"

Marina wilted.

"Out." I tapped the little bat on the bar.

He grabbed one of the bills off the floor and stomped up the stairs.

"Don't blame him," she said. "Ricky shut him down."

"He won't last long on the street without support."

She smiled sadly. "If he goes to jail, I'll have to get a raise."

"Not from me you won't."

I tipped his glass over into the dishwasher rack and scrubbed my hands with hot water and soap. As I dried them off, I eyed my face in the back bar mirror: eyes as flat and gray as fog, pouched underneath with the puffy dark flesh; the sparse pale hair inherited from my father that I couldn't keep combed. The hunched shoulders, from keeping my guard up, made me look even shorter than I was and tonight at least, I was a half a century older than thirty-seven.

CHAPTER 2

Tommy Cormier read a book one time that said the Eskimos had a hundred different words for snow. He wasn't sure his people, the Apache, had that many ways of talking about sand, but he did know one thing for sure. Icky Ricky knew a thousand ways to piss him off. At least.

"I can't believe you'd shut down all the retail trade without talking to me, Rick. What the fuck are those idiots going to do for money? I'm not paying them to stand around scratching their balls."

Ricky Maldonado's round bald head sat up on top of his round fat body like a little egg glued on top of a big one. He wore dingy polyester cook's whites with a purple V-neck T-shirt showing underneath. He narrowed his coffee-bean eyes at Tommy.

"Thomas. You forgetting who's in charge of this organization?"

As if Ricky ever gave him the chance to exercise any initiative, or understood that Tommy would have snatched the whole half-ass operation out from under him in a heartbeat, given the chance. He shifted his gaze from the deserted early-morning view of Brookline Ave. up to the grimy pressed-tin ceiling, as if Ricky might be able to read that intention in his eyes.

"Chumps like Carlos," he said. "They can't sell their product, they go do stupid things. Start robbing. Stealing things from people. Raise our visibility."

18

Tommy and Ricky hooked up about four years ago, Tommy doing frightener-duty at a club in Inman Square and trying to study for the GREs. Ricky, business friend of a business friend, unwittingly ripped off a van full of pot from the Irish mafia over in Charlestown and needed some body-guarding while he negotiated a peace. Tommy hadn't regretted the affiliation until it became clear to him that all the promises of a management position in Ricky's organization were purest bullshit.

"Let him dig his own grave. He's expendable. You, you're the heart of my organization." Ricky thumped his own chest with a fist.

Ricky's organization: two half-smart muscle men, Tesar and Donnie Spangler, and then a couple dozen street-level dealers that Tommy had to keep in line.

"You keep saying that," Tommy said. "Then you shrink the business on me, give me less and less to do."

"You short on cash?" Ricky said. "Use that money you stole from the FBI."

He walked out to the front of the luncheonette and raised the green cloth shades.

Tommy wished he'd lay off about the money. When he realized that the buy at the Mayflower Room was a sting, he'd grabbed the cash and slipped out the back. Ricky would have preferred that he hang onto the pills, which they could have resold, and he hadn't quit reminding Tommy of that for a month.

"No MBA-style advice on that score?" Ricky turned on the grill and started laying out flat white strips of bacon.

"It was instinct." Tommy hated the apology in his voice. "In six months . . ."

"You live to a hundred, that money's not going to cool off. I couldn't even sell it at a discount."

Tommy didn't believe that—this was just another way that

Ricky kept him down, punished him for showing a little initiative.

Business was business, irregardless. Tommy had read his organizational psychology, *The Corporate Mystic, Who Moved My Cheese?*, all that shit. You couldn't keep disempowering people and expect them to stay loyal. As soon as he came up with seed money, he was going to split and start his own organization, run it the way he knew was best. He'd thought this before, but what was different this time was Ricky was going to supply the capital.

"You want to be the boss, Tommy?" Ricky tucked the tails of his shirt into his pants and tied an apron behind his back. The strings barely made it. "What if I decided to retire? Hand the whole thing over to you? Would that make you happy?"

Tommy knew bullshit when he heard it. Ricky was always hinting. Although he'd never said it out loud before.

"Why would you retire?" He couldn't help himself.

"I'm a sick man. I need to slow down." Ricky pushed bacon grease into the trap. "I got the diabetes, emphysema, high blood pressure. And pills and pot isn't a big enough business anymore, for all that work."

Ricky had poor-mouthed as long as Tommy knew him, but Tommy suspected another layer of enterprise underneath. And there was the off-chance Ricky was serious.

"You know all I want's a chance." He'd eat a little shit if it got him his fuck-you money. Not a lot, though.

Ricky shrugged.

"Maybe we can work something out. You want some breakfast?"

He opened the big refrigerator and slid out a cardboard tray of eggs.

"Sure, Rick," Tommy said. "You got Wheat Chex? Or granola? Granola would be good."

CHAPTER 3

Two days later, two long days after Alison killed herself, I was still stunned by how little I understood why or how. I could have guessed that she'd keep the apartment in the Back Bay, knowing how hard it was to find decent housing in Boston, but why had she been back in the city? And why hadn't she called me? It wasn't as if we'd broken up, just that our connection had slowly frayed with the distance. The last time I'd called the number of her residence hotel in New York, she hadn't returned the message.

The Esposito was starting to develop a lunch business, which was encouraging. After the rush, around one-thirty, Burton stuck his head in the street door as if making sure someone wasn't there, then sauntered down the stairs, in a madras suit jacket that was short in the sleeves and too tight to button, a navy pinpoint cotton shirt, and an off-white tie. The jacket was purple and green and blue and he looked like a six foot tall, hundred and sixty pound bruise.

"Twice in one week," I said. "You must really like me."

He didn't comment but raised an eyebrow. I knew I looked ragged. I had managed to shave this morning but hadn't eaten anything but coffee and cigarette smoke for two days. At least I hadn't drunk.

He hefted a soft purple leather bag I recognized as one of Alison's favorites up onto the bar. The sight of it checked my throat. He reached inside and pulled out a hardcover spiral-bound notebook.

"I took this away from some weird little troll who slipped past the uniforms at the scene. Looks like she was trying to steal stuff to sell on eBay. I thought you might want them."

His thoughtfulness touched me. I didn't realize he knew that much about Alison and me. But the fact he was willing to remove what could have been evidence told me he had no doubt that Alison's death was suicide.

"Thanks," I said. Maybe some tangible memories of Alison would help me work it through.

I snapped the cap off a Heineken and passed it over. When he reached into his pocket, I waved him off. He pointed the bottle at the journal.

"You're in there," he said.

"You read it?"

"Part of the job." He drank deeply from the green bottle.

I flipped through the pages, recognizing her dense purple scrawl, then set the book up on edge in the niche, next to the glass of whiskey.

"You're drinking again?" Burton looked at the Scotch.

I shook my head. "Little tribute."

"You must have known her pretty well. I'm sorry for your loss."

The standard Irish condolence didn't make me feel any better, but the fact that he would say it did.

"I knew her well. I thought I did, at least. I didn't see this coming."

"People generally don't."

"It's hard to connect with the person I knew."

He didn't ask why, more evidence he was sure it was her own decision to go out the window.

Burton stayed, ate dinner, but left around eight, without much of a load on. The rest of the night dragged like a garageband drum solo. The later it got, the more I wanted to know what Alison's journal said about me, and the busier I got, filling glasses and serving food and trying to play the genial host, until I could finally lock up.

Home in the apartment, I tossed my coat on a hook and switched on the lamp over the armchair that faced Commonwealth Ave., leaving the notebook on the side table. I walked out to the kitchen, spiced a glass of tomato juice I didn't want, and walked back into the living room to pick out some music, before I realized I was dithering, trying to avoid what I had thought all night I wanted to do.

I sat down and folded back the hard black cover, inside of which she'd printed her name and the date, nearly nine months ago. The first entry was written the day after the first night we slept together, and the prose was detailed, overheated, and specific enough to make me blush and smile at once. I hoped Burton had skipped this part. It opened an album of memories I thought I'd archived for good: the gleam of my pale skin against her dark, the depth of her wide-set black eyes, the stubble on her scalp rasping underneath my caressing fingers.

Sipping my juice, heart rattling my rib cage, I turned the pages, skipping in and out of the months we'd spent together. Her loopy violet scrawl sang high solos of joy and long melancholic choruses of reaction and complaint, her side of the tumult we'd put ourselves through. There was an entry for the night she took me to Madame DuBarry's to tell me she was moving to New York—she was certain I wouldn't make a scene in an expensive French restaurant on Newbury Street, and she was right.

The entries turned inward and a little mordant for the first couple months in New York, then things improved: some higher-paying and higher-profile gigs, and apparently some improvement in her love life, too. I read with the fascination of someone

23

driving by a car wreck on 128—the last entry was a month ago, and it implied that she'd been back in Boston by then.

"Still love my little bird's nest in the Back Bay," she wrote. "And two men to love me, even if I only care for one of them. Singing to feed my heart and money to feed the rest—embarrassing wealth, all these ways. And no reasons anymore, not ever, to keep my sweet bird from flying. Blessed be, blessed me."

Tears spilled out of me, knowing she'd been back in the city long enough to call me if she'd wanted to, that what we'd had was as near over as my intuition had been telling me. And some of the tears were for the fact she had found stability, some actual joy, neither of which she'd known when we were together. I reread the page, wondering if I was only trying to convince myself, but I could not hear the same woman who'd written those words as suicidal. What could have happened in a month to change that?

I pushed myself up out of the armchair, chewing on the thought. I wasn't going to be able to sleep tonight either, but for different reasons. I walked back into the kitchen and ground some French roast beans from Lulu's, assembled the coffeepot, and plugged it in. Given what she'd done the day before yesterday, what had happened to Alison's life in the intervening weeks to take her down that way? All the way down.

Friday afternoon, I stood behind the bar smoking a cigarette and pondering why so few customers seemed willing to start the weekend early. I hadn't worked at a steady job for very long before taking over the bar, but when I had been on someone else's payroll, I would have taken any excuse to bail out after lunch on a Friday afternoon and not come back.

Larry Coryell played through the speakers in the corners while Marina banged around out in the kitchen. I'd been trying for two days to convince myself that Alison's last journal entry was the anomaly, the one bright day in a string of bad ones that led her up the ladder to suicide. I couldn't make it stick. She'd believed what she'd written and not just for that day and time—she'd sounded like someone who had finally walked out of a dark tunnel into the light. Which begged the question I'd been asking myself—what had happened to change that?

I wished I could bounce my ideas off of someone. Burton had already done me too big a favor by passing me Alison's things. That stretched the boundaries of our relationship. Besides, Burton's god was evidence—my intuition wouldn't cut any ice with him. Marina came out of the kitchen as I stubbed out my smoke.

"God, this coffee tastes lousy," I said. "Maybe we should get an espresso machine."

She raised one of her severely plucked eyebrows.

"Who goes to a bar for the coffee?"

The street door creaked inward. Burton shuffled his soles clean on the doormat and started down the stairs. Marine sighed and retreated to the kitchen. I thought I knew why.

More than half in the bag one night when I had a trio playing dance music, he'd put his arm around her and tried to get her out onto the floor. She'd been avoiding him ever since, though before she'd hooked up with Carlos, I would have bet she'd agree to a sober request from Burton. If Burton were ever that sober.

I had an open beer waiting for him when he reached the bar. He hesitated, then shook his head.

"Meeting with the captain at four-thirty."

"On a Friday afternoon? How does that make him anything but a prick?" I said. "Is it Alison's case?"

Burton took off his suit coat, a faded blue seersucker with bleached spots up the left arm. His shirt was snowy and the pink and purple tie so hip he could have been on Sports Center. He shook his head.

"He's acting like something's goofy."

"Goofy. About Alison?"

It might be easier to convince Burton to take another look if his boss thought there was something off about her death.

"Great word, isn't it?" he said. "How old is that coffee?"

I poured him some, not reacting to the put-off, then pulled Alison's journal out from under the bar.

"You read it all the way through?" I opened it to the last page. "She's sounding pretty upbeat for someone who was going to jump out a window a couple weeks later."

He scanned the page.

"Doesn't sound all that joyful to me. You know, I only gave you this stuff as a courtesy—and because I wasn't sure this Susan Voisine broad ought to have it. What a flake!"

"I know, and I appreciate it. You had to know her. For Alison, this was sky-high."

Burton closed the notebook and handed it back.

"Farther to fall, then," he said. "It was definitely suicide—nothing in the apartment points anywhere else. And I'm sure that's not what the captain wants to talk about anyway."

I held up my hands in defense.

"I wouldn't tell Joe Pass how to play the guitar, either. But if you get the chance, will you look again?"

He nodded, more in acknowledgment than agreement.

"If I get the chance." He stood up. "By the way, your coffee sucks."

"Who goes to a bar for the coffee?" I said.

He smiled as he headed for the stairs.

"A drunk might."

I wondered if he was talking about me, himself, or just making idle conversation. Then I wondered why he'd dropped in. To talk about why the captain had called him in? I hadn't been listening all that well.

CHAPTER 4

Even in the cold breeze, Ricky sweated like a horse as he shoved at the glass door to the Fenway Pharmacy. He'd walked the three blocks over from the luncheonette because he didn't want anyone to know what he was doing, but now he wondered if he shouldn't have had Tommy drive him. His chest ached even worse than last night and his legs felt empty, like there wasn't any blood in them.

His last check-up, this curly-head twat, no older than some of the girls whose G-strings he stuffed with bills at the Shanty Lounge, had sat up on her rolling stool and twirled the end of her stethoscope like a burlesque queen. He'd seen better moves in church, but he didn't tell her that—it seemed like a bad idea to piss off your cardiologist. Frigging doctors.

"Exercise and diet, Mr. Maldonado," she said. "There's nothing wrong with you that a better diet and some mild exercise wouldn't cure. Even now."

Fuck a bunch of killing all the lawyers—the first thing he was going to do when he was king was kill the doctors. Here he was exercising, just like she told him, and he felt like he was going to fall down on the sidewalk with a frigging heart attack.

The dark green film on the inside of the display windows blocked out most of the sun, adding to the feeling of late afternoon in someone's basement. He limped toward the back, up a narrow aisle piled with past-dated cold medicines, dusty trusses, red rubber hot-water bottles, and those old-style douche bags with the hose in their flowered plastic wrappings. No wonder the frigging vampire couldn't make a living—the place looked like he hadn't turned any inventory since the Red Sox broke the color barrier. Who would be stupid enough to buy twenty-year-old condoms, the box showing a Bobby Darin lookalike and a smiling bimbo with nose-cone tits?

He looked around, but seeing any other customers would have been a genuine miracle, witnessed by the enormous plastic crucifix on the wall above the pharmacy counter.

"Vindalia!" Ricky yelled. "Fuck are you?"

A skewer-thin man, with knots of muscle in his jaw and a face so pale it seemed to melt into the white smock he wore, hurried out from a storeroom behind the glass. His black toupee slipped just slightly as he stepped down into the aisle next to Ricky. Ricky shuddered.

"Mr. Maldonado!"

"You jerking off to the skin magazines back there?" Ricky pinched his nose against Vidalia's smell, musty blankets and un-tended teeth. "Why don't you turn on some fucking lights in here? It's like the mummy's crypt."

Vindalia fluttered like a moth as Ricky fished the note out of his shirt pocket.

"Here's the pills she said I need. Give me a hundred of each."

The pharmacist touched the plastic nameplate over his breast. "Mr. Maldonado. You don't look well."

Ricky's pain dropped into the rib cage on the left and ground at him from inside.

"Don't give me that shit. Just fill the script. I'll wait."

Vindalia threw up his hands like an Italian grandmother and walked up three stairs into the enclosed pharmacy area. He unlocked a beige metal wall-mounted cabinet and carried three huge plastic containers over to the bench, then opened the slid-ing glass window as if he didn't want to be impolite.

Ricky leaned against the steel post that ran from floor to ceiling, wondering if he was going to puke and die right here.

"Listen," he said. "I've got some new stuff coming in."

His chest didn't hurt anymore but now his throat felt as if he were being squeezed by an unseen hand. He rolled his head to ease the stiffness.

Vindalia unscrewed one of the jars and dumped pills out on the tabletop, started counting them out with a blunt plastic spatula.

"You hear me?" Ricky said. "Expect a new shipment in the next few days. Different supplier, but top-quality stuff."

Goulash boy sniffed, as if this were Bloomingdale's and Ricky had just farted.

"I had some complaints," Vindalia said. "From the last batch."

"I don't want to hear about that." His chest had started to throb again. "Customer satisfaction is your problem."

Once he discovered the Hungarian's addiction to the trotting horses at Rockingham Park, Ricky created this relationship, the secret honey pot of his business. He bootlegged prescription drugs at cut-rate prices from Mexico, where government oversight and red tape were nonexistent. Then Vindalia sold them at full price through this legitimate licensed pharmacy, kicking all the profit to Ricky, at least as long as Ricky owned his debts. It was so sweet that Ricky probably wouldn't give it up even if he did retire—he didn't tell Tommy everything.

"You know, you ought to spruce the place up a little. We could move a ton of product through here if you had more customers."

Vindalia smiled enigmatically. Ricky had a frightening thought, raised up on his tiptoes to see what the vampire was doing.

"Hey. You're giving me the FDA-approved version of those pills, right?"

Vindalia moved to the typewriter, the sound of the keys making Ricky think of machine-gun fire in third-world countries. Vindalia didn't answer.

The next shipment was coming in from South America, where the manufacturers had even less government supervision, fewer rules. Best of all, the entire batch was presold to a single customer. It would be a good deal for Ricky to go out on, maybe, twelve or fifteen million dollars. And no one would have to worry about the side effects from these drugs.

Vindalia stepped out of the enclosed area and reached across the counter with Ricky's three orange plastic pill bottles.

Ricky would have slapped the stupid smile off Vindalia's face except that, just as he reached for the pills, the pain returned with double force, clawing at the inside of his chest in rhythm with his pulse.

"Mr. Maldonado," Vindalia said. "I have to say, you look like the shit."

Ricky held himself up against the steel post.

"Don't you talk to me like that, you frigging degenerate. You hear what I said to you about a new supply?"

"I really believe you should call the 911," Vindalia said. "You are very gray and sweating piggishly."

Ricky gathered himself, ignoring the pain for a second, and straightened up to glare at Vindalia, who stepped back as if Ricky had waved a gun.

"I am fine," Ricky said. Then he had a strange thought. "Do you have a plan of succession?"

Vindalia looked confused, so Ricky spoke up louder.

"Who's going to take over your store when you can't work anymore?"

He was trying to find out whether Vindalia had thought of retiring and how he might have made an exit plan, but Vindalia's eyes popped wider and he took two more quick steps back until he butted up against the counter.

Ricky shook his head, turned, and shuffled out the pharmacy door, greasy sweat congealing on his forehead when the breeze hit it. All he'd managed to do was make the goulash boy more nervous than he'd been, not that that took a lot of effort. His people skills were going to shit, on top of everything else.

CHAPTER 5

Tommy hated hospitals almost as much as he had hated the Indian boarding school in Las Vegas, New Mexico, where he'd been sent in seventh grade. It wasn't something dramatic, like the presence of death, that put him off. He hadn't been afraid of death since he watched one of his cousins on the reservation die of rattlesnake bite.

No, what he hated was the way hospitals (and boarding schools) reduced people to the names of their parts and their problems: a bad liver here, a bad attitude there. He preferred a more holistic view of himself. In both places, too, the people with authority generally looked straight through you—even if the attention was focused, it was on the part, the specific, not your whole.

His black ostrich cowboy boots slipped on the wet marble floor and he had to stop the skid with a hand on the wall. He wouldn't have to be here long. All he needed to know was how bad off Ricky was and how long he was going to be laid up. Fortune favored the prepared, and Tommy was nothing if he was not prepared. Ricky in the hospital was an opportunity to separate the fat little shit from a significant chunk of his cash, not a chance Tommy was going to miss.

He checked the room number, shifted the bunch of ratty red carnations he'd bought in the gift shop to his left hand, and pushed the door open. He arranged his face into a smile.

"Rick."

A skinny, ancient black dude, had to be eighty, jumped up off the bed and pointed the TV remote at Tommy, who had to control an impulse to dive onto the floor. The guy was very lucky Tommy wasn't strapped.

A white curtain shrouded the far bed, but a nurse stuck her head around the edge of it and smiled.

"We'll be through here in a minute."

"Don't let him in here."

Ricky's voice was as full of bile as ever, only slightly diluted. The nurse winked at Tommy.

Ricky wasn't dead, then, if she was smiling, though considering what an asshole he could be, maybe she was smiling because he was. He sat down in a red plastic chair at the end of the bed while the old guy stared at Suzanne Somers hawking vegetable brushes on the muted TV.

Eventually, the curtain slid back and a middle-aged Latino doctor tucked his stethoscope into his pocket before gliding past Tommy and out of the room. The nurse only paused when he stood up and put his hand on her arm. She'd lost the smile.

"How is he?" He spoke in a low tone so Ricky couldn't hear.

"I can't tell you anything unless you're family." She was so pissed off, he was surprised his hand didn't burst into flame.

"I'm his mother."

The smile tickled the corners of her mouth.

"God bless the child," she said. "He'll live. But it was touch and go for a while."

"His heart?"

"His mouth."

He gave her the sleepy grin that worked better with females. "Is he going to be in here a long time?"

"Four or five days."

"Good enough," he said, and let her go.

She looked down at her arm as if she'd only just realized he was touching her, and blushed before she headed out the door.

Good enough indeed. Find the money and get out of town, he'd have that much of a head start. He walked behind the half-drawn curtain.

"Tommy." Ricky's voice was weak as water. He could have been faking, but Tommy didn't think so. "You have to get me out of here."

Tommy made sure Ricky saw the carnations, then laid them on the rolling metal table. He shook his head.

"Boss. The doc says at least three weeks. Sounds like you've got all kinds of weird shit going on inside of you."

Ricky's face almost exactly matched the faded pale blue flannel of the hospital johnny. His hair was as greasy as a crew cut could look and the neck skin above his johnny was mottled turkey red. His belly jiggled slackly as he pushed himself up into a sitting position. Bruises pocked the insides of both arms, as if he were a clumsy junkie. Tommy didn't think he'd ever seen Ricky show so much fear. He liked it.

"Bullshit," Ricky said. "I've been taking my pills, just like I was supposed to."

"You know we can't let the business ride for that long," Tommy said. "What do you want me to do?"

"I'm absolutely fine," Ricky said. "It's just indigestion. These morons don't know a dick from a douche bag. I'll be out of here tomorrow."

"What's the doctor think?"

"Fuck the doctor. Fuck the bunch of them."

"We can't afford to lose momentum while you're laid up, Rick. You want me to put the retail guys back up on the street?"

Ricky shook his head. Tommy had been counting on that. He suspected Ricky had some kind of deal going on for his own benefit that he wanted to focus on, which was why he'd shut down the street sales.

"You know I'll do whatever you tell me to do. But we have to do something. We stand pat, we're fucked."

He could almost hear Ricky's brain grind.

"Maybe one thing." Then Ricky shook his head. "Nah."

Fucker wanted to be coaxed.

"You can trust me, Rick. Just tell what it is, and I'll take care of it for you."

Ricky stared across the room at Suzanne Somers. He was only hesitating to remind Tommy how much he didn't trust him.

"There's a bag," he said finally.

Yes! Tommy stayed as nonchalant as he ever was, but he smelled his fuck-you money.

"Got it, Rick. Bag of money, bag of dope? Where's it at and what do you want me to do with it?"

Ricky coughed deeply. His belly shimmered and Tommy cringed. What a thing it would be if Ricky pegged out here and now.

"Spengler will show you where it is. I want it somewhere safe. And for God's sake, don't get into it—I need it for a deal I'm working. Wholesale gig."

Tommy's head was so tight he almost didn't recognize how much information Ricky was giving away. Spengler? Ricky trusted fucking Spengler, that bullet-headed lump of muscle, over Tommy? He took in a ragged breath.

"What kind of deal?"

That bag belonged to Tommy now, regardless. If it wasn't money, if it was dope, fine. He'd sell it. Mentally, he started packing the few things in his apartment he cared about: some clothes, his Alison Somers CDs.

Ricky flinched, then groaned as he grabbed for the call button pinned to his pillow.

"Talk to Spengler." He jammed the button again and again. "Just make sure it's safe."

CHAPTER 6

Around six-thirty, an actual dinner rush occurred, first a straggle of singles and couples that built until all but two of the tables were occupied by people eating. Most of them looked prosperous and tended to dress in black, which meant the Esposito was finally attracting a different clientele than it had started out known for—these people weren't eating just to line their stomachs for a long night's drinking. Marina and I ran flat out for the better part of two hours, but I didn't mind. Maybe we were turning a corner.

"Out of the chowder," she called from the kitchen door, then disappeared again.

She'd seemed sullen all night, though I wasn't sure why, unless Burton had tried to warn her off Carlos again. I wouldn't have minded at all if she'd dumped Carlos—beyond being a dealer, he had bad manners and that low-rent attitude of entitlement—but I doubted she embraced the prospect of replacing the boyfriend with a semi-divorced alcoholic cop, either.

Burton made it clear in a couple of elliptical conversations that he couldn't really do anything about it, but I sensed he had some questions about Alison's death. He'd gotten me a copy of the toxicology report that said there was no measurable level of anything pharmaceutical in Alison's blood. It took a couple of weeks to raise an effective level of antidepressant in the bloodstream, and even if she'd been switching from one medication to another, the levels would have shown something. She knew better than to quit taking the pills altogether, which was one of the reasons we'd made our pact in the first place.

We had a lull around nine-thirty. I punched Susan Voisine's number into the phone, and when the robot-voice told me to press the pound sign, I left the Esposito's number. When the phone rang ten minutes later, I was mixing a tray full of Tom Collins for a table of giggling grade-school teachers, men and women.

I crimped the receiver between my shoulder and my ear and dunked the toothpick spears of fruit into the foamy green juice.

"Esposito."

"Mr. Darrow, please."

Her voice was chocolate and cream, a clear announcement of its owner's satisfaction with life. I liked it anyway.

"Here."

"Susan Voisine. I hope you weren't calling to berate me for trying to take some of Alison's things—I think it's critical her genius be recognized."

Defense by offense, one of my least favorite tactics.

"I'm sorry," I said. "I meant to leave you my home phone. I'm working right now."

"What can I do to help?"

"I was a friend of Alison Somers," I said.

"I know you were." She sounded impatient, as if I were underestimating her. "Does that have something to do with how I can help?"

It was getting late and I was too tired for games. And the teachers were all waving at me for their drinks.

"Could we meet in the morning? Have coffee?"

"What time do you finish work?" she said. "I'm a night person."

"One-thirty at the earliest." That ought to put her off—I

didn't really want to schlep anywhere after a long night behind the bar.

"Fifteen Clarendon Street. Ring the doorbell twice so I know it's you."

I hesitated. "I'll be there."

But she'd already hung up, that sure of herself.

The last-call frenzy came and went. From my own drinking career, I understood the fear that compelled people to line up drinks at the end of the night: the fear that the party, however temporarily, really was over. Some nights I felt guilty pandering to it, but if I didn't make a success of the Esposito, I didn't have any prospects, so I pushed that down. Tonight, for once, people drank up and left without arguing.

Marina walked out front with her coat on, not a bit more talkative than she'd been all night.

"You need a ride?" I said.

I assumed Carlos wasn't going to change his pattern. If I could get over to Susan Voisine, find out what she could tell me, and still get home to bed at a reasonable hour, I'd be happy. Tomorrow was Sunday and I didn't want to be exhausted for my one day off a week.

She shook her head, then spoke to me as formally as if I were the family priest.

"Would you please ask Detective Burton to leave me alone? I tried to tell him he shouldn't concern himself, but he doesn't listen so well."

She had that much right about Burton. I wrung out the last of the bar rags and draped it over the faucet to dry.

"I'll try," I said. "I'm sure he'll stop if he realizes he's making you uncomfortable."

"Thank you very much."

The diesel horn on Carlos's truck blasted up in the street. She hustled up the stairs. Now there was a situation that made me grateful I wasn't dating.

The clock under the bar, the one that told the real time, said one-fifteen. I shut down all the lights except the one under the back bar and started up the stairs. I left the journal in the little niche in case Ms. Voisine saw it in my hand and decided she wanted it. I didn't want to find out how persuasive she could be.

The outside temperature had shaded back toward winter, but at least the cold kept the garbage smell in the alley behind the Esposito down. I kicked through the blowing newspapers and fast-food clamshell foam to my parking space behind the building. The Cougar's black vinyl top was shredded, the yellow paint tinged faintly green as if it were molding. The rocker panels were perforated with rust holes, but it ran and it was paid for. I still don't know how it had survived my drinking days without any dents.

There was a surprising amount of traffic for the time of night. I skirted downtown and cut up through the Northeastern campus up into the Fens. Susan Voisine's address was easy enough to find—big brass numbers identified her dark green Victorian, one house in from the corner. I parallel-parked the Cougar under a streetlight half a block away, absurdly pleased at how easy it was.

As I set my foot on the bottom step to her veranda, a prison yard–quality spotlight pinned me to the concrete. I blinked up at the front door, which opened six inches.

"Does this mean I don't have to ring the doorbell?" I said.

Mocking applause fluttered out from behind the glare.

"I would have guessed you'd be quick," she said.

The light switched off, and red and black spots streaked around in my vision. Even after they cleared, though, I wasn't sure I should believe what I was seeing.

Susan Voisine might have been the most beautiful woman I'd

seen in ten years. In Boston, natural home to good-looking women of all ages, colors, and conformations, that said a good deal. She had straight ash-blonde hair, cut asymmetrically, that hung just to her earlobes, and classic Nordic princess features: a thin sharp nose, high cheekbones, and a creamy complexion that would tan like cocoa butter in the summer. She wore a tight white wool skirt that showed a lot of leg and a scoop-necked teal pullover that displayed her collarbone and the tops of her breasts. Her eyes were pale, the blue-green of the Mediterranean Sea. She was so perfectly proportioned, in fact, that I didn't realize she was only about four feet tall until I stepped up next to her on the porch.

"At least your mouth isn't hanging open," she said. "That makes you politer than most men."

She held out a long slim hand, which I squeezed gently until I felt the power of her grip.

"Please don't confuse small with weak," she said.

"Pleased to meet you, too."

She turned and led me into the house, bolting the solid mahogany door behind us.

The foyer of the Victorian reminded me of my parents' old house in Chestnut Hill, though Susan's was decorated with better taste. The walls were painted a butter cream color, with gleaming dark wood chair rails and crown moldings. A scattering of black-shaded torchière lamps sprayed soft light up toward the twelve-foot ceilings. Marching up the wall of the staircase to the second floor was a staggered line of eight-by-ten black-and-white photos, conservation-matted and framed in black bamboo. The nearest one was the famous picture of a young Miles Davis, horn in his lap, sitting next to Charlie Parker. I wanted to look more closely at the rest, but climbing her stairs this early in the relationship seemed a little bit forward.

"The originals are in the Betteman Archives," she said, as if that should mean something to me. "Bill Gates owns them now."

I wondered whether the software mogul gave a shit about jazz or, like most rich people, only wanted to own everything of value in the universe.

She led me through a plaster archway to the left into a sitting room with the same high ceiling as the foyer. The visible wallpaper showed intertwined roses, but mostly the walls were covered with shelves, and the shelves loaded with books. The lowest ones, as well as the floor, were stacked with oversized volumes, magazines, sheet music. It was an impressive collection, bordering on the obsessive.

She pointed to two chairs covered in green and gold chintz and sat in the one closer to the bay window. A glass table already held a drink, a cigarette case, and a glass jewel-encrusted Zippo. She crossed her legs and tugged the skirt's hem down optimistically.

I looked her over more thoroughly in the favoring light. She wasn't a dwarf or a midget, whatever the politically correct term was these days—she was simply an unusually beautiful woman who happened to be about eighty percent standard size.

"I can guess what you're thinking, but don't let the outer Susan fool you," she said. "I know you don't drink anymore, but I have juice. Or club soda."

"No. Thanks." It was late and I didn't want to prolong this any longer than necessary, especially with someone who was trying so hard to impress me with how much she knew about me.

She took out a thick filterless cigarette, something like a Gitanes or a Gaulois. There were so few places I could smoke unmolested nowadays, I would have joined her even if I wasn't craving the nicotine. I let her light me up.

"This lighter once belonged to Janis Ian." She clicked the

Zippo shut.

I smiled, not sure what she wanted me to say. Hooray?

"I wanted to apologize," she said.

"For?"

"Stealing your memories of Alison. I don't really know what came over me. None of it was really saleable material."

"Not to mention you got caught with it? How did you happen to be there?"

Surely Burton had asked her the question, too, but it would be useful to compare the answers.

She waved the hand with the cigarette, tumbling ash to the floor.

"I'm a legitimate businesswoman."

"And that's how you came to be in Alison's apartment right after she died?"

She stubbed out the cigarette as if it had annoyed her and leaned forward. I kept my eyes up.

"Alison and I were soul sisters, Elder. Do you mind if I call you Elder?"

Even if I did, the question was clearly rhetorical as far as she was concerned. And as far as any kind of sisterhood between the two of them went, it would have been all one way. She saw what I was thinking.

"Not physically. Under the skin," she said.

No duh. "Is that so."

I glanced at the windows. The weirdness level was rising and I'd never been very patient with that. She took a sip of her drink, something very dark brown.

"Don't criticize it if you don't understand," she said. "We had more in common than you might think. The first time I heard her sing, I felt like something I'd been missing my whole life dropped into place. Didn't you ever feel like that?"

Inevitably, maybe, I remembered my first taste of Scotch, in a milk glass stolen from the dining hall at St. Paul's. I remembered the dares of my roommates, the relief when all three of us had drunk and were all equally at risk of getting suspended. One of them was now a federal judge in Richmond, Virginia, the other a software entrepreneur up in Chelmsford.

"I think I know what you mean," I said.

She leaned forward some more. I concentrated on the faint blue vein throbbing on the side of her throat.

"I admired Alison, Elder."

"Did the two of you ever meet?" I still wasn't sure what brand of wackiness I was dealing with here, though it was clear that coming here was a waste of my time.

She shrugged and the hair brushed the sapphire studs in her earlobes.

"After a show once or twice. I saw her a month ago with the boyfriend."

"Boyfriend."

"A man named desRosiers? Tall and thin, very well dressed. I think he's a psychiatrist. Still jealous after all this time?"

"I can see why Burton doesn't like you."

She pouted. "Is he the man with the bad taste in jackets? Women have done him mischief, I think."

That didn't impress me particularly. Being hard to read wasn't one of Burton's faults.

"You know if she was seeing anyone else, besides desRosiers? I'm trying to understand why she would suddenly decide to kill herself."

"What makes you think I'd know that?"

I stared at her until she got defensive.

"I'm not a stalker, you know. Her apartment's, like, five blocks from here. We shop at the same Star Market and use the same post office."

"Was she working much?"

"The gig she had at the Mayflower Room got cancelled when they were closed down, maybe a month ago."

Losing a job wouldn't have pushed her over the edge—uncertainty was about the only certainty for a performing musician.

"She was a huge talent." Her voice cracked.

"She had a good voice." I wasn't sure where all the hero worship was coming from—Alison would have been the first to admit she wasn't Ella Fitzgerald. I stood up. "I need to get going."

I'd gleaned a little out of coming here, but not enough to lose sleep over.

"So soon?"

In the foyer, I looked over the top of her head at myself in the mirror. Graying hair stuck out in wings from my temples and my face looked tired and pale.

"It's late."

"Maybe you'd like to see the rest of my photographs."

She pointed at the images marching up the stairway wall. I'd half-expected something like this, but she was a little too desperate about it for me to feel comfortable. Before I could control it, though, I had a mental image of her posting on top of me, a tiny naked rider on a horse. I shook my head.

"That's a nice offer," I said. "But I think I might feel a little too much like Alison was watching us."

Which in some weird form was exactly what she wanted.

"If you think it best." She drank again. She probably didn't get denied very often.

A familiar face stared up from a photo propped on a small oak table. The background looked like the old Paul's Mall on Boylston Street.

"You know Cy Nance?"

"I've lived in Boston for fifteen years, Elder. I go to jazz clubs. How could I not know Cy?"

He was seated at the piano in a tux, Susan's hands resting on his shoulders in a proprietary way.

She let me out and locked the door behind me. As I walked back up the block to my car, I felt disturbed, without really understanding why. Susan knew Cy, Cy knew Alison. What of it?

As I drove home through the city's blackness, I lost myself in complicated daydreams, miniature horses running through turquoise surf, midgets and mangoes and tropical winds, bare flesh, hot sand. Some self-protective instinct had kept me from following Susan upstairs. She was the woman the adage warned about: "Never sleep with someone who's crazier than you are." Beyond that, she wanted something from me, and I didn't have a clue what that was. That didn't mean I wouldn't want to know someday.

CHAPTER 7

I slapped blindly at the screaming alarm clock and managed to shove it off the bedside table, but that didn't kill it. A distant bell bing-bonged right along with it, but it wasn't until I managed to untangle my brain from the black twisted remnants of my dreams that I realized the doorbell was ringing too. I kicked the clock to silence as I unwrapped myself from the sheets. They were damp and cold.

"What?"

"Mr. Darrow." Dorothea Rinaldi's reedy voice piped outside my apartment door. "It's after seven-thirty. Are you ready to leave?"

I groaned, but not so loudly that she'd hear me. The good news was that the Esposito had done a steady business all Saturday night long. The bad news was that my back and shoulders felt as if I'd been shot-putting concrete blocks and I had completely forgotten that I'd agreed to drive Mrs. Rinaldi to eight o'clock Mass in Hyde Park.

"Three minutes," I called through the door. "I'll meet you at the bottom of the stairs." I didn't want her hovering outside the apartment until I got myself together.

Shaved, dressed, and half-comforted with a travel mug of French roast, I eased myself down the stairs, trying not to bounce too much. One of the many enduring oddities of having been a drunk so long was that I still got hangovers. If I'd been spending my evenings in a place where they smoked pot all night long, I would have suspected a contact high. But just because it didn't make any physiological sense didn't mean I didn't have a head.

Dorothea stood on the landing outside her ground-floor apartment, wearing a dusty brown coat with a raccoon fur collar and carrying a tan plastic purse. A small beige pillbox hat completed the ensemble. She was seventy-five if she was a day, slender enough to have been a dancer, and though the skin of her face was papery and wrinkled, I was certain she was the belle of the Columbus Ave. Senior Center. I could imagine old men watching her with their memories in their eyes, thinking: "Class. Real class."

"Good morning, Mrs. Rinaldi."

"Thank you for being willing to drive me," she said. "But shouldn't we get going? I don't like to come into the church late."

"Absolutely." I held the door open for her.

"And haven't I told you to call me Dorothea?"

"But never Dot."

The dimple in her right cheek deepened. "Correct."

The morning was cold but brilliant with sunshine, and an early green scent of growth rose from the flower boxes along the front bay windows. In the rough squares of earth between the sections of sidewalk, the skinny maples showed a red haze around the tiny buds.

I helped her into the front seat of the Cougar and drove through the light traffic across town to pick up the Jamaicaway.

"I was very sorry to hear about your friend," she said as we turned into the parking lot at Most Precious Blood Church. "Sometimes I think it's more difficult to lose a friend than a family member."

I was surprised she knew about Alison, and touched she would say something.

"Thank you," I said. "It's harder than I thought, considering how long it's been."

A red-nosed man in a Harris tweed jacket headed toward the Cougar with a smile lighting his face. Dorothea looked at him without delight.

"I remember when I lost my Jack." She clutched her purse. "I found myself saying and doing things I never thought I would. There tends to be a vacuum, you know. You have to be careful not to let the wrong things rush in to fill it." She opened the car door. "And you don't ever stop missing them."

My throat felt congested, as if I was having trouble breathing. I walked around the back of the car and handed her off to the beaming jockey in tweed.

After my father died, I had as little use for churches as I did for hospitals, so I didn't go in with her. I leaned on the sagging chain-link fence and smoked and stared at the brown grass on the ball field, thinking about the vacuum Dorothea had described and wondering if I was fooling myself into thinking there was something suspicious about Alison's death, using it as a way to keep from accepting that she'd killed herself. The absence of antidepressants in her blood could be explained any number of ways. Maybe she'd been using the journal to try and convince herself she was happy.

And I wondered about the Indian with the sunlamp tan hustling my pianist Eric's girlfriend the other night. Eric said he used to book talent for the Mayflower Room, where Alison had played off and on. Maybe I should talk to him. Maybe he'd known her well enough to understand where her head was in the last few months.

As the church doors opened, I crushed the cigarette butt under the sole of my boot. I had something invested in the idea that Alison had not killed herself, but I had to believe that I might have been trying to wish a fantasy into fact.

"Nice service?" I said as we drove past Jamaica Pond.

Dorothea sat stiffly, as if she'd had bad news, though at her age, death and illness barked at the heels of many of her friends.

"The rituals don't impress me like they used to," she said. "I suppose you think that's awful."

"Religion's not my department." I wondered if I had anything close.

"Really," she said. "The only thing that gives me pleasure anymore is building my sets. Even if I can't get anyone to take them seriously."

She stared at the boathouse passing, the greening lawns on the bank of the pond.

"I thought that was more of a hobby," I said.

"It's my work," she said. "But if nobody else ever looks at it, I might as well be masturbating."

Not the word I would have expected out of a nice old lady on a bright morning after Mass. But I understood what she was saying.

"I don't know anyone in the opera world," I said. "I can ask around."

"How about in publishing? I'm writing a book about my years in the company, too."

"Sorry. No."

She sat forward, more animated.

"I have a great deal of original material. Programs notes, photos. Even autographs."

"That's terrific."

We pulled up in front of the building. I was aching for a nap, but I didn't want to dump her and run.

"Can I offer you some lunch?" she said.

"Not today, Dorothea. But thank you. Maybe another time."

She cut me a look from under her hat. "We should do it soon, then."

Upstairs, I collapsed in a wing chair, so exhausted I didn't even put on any music, and when I woke, the sunlight was slanting high through the big front window. I was scratchy-eyed and hungry, but oddly elated, too, as my brain had been doing something productive while I slept.

But I knew better than to trust the feeling. In the process of drying out, I'd learned that pretty much all my moods were self-generated, the highs as suspect as the low, and maybe more so. These days the best thing I could do was cruise a middle lane between them, focus on a long-term sanity.

I walked down the corner to Angelo's and had them box up a couple of pieces of white clam pizza and a Caesar salad. I almost sat down and ate my dinner there, just for the illusion of having company, but I wanted to think.

Back in the apartment, I set the table with a plate and knife and fork, turned on Wes Montgomery's *California Dreamin'*, and tried to sort what I knew from what I felt.

I did believe that Alison had been happy three or four weeks before she died. And I knew that there weren't any anti-depressants in her system when she did go out the window. I also knew, if I believed Burton, that there wasn't any evidence she did not go out the window voluntarily.

But what I felt seemed more persuasive. I had believed her when she said she wouldn't quit taking her pills as long as I didn't drink—her going to New York wouldn't have voided our agreement. And if she'd been writing so faithfully in her journal all these months—wouldn't she have talked about suicidal thoughts if she'd had them? I thought so.

I quit struggling with it after a while, and settled down to what was usually my most difficult night of the week, Sunday. As long as I could occupy myself without drinking until I got sleepy, I considered it a success.

I drank a cup of coffee, smoked, and tried to read an

Umberto Eco novel, but my attention span wasn't up to anything that rich and convoluted. About a quarter to ten, I woke up in the chair with a stiff neck and a thirst for a glass of Scotch so strong I wobbled as I walked to the bathroom.

I drank a glass of tap water, brushed my fuzzy teeth, and carried myself off to bed. As I lay there, repetitive thoughts carving ruts in my brain, I realized that somehow I was going to have to satisfy myself about Alison's life and her death and having firmed that decision, I slept like a stone.

CHAPTER 8

On Monday morning, I returned to the comfortable territory of the Esposito. To prove to myself that I wasn't turning into a coffee snob, I stopped at the Dunkin' Donuts two blocks from the bar and bought myself a large regular and two Boston Kreme doughnuts.

I parked behind the building and kicked my way through the trash up to the street, balancing the bag and the cup with my keys. A bum was huddled in the Esposito's doorway and I was all ready to kick him awake and run him off until I recognized the cheap gold bracelet with the Marine Corps anchor around the thin brown wrist that extended from the greasy leather jacket. He had the hood of his thermal sweatshirt pulled so tight I couldn't see much of his face, but I knew who it was.

"Delford?"

His turned his head, his spit-colored eyes full of pharmaceutical cloud.

"Jesus, Elder. You're running a little late this morning. I could have used a drink a couple hours ago."

His normally cocoa-colored complexion was gray as cigar ash. One eye was swollen shut and a black crust of dried blood stained the corner of his mouth. His two front teeth on top were broken off square, leaving a gap the shape of a Chiclet, but I didn't know if that was new damage or old. His lower lip bumped out, as if a grape had grown under the skin.

"Can you stand up?" I put my hand down, though I didn't

particularly want to touch him.

He slapped at it, his broken teeth mashing the words into a messy sibilance.

"S'my own fault," he said. "Wasn't sposed to be selling no pills."

He scooched himself up against the door frame as I unlocked the door and ran downstairs to call 911. The alarm was starting to chirp by the time I got back up the stairs and I keyed it off as I handed Delford a wet bar towel.

He held his right hand away from his body as if it were a small rabid animal that wanted to bite him, and dabbed at his face with the left. As the dried blood softened and wiped away, some of his natural color started to return and he didn't look quite so shocky.

"Don't get no nine eleven down here." He spat darkly into the gutter. "Not for a black man's mugging."

"Why would anyone mug you?"

Delford looked and acted streetwise—more to the point, he didn't look as if he owned the proverbial pot to piss in.

"Shouldn't a been there." He stared up into the cold gray sky. "And I shouldn't a been doing what I was doing there neither."

"It didn't happen here?" It was selfish, but the fewer police callouts associated with the Esposito, the better.

He shook his head.

"I was selling my dukes down on east Berkeley, near the cab stand? 'Sposed to be this mortatorium."

"You sell dope?"

It sounds stupid, but it hadn't occurred to me, and if I followed my own rules, it meant I was going to have to bar Delford, too. He looked at me sideways from inside the hoodie.

"You think I was a stockbroker?"

I hated to think he was right about the paramedics, but I

wasn't hearing sirens.

A red-haired woman, sleek in black and white pants, walked by on the far outside of the curb, trying to ignore us. Her soap sweetened the air.

"Try standing up?" I said.

He used my anchored weight to climb himself vertical, then bent and grabbed at his ribs.

"Come on," I said. "I'll drive you to the emergency room."

"Elder . . ."

I knew one reason why he hated the idea. The other was that the nurses and doctors would lecture him about his drinking.

"I'll cover it. You need some X-rays at least."

He pushed his hood back. Sweat glistened on his forehead and he shuddered.

"I'll pay you back," he said.

How well I knew the good intentions of a drunk, the same pure gratitude I'd always felt when I was drinking and someone helped me out, even if it was only by lighting my cigarette.

"Sure thing, Del."

I locked the door to the bar and helped him back down the alley into the Cougar's bucket seat. His odor dominated the interior. I cracked my window.

"You got beat up for selling pills you weren't supposed to?"

He stared through the windshield as I exited the alley onto Mercy Street. I remembered my coffee and doughnuts sitting on the stoop as I headed downtown.

"My own fault," he said. "I knew. But I needed some cash."

"Knew what?"

"I wasn't 'sposed to."

"You have a boss?"

He shut his mouth in a tight line, except for the lump.

"Someone knocked you around pretty good, for a warning. You want to say who?"

Dead silence. His breath was rotting melons, untended gums. "Couple spics."

"Carlos Tinto one of them?"

He made the barest nod as we pulled into the visitors' lot at Mass General. I didn't know what I would do with the information, but I might find a use for it somewhere, sometime.

While I waited for them to get around to examining Delford, I called Marina. She drove down and picked up the keys to the Esposito. She was ready for work, dressed in pleated high-waisted khakis and a short-sleeved white shirt.

"You could break down and give me a set, you know," she said, plucking them out of my hand. "Then I wouldn't have to run around like a chicken with my head cut off every time you were late. It's like you don't trust me."

She knew it wasn't her I didn't trust, or at least she would have if she was thinking. She was at the stage with Carlos where he could talk her into anything.

As Marina walked away, a short, slope-shouldered nurse with dyed black hair walked up, bouncing a clipboard off her thigh like a football coach.

"Mr. Darrow?"

I nodded. I'd had just about all I ever wanted to do with medical types when my father died.

"You're listed on the paperwork as the responsible party?"

"I'm good for your bill," I said.

Her malachite-green eyes were full of anger, quite a bit of it for this early in the morning.

"That's not what I'm worried about. Someone will have to either stay here with Mr. Woodley or come back and pick him up. We're not going to admit him, but it will take a while to get to him, and he will be medicated."

"Fine. What time?"

"Sometime after five," she said. "If it's not too much trouble for you."

She spun on a soft-soled shoe and headed for the nurse's station. I guess it wasn't my day to make anyone happy, or to get any smarter myself. Even though I knew who'd beaten Delford up, I didn't know what I was going to be able to do with it.

It had surprised me, once I was reliably sober, how much a predictable schedule made it easier to stay that way. One of the reasons I lost all those years to booze, I was convinced, was that until I ran the bar, I didn't have to get up every morning and go to a job. In a way I couldn't have five or six years ago, I sympathized with Dorothea's need to be productive.

The next morning, Delford wasn't anywhere in evidence. I'd dropped him outside the bar last night, and I hoped the fact he wasn't here for his morning eye-opener meant he was somewhere healing up.

Marina didn't show up on time, and I wondered if she were still pissed off at me. After I picked Delford up at the emergency room, I hadn't gotten back to the Esposito until well after the dinner rush and she was so angry at having to run the place by herself that she slammed out the minute she saw me walk in, leaving me alone for the rest of the night. I waited until the beginning of the lunch rush before I started to worry. In the past, she'd always called, even if she were only going to be an hour late. I called her mother.

"Carmen? Hi. Marina there?"

Marina's mother sighed like a teakettle. She saw herself as her only child's only protection against the chills and aches of life. In her eyes, Marina did not have the sense, intelligence, or skills to do anything more challenging with her life than cook in a bar. Nor did she have the good looks to attract a marriageable man in order to give Carmen and Frank grandbabies to spoil.

Carlos Tinto actually made a little more sense to me when I thought about the pressure Marina's home life put her under.

"She didn't come home," Carmen said, sounding scandalized, not worried, and I didn't doubt the fact that Marina slipped the leash as often as she could.

"Saturday and Sunday night both," she said. "She missed early Mass."

My anxiety notched up at that—Marina was regular, if not devout, and always dutiful about getting her mother to mass. It cost her too much aggravation not to be.

"She probably got busy," I said. "Forgot to call. But I need someone to cook for my lunch crowd." She'd done it once before, when Marina was sick.

Carmen sighed. Mentally I apologized to Marina. This would only increase the amount of shit Carmen would send her way.

"You'll pay for my taxi?" she said.

The bar was filling up, getting raucous.

"I'll call you one myself."

"You have fresh garlic? None of that powdered business?"

If I let her, she would go on all afternoon like this.

"Come and see for yourself," I said.

One more sigh, operatic in duration.

"Send the taxi."

"Mille grazie."

"Your accent is terrible."

Two hours later, I walked back into the kitchen to see how she was doing. Her cheeks were flushed from the heat and the excitement and scraps of her suspiciously black hair were escaping from her hairnet, but for all the muttering, she seemed to be enjoying herself.

When she saw me, she slammed an industrial-sized shaker of oregano onto the shelf with a look that could have curdled vinegar.

"Marina always calls if she's going to stay out all night. She knows how much I worry."

I poured her a cup of coffee.

"What? You don't have espresso?" she said.

"I can't afford a real machine. You want it or not?"

She took it and looked down into the blackness as if it might hold leaves to read.

"She didn't call you?"

I shook my head. "She slammed out of here on Saturday night. Mad at me."

"I even called that Carlos boy of hers. To me, he pretends he doesn't speak any English."

"You want me to talk to him?"

She frowned as if she weren't sure I was up to it, then nodded.

"Don't worry," I said. "She's probably just still mad at me."

Marina still hadn't shown up by dinnertime, but rather than call Carmen again, I closed the kitchen. Monday night wasn't much of a night for people eating out, and I was still worn out from dealing with Carmen's kitchen diva act at noontime. I doubted anything serious was wrong with Marina—if she hadn't called Carmen to keep her from worrying, she wouldn't have called me. She was probably sulking.

Bar business built steadily through the early evening, which kept me from worrying about Marina or thinking about Alison. I wasn't confident that even if I found some evidence that would interest Burton, he'd be able to follow up. His need to do the right thing didn't always trump his sense of survival—he needed being on the cops as much as the cops needed him.

I leaned on my bar and listened to Ibrahim Ferrer sing in Spanish about love and pain and loneliness. A matched pair of yuppies sitting near the cash register was talking, and when I heard the conversation turn to music I walked in their direction, pointed at their half-empty glasses, and raised my eyebrows. I was always interested in music talk.

The female of the two wore horn-rimmed black glasses, a black wool suit over a frilly white blouse—she placed a ringless hand over the top of her glass. The male was dressed a little more sportily, in the pleated pants to a glen plaid suit, a lavender shirt, and yellow Curious George suspenders. He frowned as if I'd just asked him for spare change, then both went back to ignoring me.

"Closed them down for at least a month," the she-yup was saying. "Nonpayment of taxes, I think. Or maybe there was a bust."

"How is anyone supposed to make money if they have to pay taxes?" he said.

I liked the way he thought.

She bit her lower lip, which was the color of a ripe Bing cherry.

"I think they had trouble with people dealing inside the club."

He snorted. "The Mayflower was retro. Way too, if you know what I mean. I know this killer techno club in Saugus, up behind the steakhouse. You want to check it out?"

"Sure. Beats listening to this National Geographic shit."

I picked up their glasses after they left, racked them in the dishwasher, and washed my hands in case their bad taste was contagious. I had been hearing a lot about the Mayflower Room lately, and on the principle that coincidence was the way the universe checked to see if you were paying attention, I thought it might be time to check into the place.

Burton dropped in around nine-thirty.

"Where's Marina?"

"Night off," I said.

She'd been pretty clear about not wanting Burton in her

business, and I wondered what the attraction was for him. He was a white-bread boy from Charlestown, the most provincial section of Boston there was—the different branches of the Irish families barely spoke to each other, let alone to the Jews or the Italians. Then that made me think of Alison.

Beyond the obvious, the racial difference, the disparity in our backgrounds had been wide. She'd grown up in Roxbury, the poorest part of the city, and had been lucky to finish high school in an educational system for which being black implied inferior intellectual talents. My family had been in investment banking since the Revolution, and at thirteen I was off to a New Hampshire prep school, then Harvard, to learn the mores and manners of the ruling caste. I had to wonder if the differences would have sunk us sooner or later anyway.

"I went all the way back through it," Burton said, ticking off points on his pudgy fingers. "There's no evidence anyone else was in the apartment at the time. She had a well-documented problem with depression and some recent professional setbacks. And she wasn't taking her meds. I'm not going to be surprised if we close it as suicide."

I felt a tendril of panic, not least because if they closed the case, I was going to have to accept the unacceptable. I'd been feeling more frequent urges to drink, struggling with the need I thought I'd tamed—I hadn't broken yet, but I could feel the pressure building.

"I still don't believe it," I said. "But I'm goddamned if I could prove it to you."

And I had to wonder if I were trying too hard to erect a logical scaffold around my intuition. One of the more pleasant aspects of being an alcoholic was indulging your emotions. No one expected a drunk to have any kind of impulse control. But maybe I'd gone too far the other way, relying too much on logic: If I do this, I drink. If I drink, I die.

"You met with this Susan Voisine woman," Burton said.

I stopped at the end of the bar with my hands full of dirty dishes.

"Where'd you hear that?" I felt vaguely violated.

"We had her in to sign her statement," he said. "She was pretty good about cooperating, once we pointed out the downside."

"You caught her stealing from a dead woman." I stacked the dishwasher. "She had good reason to cooperate. If you're still talking to witnesses, you must have doubts."

Burton shook his head.

"Tying up the loose ends. She was present when the uniforms arrived, hence a potential witness."

"She was in the apartment?"

Burton snapped his fingers in front of my face. "Are you listening to me? The door was locked. Voisine walked in with the patrol guys, told them she was the victim's sister."

"So she couldn't have pushed Alison."

It must have showed that I was relieved, because Burton grinned.

"You've got it, too."

"What?"

"Whatever it is she's selling. The desk guys almost scuffled over who was going to escort her up the stairs."

"She's a good-looking woman," I said.

"She's a fucking ghoul, not to mention a little unusual-looking."

"Nothing wrong with that."

"Which part?"

Burton drank some beer. I wiped down the table with a wet rag.

"How come you gave Marina the night off? So you could do all the shit work?"

I spoke before I thought. "She didn't come in this morning."

His face flushed a deep dark red. When he stood up, the stool tipped over. Conversation at the tables lulled, then picked up again.

He slammed back the rest of his beer and yanked the cell phone off his belt.

"What's up?" I said.

His face was a study in fear and anger.

"Narco arrested Carlos Tinto on Saturday night. Could she have been with him?"

I shrugged. If she'd been arrested, she probably would have called me, not Carmen—I doubted she would have anyone else to call. But before I could say anything to calm him down, Burton was halfway up the stairs, punching numbers into his cell phone with a spastic finger.

CHAPTER 9

Donnie Spengler, the brighter of Ricky's two muscle-twins, was dangerous mainly because he was so single-minded. As much as his one-pointedness drove Tommy crazy, he had to admit it was a good thing for Ricky. You couldn't convince a single-minded person of anything he didn't know already.

He and Donnie were sitting among the fifty-pound sacks of pancake mix and cases of canned tomatoes in the back of Ricky's luncheonette. The conversation reminded Tommy of trying to dig a garden plot in the sunbaked clay of his uncle's land on the Ramah Navajo reservation.

"Spengs. Ricky told me specifically to pick up the bag from wherever you had it."

Donnie was dressed like the young Gene Kelly this morning, white pocket T-shirt, high-waisted khaki chinos with a plain cordovan belt, white socks, penny loafers. He sported a red heart tattoo the size of a silver dollar on his left forearm, and he weighed about thirty pounds less than he should have for his six and a quarter feet tall. Tommy was pretty sure Ricky didn't realize the man he'd trusted to hold his precious bag was probably an Olympic-class speed freak.

Spengler hooked the heels of his shoes over the rung of the kitchen stool and ran his hands through the close black stubble on his scalp. He looked like a magazine ad for the Gap.

"But he didn't say nothing to me about it, Tommy. I'm sorry."

Tommy understood that Spengler wasn't sorry at all, that like everyone else around here, he apparently didn't trust Tommy. That was Spengler's rule for filling his role—trust no one—and it was just one more reason Ricky's organization was so weak. No one could trust anyone else.

He wouldn't have pushed so hard, except that he had convinced himself the bag was going to be full of money. Ricky didn't need to hide any dope away. Maybe a little executive-level honesty was called for in this situation.

"Spengs. I know you don't trust me. Some days I don't trust me. But how would I even know about the bag if Ricky hadn't told me?"

The bodyguard's little yellow lizard eyes blinked rapidly as he tried to follow the logic, and when he sighed at last, Tommy knew he had him. Time to give a little more.

"He's always trusted you more than he has me."

"If he trusts me so much," Spengler said, "why didn't he call me and tell me to move it myself?"

Tommy had been asking himself the same question. He wasn't in such a hurry to get his hands on the bag that he didn't wonder if Ricky could be setting him up, but he finally decided that too much paranoia was as bad as not enough. Ricky was too sick to be playing head games.

"I think he was trying to protect you, man. People, they start feeling sick, they don't always act the way you expect. I don't even know what's in the bag. Ricky just wanted me to hide it somewhere away from here."

"I still don't like it."

Good instincts, Spengs. But here was the weakness—because his instincts were always telling him not to trust Tommy, he had no way of knowing that this one time, he was right.

"Call him and ask, if you want."

Before he'd left the hospital, Tommy had made sure that

Ricky would be out of the room—they were running tests all afternoon.

"Maybe I should." Spengler was pacing the storeroom, his body language that of a little kid who had to pee.

Tommy spread his hands.

"OK," he said. "Then you can explain to Ricky what happened when this very important bag gets ripped off or lost or whatever."

That was his second act of executive genius this morning, pushing Spengler's threshold of responsibility. The last thing a guy with the flunky mentality wants is to wind up holding the bag, either literally or figuratively.

Donnie flowed to the door of the walk-in cooler, which was always padlocked shut.

"Ricky said this has something to do with a big deal he's working on. You have any insight into that?" Tommy said.

Spengler gave him a flat unhappy look, then unlocked the lock with a small brass key from his wallet. He held the door open for Tommy, who shivered in the blast of cold fog.

"Go ahead." Tommy wasn't going to walk into the cooler and leave Spengler behind him.

Donnie kicked a bulk-pack of frozen franks over to prop the door, then shifted cases of frozen French fries and hamburger patties until he uncovered a green plaid gym bag trimmed in vinyl. It was gray with a thick layer of frost.

Tommy was far more comfortable outside the cooler, and it wasn't just the warmth. Spengler didn't show even a goose bump, one more advertisement for the power of speed. He held the bag a few seconds longer than he had to before he handed it over.

"I am calling Ricky later," he said. "Just to be sure."

Tommy headed for the door to the alley where he'd parked the Navigator. Unlikely.

"Sure thing, Spengs. And you'll find out that everything is just fine."

Shielding the bag with his body, Tommy looked up and down the alley before he pulled the zipper back a couple inches. His heart thumped.

Shit. The frost left marks on his silk shirt. And the bag was full of pills, not money, thousands of assorted capsules and tabs, all separated by type into thick plastic bags.

He rethought his disappointment quickly. It wasn't money, but it was only one step away. It might take him a little longer to get the money from the pills, but Ricky was in the hospital for a few more days too. As long as Tommy got his fuck-you money in time to get out of town, he didn't care.

He tossed the duffel in the back seat of the truck and backed out of the alley, starting to think for the first time that he had a legitimate chance at making this work out. Thinking positively about his relationship with Icky Ricky for the first time in a while.

CHAPTER 10

Before I left for the Esposito the next morning, I called Cy Nance and asked him to meet me at the coffee shop. I wanted to ask him what he knew about the Mayflower Room and, incidentally, how he knew Susan Voisine. I still hadn't heard from Marina, but she was probably hiding from Carmen now. I doubted that she had been unlucky enough to get arrested with Carlos, and Burton would have covered that possibility anyway.

As I stepped off the bottom step into the foyer of my building, the door of the ground-floor apartment swung inward. I smiled.

"Henri?" I stepped closer to the doorway, braced myself.

A tall gaunt man in sharply pressed khaki pants and a tattersall shirt jumped out at me, flailing his arms and legs.

"Kung-fu fighting! Kung-fu fighting!"

When he saw it was me, he dropped his arms to his sides and morphed from martial-arts wizard into normal-looking seventy-year-old man. Aside from a vague paranoia, which I thought was completely justified if you were a certain age and walking the streets of Boston looking like you had money in your pocket, Henri was in pretty good shape. Recently, he'd started to act a little drifty, though, and I wasn't sure if his mind was starting to go or he was just bored as hell by being retired.

For many years, he'd run one of Boston's premier rare book restoration businesses. His clients included old-line Boston institutions like Brattle Street Books and the Old Corner Bookstore. Until last year, he'd even maintained a workshop about three blocks from here, but gave it up when the rents went up too far.

"It is you," he said.

"It is I. Disappointed?"

His eyes were rheumy, as if he had a cold. He'd moved into my building in 1994, a year after Mrs. Rinaldi, and I only realized how enamored of her he was when she spoke to me about his staring through the peephole in his door every time she passed. Since he lived on the ground floor, that meant every time she left the building. He hadn't admitted a thing, but I'd had a word with him regardless.

"When are we going to have a game, then?" he said.

Whatever else was or wasn't working, his brain was still sharp enough to play a cutthroat game of backgammon. Unfortunately, he loved to drink Fonseca's Bin No. 27 while he played and got miffed when I wouldn't drink along with him. I don't think we'd played more than four or five games since I got sober.

"Any time, Henri. Friday morning?" He'd probably forget.

He shook his big bald head, dotted with skin tags.

"Not so soon. I have a rush job for Baroni."

Paul Baroni dealt rare books out of his attic in Brookline for thirty years, but he'd died several months ago. I wondered if it wasn't time for me to check on Henri's next of kin, maybe get them to have him looked at by a gerontologist.

"When you have a chance, then," I said. "Just leave a note on my door."

Henri bowed like one of the Three Musketeers and swept his arm to one side.

"Until we meet again, *mon ami*." His door slammed with a bang that shuddered dust motes out of the wallpaper.

Stepping out into the morning bustle of Commonwealth Ave.,

I shook my head. Sometimes it felt like I was living in a Coen Brothers movie.

Cy was more than forty minutes late, which left me wondering if I'd overestimated his friendship, misremembered what I'd thought were good nights he and Alison and I had spent together. Maybe I was just a business relationship to him.

When he finally wandered in, just as I was pulling my paper plate and cup together and getting ready to give up my table, his face looked as if he hadn't slept for days. He'd washed the pomade out of his hair, so that it looked more like fine steel wool. Now he looked less like Cab Calloway and more like an older version of Delford Woodley.

A New Age-y version of "Luckenbach, Texas" oozed through the sound system. Willie would have shot out the speakers. I moved my empty cappuccino cup over to make room for Cy at the tiny metal table.

"New 'do?" I said.

He lifted his mug with a shaky hand. His tea was some herbal decoction, green and slimy.

"Feeling lousy," he said. "Flu or something."

"Keep it to yourself."

I made a cross with my fingers and held it up in his face. He grunted.

"You ever do any business with the people who book the Mayflower Room?" I said.

"Business? What's that mean? I do favors sometimes, the same way I do for you. Doesn't mean it's business."

That seemed a little disingenuous, but maybe Cy was worried about his own tax problems, if that truly was why the Mayflower Room had closed. I could understand him not paying taxes on any cash that stuck to his hands.

"I know they got closed down," I said. "That's not what I

wanted to talk about."

" 'Closed'?" His eyes were webbed with red capillaries.

"Alison worked the room there off and on, right? I want to talk to whoever hired her."

He relaxed a fraction.

"I heard they're going to be closed a long, long time," he said. "The FBI tried a drug buy, but it went south."

I drank the cold dregs of my coffee and let the silence push on him. He sipped the tea with the unsteady hand of an older man.

"You need to talk to Tommy Cormier," he said. "He used to book their talent, but I don't know where you'd find him now."

"Indian-looking guy with a sunlamp tan?"

"Tropical Tommy." Cy snorted. "I think he wishes he was born a brother."

Cy must have been feeling shitty. He never made jokes about race.

"You didn't tell me you knew Susan Voisine, either," I said.

He drank more of the evil-looking liquid.

"Where'd you run into her?"

"She tried to rip off stuff from the apartment, the night Alison supposedly killed herself."

He was surprised.

"All I know was that she used to trawl after musicians. In a previous life. 'Supposedly'?"

I ignored him.

"How did you know her?"

"She's like a junk dealer now, right? Sells people's shit on eBay? She used to be a rabble-dabbler."

Cy's pet term described the young women who liked to hang out with artists and musicians for a while, but only until it was time to get serious about husbands and babies and houses in Newton.

"Memorabilia," I said.

He closed his eyes and swayed back in the chair.

"What's the matter, Cy?"

He pushed on the bridge of his nose. "One of my kids—I was up all night."

He didn't have kids of his own—he must have been talking about someone from the music school.

"Not Eric?"

I assumed it would be a drug thing, and I'd have thought Eric was too smart for that. He shook his head.

"Guitar player. Got herself into some X out at one of those rave-up things."

"Using? Selling?"

He sat up straight. "Just using. What do you know about X?"

"What I read in the papers," I said.

"This little girl's in a coma. Severely dehydrated."

"Jesus."

That the kid was a good enough musician for Berklee made things worse for Cy—he believed that people with talent had more right to survive their mistakes.

"I spent most of the night at Mass General," he said.

"High level of service for an admissions officer."

"Her daddy played with me in the All-Stars."

"I'm sorry."

My shoulders twitched. He stared into the seaweed dregs of his cup.

"Nothing to do about it. Little thing called life."

"That's what all the people say."

He didn't catch the joke and I didn't repeat it. He didn't need my sarcasm.

I left him staring into his mug and pushed my way out through the heavy glass doors. Except for Tommy Cormier's name, he hadn't been much help. I suspected the song and dance about his student was a way to divert me from questions about Susan Voisine and the Mayflower Room. But it was still only nine-thirty, which gave me time to run by and check out what I could of the Mayflower before I had to go open up my own bar.

I zipped up my purple and white letterman's jacket and crossed the street, walked up half a block and down the stairs into the T station, thinking about conventional wisdom and what it could and couldn't do.

Because of my own history, I'd gotten interested in the nature of addiction. My drinking days had always felt more real than unmedicated daily life: brighter, more colorful, more satisfying. Except for the physical damage it caused, I wasn't sure I believed that chemical addiction was any less worthwhile than an addiction to vibrating crystals or high colonics. The pursuit of any kind of living beyond the mundane seemed like a laudable goal, even if it had its risks.

The conventional therapeutic wisdom says that addicts are fleeing something in themselves. But what if they were traveling toward something, risking themselves for insights the rest of the world doesn't want to risk? What if addicts were pioneers of a kind?

The subway platform was deserted, except for an obese white man in his fifties with a guitar case at his feet, finger-picking a Delta blues. Pulling in, the train rushed a gritty warm wind past my face.

Drugs and kids. The train wheels screeched on the curve out of the station. Jazz was rife with the lives and careers shortened by drugs: Billie Holliday, Charlie Parker, Chet Baker only the best-known names. How many anonymous sidemen and singers, trying to emulate their heroes, had succumbed?

Today's drug of choice was money, though. You weren't likely to die in an SRO hotel from an excess of hundred-dollar bills, but making all your decisions in financial terms, the way Cy did, made you as much of a junkie as any sad soul plotting his next fix.

The train doors sighed open at Boylston and I walked up the concrete stairs and stopped next to the newspaper kiosk. The air was cold and stank of truck exhaust, but the Common was starting to show patches of green through the matted winter browns. I headed down the sidewalk toward the John Alden Hotel on the far side of Park Square.

The Alden's lobby had a genteel but shabby feel, despite all the money that had poured into the big hotels in this part of town. Whoever owned it pretended that synthetic fabrics and air conditioning were still too recent an innovation to trust. When I was a child, my mother's relatives always stayed here when they visited, and I knew from that what the two infallible identifiers for places frequented by the quiet rich were. The floors were always carpeted with ancient worn and patched Oriental rugs, and there were always crystal vases full of fresh flowers on the check-in desk. The red Bokhara runner muffled my footsteps as I stepped up to the front.

The desk clerk was stiff and thin as copper pipe. His eyebrows lifted at the condition of my topcoat, but he maintained a reserved politeness. Doubtless he'd been dressed down by more than one rich Yankee eccentric who wore the same clothes he'd worn in college.

"Mayflower Room?"

"The outside entrance is around the corner, sir. On Providence Street."

He might have been implying there was an inside entrance, too, or maybe he was being nonspecifically passive-aggressive. It was the kind of classist bullshit the city was full of, and it drove me crazy, but I didn't see a profit in paying attention to it.

I pushed my way back out through the revolving door, around

the corner, and found a set of double glass doors with the single word "Mayflower" painted on the left one in gold script. But the heavy brass handles had been looped together with a chain and padlocked. I banged the heel of my hand on the glass. I knew it had been closed, but I didn't expect it to have stayed that way for long.

Back in the Alden's lobby, the clerk was bent behind the counter, stuffing letters into slots. I slammed the call bell so hard it skittered along the mahogany counter and bounced off the wall. As he straightened up, he knocked his head, then glared at me as he rubbed his bald spot.

"The Mayflower Room seems to be closed," I said. "Which you could probably have told me before I went back out there."

His superior attitude threatened to recur until I thumped the top of the counter. A bellman stepped out of the cloakroom behind the desk, adjusted the chinstrap on his hat, and stepped back inside.

"Please," I said, "don't assume I'm playing by the rules of your normal customers. What happened?"

He smoothed the front of his maroon jacket as if I'd grabbed him by it.

"The FBI closed it down a week ago."

"Not the IRS."

The two yuppies in the Esposito had talked authoritatively about tax problems, but their story could have been garbled.

He shuffled the rest of the envelopes from hand to hand. The mole next to his mouth made him look like a movie ingénue.

"Where do I find Tommy Cormier, then?"

He sneered, then covered his mouth, as if ashamed of his teeth.

"I really wouldn't know. Mr. Cormier lived in the hotel off and on, but he moved out a couple of weeks ago. In advance of the dogs, you might say."

I thought about anything else this supercilious asshole might have that I needed to know. I didn't want to get back to the Esposito and remember questions I should have asked.

"How well did you know Alison Somers?"

An emotion flicked across his narrow face, almost too quickly to identify, but I thought it was regret.

"Very talented woman," he said. "Well thought of. She stayed in the hotel occasionally."

"When she had an apartment in the Back Bay?"

He nodded. "Usually when she'd had a difficult night."

Which meant whenever she felt too high or too low to be at home by herself.

"And whenever she stayed with Mr. Cormier, of course."

"When she what?"

He was inordinately glad to tell me something I didn't know already.

"They were quite close, for a little while."

I stared at a painting that hung behind the desk, children skating on the Frog Pond. Alison Somers and Tommy Cormier. I wasn't sure how I felt about that.

By the time I was standing out on the sidewalk, though, I had a better idea. It was embarrassing, but I was jealous of her relationship with a man I'd never met, even after we'd been apart for many months. And identifying my feeling didn't take out the sting.

The Alden's doorman gestured at the line of cabs waiting. I shook my head and started walking south and east. The warmth of the sun increased the odors of Park Square—urine in the alleys, the garbage behind McDonald's, the bus exhaust. A red-haired woman passed me going the other way, trailing a cloud of Joy.

As I walked across town toward my bar, I found myself mourning the time I'd missed out of her life, the times we'd never have, and every other bar I saw along the way called out to me in passing, singing a low sweet song I knew by heart.

CHAPTER 11

I made it back to the Esposito without stopping in anyone else's bar, and as if she were the reward, I found Marina leaning against the brick wall on Mercy Street in her long green wool coat. I was so relieved to see her that I almost didn't notice the angry scrape along the outside of her right eye or the way she limped as she descended the stairs. I keyed off the alarm and followed her.

"What happened to you?" I said.

I wasn't talking about the injuries so much as her disappearing act, but she didn't appear to be taking questions today. At the bottom of the stairs, I stepped around in front of her. Her lower lip was puffed out and a burst blood vessel in her right eye made her look deranged.

"Carlos." I wasn't asking.

She tilted her chin down, not quite a nod, and I was shocked by a rush of anger pumping through me. There was nothing I could say to her that wouldn't sound like I-told-you-so, but I felt some responsibility myself. Maybe if I'd taken a harder line on keeping him out of the Esposito, he would have left her alone.

She retreated to the kitchen, still without a word. I turned on the radio and found it was pledge week. WGBH was playing an old tape of Ron della Chiesa's *Music America* show. As I listened to Coltrane blow on "My Favorite Things," my anger banked down into something less fierce, a deep sadness on Marina's behalf. I was afraid that she thought the only way to wrench herself out of Carmen's orbit was by way of a man, any man. But she had too many other positives—her work ethic, her good nature, her cooking talent—to settle for Carlos Tinto.

As if to prove me right, she outdid herself at lunch with a cioppino of tomatoes, some cod ends, mussels, and manila clams. Around twelve-thirty, I sat at the bar and ate a bowl of it with a hunk of French bread and remembered the winter after I graduated from Harvard, when I'd lived in North Beach and drunk a bottle of red wine every afternoon, sitting at a sidewalk café. Some people went to San Francisco to be poets. I'd left home to find new and more pleasurable places to be drunk.

I was slipping a Paul Butterfield bootleg tape into the deck when Burton walked in.

"Changing your luck?" he said as the harp started up. "I'd hate to think I was going to walk in here and hear Blind Lemon Chitlins someday."

" 'Blues ain't nothing but a good boy gone bad.' "

"Grace Slick."

He was guessing and he was wrong, but I gave it to him anyway, went out to the kitchen, and ladled up a mug of the cioppino. The alley door was open and I smelled cigarettes—I didn't know Marina smoked.

"Try this." I slid Burton the mug, a napkin, and a spoon, then cracked open a green bottle of beer.

He didn't move, staring at the back bar with his face drooped down like a disconsolate hound.

"Bad day?" I said.

"What are you, my mother?"

Nothing to do with that but walk away. I slid down the bar, unloaded the glass washer, and whistled along with Butterfield's harp break. The glass of whiskey up in Alison's niche was down a half an inch, evaporating into the air.

Marina walked out of the kitchen holding a saucepan up to the light. Her thick lip made her lisp.

"Elder. There's a hole in this."

The overhead lights exposed her bruises mercilessly, the lump in her cheek darkened blue and her lip doubly swollen by the shadow it cast.

Burton went still as the monument in Charlestown, then backed off his stool as she might not notice him if he were stealthy enough. I caught his expression, like a gargoyle, as he turned and walked toward the men's room.

"Shit," Marina said.

I shook my head. "Throw the damn thing out. I'll buy a new one."

When he returned, Marina was back in the kitchen and I doubted she'd be out until she was sure he'd left. Burton wore a brittle calm. When I reached into the beer cooler, he shook his head.

"I wanted to tell you face to face," he said. "We're closing the Somers case as suicide. I know you thought it was something different, but it just isn't there."

I'd known it was coming, but my stomach dropped out anyway. Apparently the only evidence that Alison hadn't killed herself was in my heart.

"Not surprised." I gave him the benefit of the doubt. "Though I am disappointed."

He pinched balls of bread dough from inside the crust, rolled them into pellets, and stacked them on the bar like miniature cannonballs. The inside rims of his eyes were red, the color of the artificial jelly in doughnuts.

"I agree that something doesn't smell right." He stared at his pile of ammunition. "I just can't see what it is."

The assertion carried the weight of his experience and it only increased the itchy feeling I'd had about Alison's death.

"What do you really think?"

He turned the empty bottle on its side and spun it.

"Lieutenant Costain is smarter than the average bear. He yanked me off this so hard, it was like he wanted me to complain."

"He didn't encourage you to keep it open?"

"This is longer than we'd normally keep a suicide open without any evidence to the contrary."

"I know the journal doesn't count, but the lack of anti-depressants in her blood?"

He stood the bottle up. "Not compelling."

"Can you do anything else?"

"Not a goddamn thing, pally. Not if I want to keep my job."

"What if Costain was trying to keep you interested for some reason?"

"It wouldn't be criminal," he said. "Costain is all about politics. It would have to be someone with power and a wild hair across his ass. Probably nothing to do with the Somers woman *per se*."

The finality of his words nailed me to the floor. He'd been my main hope for official action. I still believed that Alison would not have broken our pact voluntarily, but if I were ever going to be sure of that, I was going to have to find out for myself. Because I was afraid that if she had killed herself, then I would find my own reason to start drinking again, and then both of our stories would be over. If I didn't do something, I was failing her memory and probably obliterating my own.

It was barely nine-fifteen the next morning, but I was awake. I'd been sleeping fewer and fewer hours a night over the last few weeks, which I thought might be another mark of my body's adjusting to the sober life. It gave me more time to fill, a seriously mixed blessing.

As I washed out the French press and turned it upside down on the drain board, I wondered why Diana Krall had layered all those strings over the beautiful glass of her voice in the new CD. Every one of the songs felt sticky, and it wasn't so much that I hated it. I just wanted to understand why she'd do it, she with the voice of a goddess.

Overnight, my attitude had shifted. I didn't see what I could do to prove whether Alison's death was suicide or not. I was more inclined to accept it and get on with the life I was trying to build. If I was stupid enough to let myself drink, I would drink, and no pact with her would keep me from it. It seemed much more intelligent to focus on what I could control: building the Esposito up as a legitimate jazz club, tending to my own business.

As I headed for the door, the telephone rang. I assumed Marina was calling in sick—yesterday she'd been moving as if she were in pain and bruises hurt even more the second day. I could get along without her for a day, though.

"This is Elder."

"Mr. Elder Darrow?"

The voice sounded starched, either a lawyer or someone else who took himself too seriously.

"Mr. Darrow, we haven't met, I don't believe . . ."

"Excuse me. Is this a solicitation call?"

The caller puffed into the mouthpiece.

"Certainly not. This is Daniel Markham, from Markham and Beane. I assume you've heard of us."

Markham and Beane had been a specialty law firm in Boston, small and highly exclusive, for almost as long as my mother's family's bank had been around. In fact, my father had used them for years as his personal attorney. My pulse started to bump—maybe this had something to do with my going to work for the bank.

"Mr. Markham. I apologize. I get a lot of unsolicited calls. How can I help you?"

"One of our clients died recently. She hadn't been with us long, but I understand you knew her. A Ms. Alison Somers."

"I knew Alison," I said. Not well enough, apparently. She must have been doing better than I thought if she could afford Markham and Beane.

"Evidently you did."

The dry humor made me like him a little better. "And why would you say that?"

"She designated you as the executor of her estate." Mr. Markham cleared his throat.

"Say again, please."

Markham blew another puff of impatience.

"Are you free this morning? I could see you at ten and explain in person."

"Sure. Where's your office?"

He gave me an address on Congress Street, in the financial district, and I wrote it down on the back of an envelope.

Driving downtown, I tried to parse why Alison might have chosen me to be her executor. Our relationship had never gotten to the point where we'd had to talk about money, though I was pretty sure she knew that my family had a bank. I supposed that she hadn't been able to think of anyone else—her mother had died fifteen years ago and she was an only child—but that begged the question of where a young woman from Roxbury in her twenties had come up with enough money to warrant a will.

And being represented by Markham and Beane? When we'd been together, she'd lived from gig to gig, without any cushion to hold her up in rough financial spots. I'd even lent her small sums once in a while, which she'd always paid back. If she'd been making that kind of money from her career, I would have heard. The Boston media would have made a far bigger deal out of her if she was singing and recording a lot in New York than if she'd stayed here.

The law offices of Markham and Beane were aggressively generic: beige walls, fuzzy impressionistic prints, silk plants in pots. I stepped inside the door and around a drywall partition into the reception area, where a man around forty-five stood waiting.

"Donald Markham." He put out his hand.

"Elder Darrow."

His dress echoed the office's plain style: charcoal slacks, white shirt, a blue and red repp tie, and a navy double-breasted blazer. It was a professional uniform so common in Boston he would have been completely camouflaged in a lunchtime crowd at Locke Ober's. His thinning blonde hair was brushed straight back and his weathered cheeks made me think he was probably a weekend sailor.

"Thanks for coming down," he said. "It took a little while to track you down."

Considering that lawyers got paid by the hour, a couple weeks seemed like breakneck speed to me, but I didn't know him well enough to give him any compliments.

"Sorry if I was a little foggy this morning," I said. "I'm not usually awake at that hour."

"Yes," he said. "You own a restaurant?"

A nicely modulated description, one that wouldn't have survived his first visit to the Esposito. I appreciated the effort.

He led me through a hollow-core door into a deep and narrow office, two walls of bookcases and one wall of glass, with a view of Government Center. The room was furnished with a farm table, a scatter of mismatched stuffed chairs, and a half-dozen orchids, several blooming. He touched the red and yellow blossom on one, then sat down behind the table and opened a manila folder.

I sat down in a straight wooden chair as he thumbed through the papers.

"Are you familiar with the duties of an executor?" he said.

I'd done it for my mother and my father both, and I was happy to do it for Alison, too. Maybe it would give me some measure of the closure I seemed to be trying so hard to find.

"Pay outstanding bills," I said. "Dispose of the assets, disburse the remainder."

Markham nodded approvingly and extended a mono-grammed gold key ring in my direction.

"Here are the keys to Ms. Somers's apartment. Can I assume you know the address?"

I nodded, trying to figure out how to frame the question so it wouldn't sound clumsy.

"Does the will say . . ."

"Yes?"

"Do you have any idea why she selected me? We were involved at one time, but we haven't been in contact for almost a year."

He shrugged. "I can't be sure, but my impression was that Ms. Somers didn't trust anyone easily. There was family?"

"An uncle and an aunt. But she was estranged." Neither of whom had supported her decision to try and sing for a living. I understood; I was more likely to ask Burton or Marina to take care of my last wishes, even if I'd had any family alive.

"Here are several modest bequests."

He handed me a typed list of five names and addresses. I recognized Tommy Cormier and Cy Nance, but that was all. No amounts were listed, which made me wonder how modest mod-est was.

Markham frowned as he passed over the next list.

"Outstanding payments for performances given in the last six months. That's quite a lot of money. You'd better contact her agent for the details and a full accounting."

"Agent?" Something else new. She'd always handled her own booking and finances. I wondered what had changed her mind.

"His name and address are in the file, which you can take with you."

He handed me a sheaf of printed forms.

"Brokerage account statements, IRAs, mutual funds."

I felt my eyebrows climb. They were year-end statements and didn't show when the accounts had been opened, but the numbers were big. Had she had all this money when we were together, and I'd been too drunk to know?

"You didn't know about any of this," Markham said.

"I am surprised. But I'm happy to help."

Markham touched the knot of his tie and stretched his neck as if I made him nervous.

"Ms. Somers did not specify an executor's fee, but you are the residual beneficiary."

"Pardon me?" Surprise number two.

"Once you've made all the bequests, you'll receive the remainder of the estate. It is a rather significant amount."

I was busy enough absorbing the fact that I was an heir that I didn't want to ask how much, but Markham obviously was enjoying this.

"How significant?" I said finally.

"High six figures."

I breathed in through my nose and clamped my mouth shut. There was nothing I could say that would have adequately expressed my astonishment.

Markham tapped the stack of papers into alignment, slipped them back into the folder, and handed them to me.

"If you have any questions, don't hesitate to call," he said. "I would have to say that Alison was one of my more interesting clients."

Still fuzzy with the revelations, I accepted the folder.

"I'm not quite sure where to start," I said.

I was grateful enough that she'd left me the money, though I would rather have had her. And it was sad she hadn't had anyone closer to her to do this. I wondered if I should use the money to rest my questions about how she'd died.

"It's almost the end of the month," Markham said. "I would say the first step is probably to clean out her apartment. Then the estate won't have to continue to pay rent. The landlord has been in touch with me already—apparently she had a very generous lease."

Having a specific task helped me to concentrate. I jotted notes on the back of my folder as Markham continued.

"Then I'd pay off the few bills outstanding and clear up any payments she was owed. The rest of the estate isn't going anywhere. I can schedule a meeting to take care of all the bequests at once, or you can handle them individually."

"I think one meeting," I said, relieved to make at least one decision. "I can call on you for help?"

Markham gave me a genuine smile. "I hope you do. The firm is on retainer until the estate is completely settled."

I got up, feeling shaky and sad. "Thank you."

He stood up and walked around the desk, and although he wasn't any older than I was, he gave off an avuncular sense.

"Don't let it throw you," he said. "In my experience, people are shocked, even when they've been notified ahead of time. There's no hurry to any of this."

He shook my hand.

"I will warn you, though. You will get phone calls: financial advisors, tax attorneys, anyone else who prospects in the obituaries." His mouth twitched in distaste. "And once the will is probated, your name becomes public."

"Thanks for the warning," I said.

As I headed for the elevator, I thought that after throwing

drunks and drug dealers out of the Esposito for the last few months, telemarketers wouldn't be much of a challenge. And aside from using some portion of Alison's money to figure out what really had happened, I didn't need money so much I needed to start spending it right away. I drove back to work, mulling the possibilities. Life turned on a dime.

Chapter 12

Tommy backed the black Navigator into a space on a side street, far enough away from Alison's building that no one would connect him with it. It had been a stroke of foresight to have her keys copied the day she asked him to let the furniture delivery guys in, although he'd had other reasons while she was alive. He wasn't surprised when he heard she'd dived out a window—when they'd been together, he was always having to remind her to take her pills. Otherwise, she got flaky as shit.

Her apartment was about the safest place in Boston to hide anything from the police right now, though. She'd always kept her private space to herself—he didn't think the people she hung out with in clubs knew she even lived in town—and the apartment would probably sit empty until the end of the month. And if his deal with Ricky's dope didn't work out in the next week, he'd have to be leaving town anyway, at high speed.

He grabbed the ugly green plaid bag out of the back of the SUV. The frost had melted and stained the leather seat and he cursed himself for not putting a towel under it. The details sometimes skipped him. He walked down the block, around the corner, and up the granite stairs to her building, and unlocked the street door.

Inside, he sat down on one of the plush white sectionals, having worked out the mechanics of what Ricky was planning. The reason he'd closed down all the retail drug sales had been to lull the cops from thinking about him while he put together this

bigger deal. The only guy they'd left in place was the dude dealing pot at the music school. The cops never got any information
out of college kids anyway, and well, it was pot. Hardly anyone
cared.

But if the deal was big enough to make up for the loss of a
couple months' income from the street dealers—no wonder
Ricky wanted him to discipline Carlos for ignoring the ban.

When someone knocked on the door, he jumped up and
stepped to the peephole. Then he sighed—think of the man and
he appeared.

He opened the door and yanked Carlos into Alison's living
room with a fistful of his cheap leather jacket.

"You followed me?" He breathed in Carlos's ear. "You fucking
followed me here?"

He backhanded the little shit across the face, and Carlos
staggered back toward the bookcases, caught himself on the
wall.

"You fucking moron."

Tommy hit him again, twisting in the edge of his silver and
turquoise ring. Carlos was in love with his own face. Maybe a
little scar would help him grow some brains.

"Tommy. Hey. What the fuck?" Carlos backed away. "I'm
only trying to help. I wanted to report."

Carlos also had this college boy thing going, which Tommy
hated, mostly on principle. Raspberry Ralph Lauren polo shirt,
pleated poplin pants, the Topsiders without socks. In April, for
fuck's sake.

"Report what, you asshole?"

"One of the guys was selling. I got him off the street for you.
Beat the shit out of him."

Tommy sighed. Complications he didn't need.

"Who?"

"Woodley? The bum?"

Carlos looked so proud of himself that Tommy wanted to whack him again.

"You beat up some hapless nigger because he sold a couple of hits of speed to a truck driver?"

Tommy liked the sound of "hapless." He started to raise his hand, then decided not to hit Carlos again just yet. He didn't want the kid so fucked up he wouldn't listen.

"You put him in the hospital, you moron. Which means paperwork. Reports."

Carlos pulled a starched white handkerchief out of his back pocket and wiped at the corner of his mouth. Tommy thought he might need a stitch or two there. Good.

"It's that fucking Darrow's fault," he whined. "The guy who owns the bar? He's the one who needs to mind his own fucking business. He's the one who took the nig to Mass General."

Tommy feinted a slap. Carlos cringed away.

"My friend. Let me take care of Mr. Darrow." He was smiling to himself at Carlos's unconscious surrender, the white flag of his hankie.

"Look, you think I enjoy whaling on you? I'm trying to do some other business here."

Ricky's bag of pills sat on the small Oriental rug by the door. Tommy was starting to form the plan that would get him out of town without any blowback from Ricky.

"You guys keep thinking we shut down the street because we can't get product," Tommy said. "That's not the case."

Carlos looked down. The logic was lame, but no one in the lower levels of these organizations thought in anything but the shortest of terms.

Tommy unzipped the bag and opened the top so Carlos could see. Greed lit up the kid's eyes.

"As you can see," Tommy said. "There is plenty of product. This freeze is a short-term decision, a tactical shutdown. You're a leader to these guys—tell them they have to be patient."

Carlos grinned in an evil way that put Tommy on alert.

"What?" Tommy said.

"I want in."

"In what?" Tommy truly hated when people assumed more than they were entitled to, as much as he hated people with bigger ideas than their brains could handle.

"Ricky's in the hospital," Carlos said. "I hear he might not make it."

Rage flashed like fireworks behind Tommy's closed eyelids. He read the subtext perfectly. This little greaseball didn't think Tommy was going to rob Ricky, he thought Tommy was going to kill him. It was insulting.

He didn't need to hurt Ricky to get what he wanted. He was obeying the laws of nature and capitalism: The young take from the old, the strong from the weak, whenever and whatever they got away with. It didn't mean you had to take anyone out.

He folded over his knuckles and punched Carlos lightly in the Adam's apple. Carlos dropped to the floor like a tree, hacking for air.

"You little prick," Tommy said.

This little prick had some heart, though. He staggered his way upright and threw a soft looping punch at Tommy, who grabbed Carlos's upper arm and broke his nose with the heel of his hand. Carlos was too smart for his own good and too dumb to be dangerous, but Tommy gave him credit for sack.

"You run around telling people that I'm going to kill Ricky," he said, "I'm going to come and kill you. Nothing could be farther from the truth."

"Right," Carlos said.

Tommy didn't like the tone, but blood was starting to leak from Carlos's nostrils. He spun the kid toward the door and opened it.

"Don't dribble on the rug. Look—everything will be back to normal soon. OK? Now get the fuck out of my sight."

Carlos nodded, but he didn't look hangdog enough for Tommy. While he hadn't planned to clip anybody, maybe that would be cleaner all around. Leave Carlos somewhere for Ricky to find, along with the green plaid bag. Empty.

He dead-bolted the door and carried the bag into Alison's bedroom. When he opened the closet, the faint cinnamon smell of her perfume hit him in the stomach.

He checked to be sure the leather satchel was still here, the marked money from the FBI's aborted buy at the Mayflower. He'd left it here the last time they'd been together, knowing he could get at it anytime. How the hell could he have known she was going to kill herself a week later? He was lucky the cops hadn't found it.

Maybe there would be a way to wash the money while he was pinch-hitting Ricky's big deal. He hated to waste any genuine currency. If he wasn't coming back to Boston, he was less likely to get caught.

He kicked both bags as far back into the corner of the closet as they'd go, behind the jumble of shoes and shoe boxes. Woman had loved her footwear.

The vague ache he'd felt off and on since Alison died made a reappearance. He wasn't soft or sentimental enough to pretend it was love on either side, but the bitch could sing. And she'd been nicer to him than any woman he'd hung out with for that length of time. While it lasted, it had been good. All good.

Chapter 13

While I worked the bar that afternoon, I couldn't stop thinking about the fact that Alison had so much money and that I hadn't had a clue. It implied other things I didn't know about her, more important things than her net worth, and I didn't like that, either. The next morning, I started to earn my keep as executor.

At ten in the morning, it was easy finding a parking space in her neighborhood. I tucked the folder full of documentation from Markham under my arm and locked the Cougar. Although it was over sixty-five degrees, hardly anyone was out on the street. Everyone working the day shift, I suppose. I jogged up the granite stairs of her building two at a time, feeling strangely anxious.

The key was stiff in the outside lock, as if it had been cut and never used. As I was fumbling with it, a willowy young man with blue eyes and bright bleached hair cruised out, holding the door open for me. He smiled, but I didn't encourage him.

"Thanks."

I paused for a second in the foyer, the slow waves of memory rolling over me: the musty smell of the old wool carpet, the dim yellow sconces, converted from gas to electricity in the twenties, mounted high on the walls. The stairs and banisters and wainscoting were still that dark mahogany, the varnish rubbed dull with hands and feet. I climbed to the fourth floor and unlocked the door.

95

On the southeast corner of the building, Alison's apartment drowned in sunlight. I bolted the door behind me, unsurprised by the memories of some of the mornings we'd spent with papers and coffee and instrumental jazz in the background. She didn't like listening to singers—she was always judging, she said.

Things hadn't changed that much in the year or so since I'd been here. She certainly hadn't been using the money she'd accumulated to redecorate.

The living room held the same two overstuffed wheat-colored sofas and a half dozen of those prep school chairs with the black bodies, cherry arms, and gold seals from Harvard and Exeter on the backs. She had a friend who worked at the factory in Fitchburg who'd sold her some seconds. A huge plasma TV, DVD player, cable box, TiVo, and a stereo complex enough to direct a moon shot were the only new items. A film of dust shrouded them all.

I stepped across the polished hardwood floor of the hall to the master bedroom, scene of so much of the pleasure we'd had together. The door stuck when I opened it, triggering a memory of my being so drunk I could hardly stand, trying to carry her into the bedroom. She'd stuck her tongue in my ear at just the wrong time and we'd almost wound up on the floor.

The bedroom was bright with sun, too, the white chenille spread smooth as snow over the four poster bed. I used to tease her, a black girl from the projects, about her taste for furniture from an era of American history that included slaves, but she didn't do irony. All she'd said was that she'd wanted a bed like that ever since she was a little girl.

To hold off the flood of memories, I picked up a pad of paper and a ballpoint. *Movers*, I wrote. *Pack up music, books.* I tossed the pad on the bed. I'd hire someone to do all that. I might have been the executor, but I didn't think that carried any obligation to let my memories rub me raw.

I opened the walk-in closet and the scent from her dresses, her perfume, and her skin made my chest hurt. I stepped inside, wondering whether Goodwill had ever been so blessed as they were going to be with the gift of all the clothes she'd ever owned.

In the back of the closet, a leather strap peeked out. When I pulled on it, a black Coach briefcase surfaced out from under a pile of shoes. I kicked it free. It didn't look familiar and I wondered why she'd store it in the clothes closet. I carried it out and set it on the bed and unlatched it.

"Jesus Christ."

Tens of thousands of dollars, maybe hundreds, banded bricks of American currency in fifty- and hundred-dollar bills. My heart fell. There couldn't be any legal way for her to have come by this.

I dug back into the closet, and in the farthest corner, behind where the money had been, found a green plaid gym bag. If this was full of money, too, I was going to think seriously about closing the bar and moving to Switzerland. The vinyl trim was strangely cold to the touch as I unzipped the top.

This bag, though, was stuffed with drugs, hundreds of thick plastic reclosable bags of capsules and tablets, all colors and shapes and sizes. I recognized none of them, but that didn't mean much since pills were never my choice of intoxicant. Depressed, I zipped the bag shut and brought it out and tossed it on the bed next to the money.

This had to be the explanation for Alison's money, where her small fortune had come from. Interesting that she'd invested it, though—if the tax folks got wind of it, there'd be all kinds of trouble if she didn't have the income to support the investments. In fact, maybe trouble like that had caused her to kill herself. Maybe she was being investigated. I sat down on the edge of the bed, trying to take it in.

She had always appreciated the finer things. Maybe she'd gotten tired of waiting for her art to bring them to her. If she had been dealing, it was obviously wholesale quantities too, not like Delford Woodley down on the corner of Exeter Street.

Or maybe she had been murdered, for reasons having to do with the drug dealing. In any event, I had to take the bags to Burton. He'd know the right thing to do, though I had to wonder how the police had missed them the first time around.

The deadbolt on the apartment door clicked and the door opened. Whoever it was wasn't trying to be stealthy, but I shoved the bags under the bed anyway. I had every legal right to be in the apartment, but it would be inconvenient to try and explain to any official presence why I was holding drugs and money. I only needed a gun for the perfect trifecta. On impulse, I grabbed an umbrella with a solid wooden handle hanging behind the door.

"Alison?" A basso male voice called down the hallway. "Are you here, love?"

I shoved open the bedroom door and it bumped into the man, who dropped a bunch of red and white carnations and splattered drops of water all over the hardwood.

"Was there something I could help you with?" I said.

He was very cool, though he had to be surprised. He knelt and collected the scattered blooms.

"You are?" he said.

He stood up, his eyes a malachite green and their affect as flat as an animal's. He was a couple of inches taller than me, maybe six-three or four, and slender. His mother had probably told him every morning of his life to stand up straight, and he stood erect, though his narrow shoulders sloped down. His blonde hair was buzzed the way I'd seen men try to hide male pattern baldness, and he wore a knee-length black topcoat from which a triangle of white shirt and the knot of a sky-blue tie peeked. A brown Scollay cap, down-market beside the rest of his tailoring, dangled from his hand.

I looked out the window. It was still too sunny for a coat and hat, but I didn't start to dislike him intensely until I noticed a thick gold wedding band on the appropriate finger.

"A friend of Alison's," I said. "As I suppose you must be."

He nodded absently, looking around in a proprietary way. He was closer to forty than thirty and his features had a set to them, the way some people's faces get when they don't expect life to change them anymore.

"You don't happen to know where I could find her?" he said.

His reaction was all off—if he were her lover, he should have been demanding, at least, to know what I was doing there, who I was to her. I leaned the umbrella against the wall and gestured toward the living room. He followed me obediently, like a dog.

"I'm Elder Darrow."

He shifted his cap to the hand with the flowers and shook my hand.

"Cameron desRosiers. Why are you here again?"

This must be the most recent boyfriend, then, the one Susan Voisine had been talking about. There was no soft way to deliver the news, if he didn't know.

"I'm Alison's executor."

His knees sagged enough to wrinkle his trousers, but his steady gaze never broke from me.

"She finally did it," he said.

"Supposedly."

"You don't think so?"

"We were old friends," I said. "I'm having a hard time believing it."

DesRosiers unbuttoned his coat and sat on the arm of one of the couches, showing off an olive wool suit.

"I've been away at a conference," he said. "In Oslo. I'm a

psychiatrist."

Alison had stepped up a class in men, at least in professional terms. But my very next thought was about pills and how easily psychiatrists could acquire them.

"This happened almost a week ago," I said.

"No one thought to let me know," he said. "There weren't a lot of people who knew about us."

I glanced at his ring. "No doubt."

He flushed dark. His anger meant the loss was starting to penetrate. I thought I wanted him out of my sight before the full impact of Alison's death hit him.

"I'll be in touch," I said. "But I'll need to have your keys."

DesRosiers looked at me blankly.

"In touch."

"About the will," I said.

His name was on the list of beneficiaries, but I hoped he wouldn't ask me today what he was getting.

He pushed past me to the bedroom.

"I need to find something."

I followed, mainly to discover if it was the money or the pills that he was talking about. I wouldn't try and keep him from taking them, but I'd know what happened to them. And I'd have more information about whatever Alison had been doing.

In the bedroom, he went directly to the bedside table, opened the drawer, and slipped a small square box into his pocket. My view from the doorway was blocked, but it looked like a three-pack of condoms. I couldn't imagine why he'd be worried about that. When he opened the closet door, I stiffened. Maybe he was going after the bags. But he only ruffled his hand across the rack of dresses, closed his eyes, and inhaled deeply.

"That's enough," I said, but he ignored me. I wondered if my executorship was going to get physical.

"Mr. desRosiers."

"Doctor."

At least I had his attention.

"Did you prescribe antidepressants for Alison?"

"Of course not," he said. "That would be unethical. We were lovers, not doctor and patient."

"Never helped her out if she forgot to renew her prescription?"

He shook his head.

"The reason I ask is that her bloodstream was clear of drugs when she died."

His eyes darkened, but more like shock than surprise.

"Impossible," he said. "She was taking Effexor. You don't piss that stuff out overnight."

The sudden crudity made me wonder if he was trying to distract me.

"I worked in the Medical Examiner's office during med school," he said. "It isn't the most efficient operation in the state."

He closed the closet door as if finally getting ready to leave.

"I'll call you about any bequest," I said.

He reached inside his suit, took out a gold-chased case, and handed me a card.

"Please communicate through my clinic," he said. "I'm rarely found at home these days."

No wonder, if he dated jazz singers behind his wife's back. The address was on Hereford Street, though, which I thought was residential.

"You don't seem surprised to find Alison dead." I was irked by how quickly he'd recovered his equanimity.

"I'm not accustomed to expressing my emotions to strangers," he said. "So if there is anything else, please telephone."

"If you haven't heard from the police, I'd expect to," I said. "For a while, they were treating her death as murder."

Not technically true, but Burton might perpetuate the story if it helped him get some truth out of desRosiers.

Whose mouth cinched up.

"Your name again? Darrow?"

Then he stalked out the door.

I hustled back to the bedroom window and looked down into the alley. A figure in a brown Scollay cap got into an illegally parked Jaguar and drove off. I realized I hadn't retrieved his keys to the apartment.

I pulled the two bags out from under the bed and carried them out into the living room. Then I opened the top drawer of the file cabinet, but I'd lost my momentum. Another time for that.

I double-locked the apartment after me, though that didn't mean much if there were keys floating around out there. I didn't know what I had to suspect desRosiers of, but it seemed stupid to leave the pills and the money there.

Carrying them downstairs, I wondered whether this meant Alison had brought her own death on herself. The fact that she might have been murdered wasn't helpful—even the fact that she hadn't broken our pact wasn't much comfort. I couldn't think of one innocent reason for her to have so much money, so many drugs.

CHAPTER 14

Even for a Thursday night, which is traditionally the slowest of the week in the restaurant business, the Esposito was dead, and we closed up on the dot of one. Carlos hadn't shown himself in the last few days and Marina took a cab home, but it was warm out, almost spring-like, and I decided to walk.

I headed north on Mercy Street, then crossed over to Columbus Ave. toward my neighborhood. As I passed Kresge's doorway, a mound of rags next to a shopping cart shifted and moaned. I thought about Delford Woodley and hoped he was sleeping somewhere safe. Every year in this shoulder season, people on the street died of hypothermia, trying to push the boundaries. It could still get below freezing in April.

As I stepped onto the second-floor landing going up to my apartment, the security chain on Mrs. Rinaldi's door rattled.

"Mr. Darrow? Is that you?"

"At two in the morning?" I said. "I certainly hope so."

She opened the door wider and my smile dropped. She looked as if she had lost ten pounds and aged ten years since I'd seen her last Sunday. Her face was mottled, as if she were exhausted, and she shivered despite the thick flannel robe.

"Dorothea," I said. "What's wrong?"

"I'm a little fussed by something. Can you stop in for a minute?"

A little fussed. She was the kind of woman who wouldn't complain at gunpoint.

"Are you ill? Should I call someone?"

She made a sound that I interpreted to mean it was none of my business if she was and that she wouldn't tell me anyway.

"Tea?" she said once we were inside.

"Thanks." I didn't really want anything but my own bed but moving around the kitchen seemed to calm her down.

When she finally sat down, two mugs in front of us, her hands were trembling so badly I wanted to light a cigarette.

"I think someone's been in my apartment." She cupped both hands around her mug and breathed the steam.

I did my best to keep the building secure, but this was also a neighborhood junkies and muggers sometimes cruised for opportunities. And occasionally one of my forgetful tenants would leave the street door unlocked.

"What's missing?" The idea I had failed to protect her made me feel sick.

She pulled the lapels of the robe across her birdy chest. The tea had stopped her shivering and brought a little peach color to her cheeks.

"That's what I find strange," she said. "All my silver is still there, and all the bits of jewelry I haven't given away to my nieces. The only thing missing is my box of materials from the Opera."

"Your program notes?"

"Programs, my notes, photographs. Autographs. All the source material I'd amassed for my book."

I still believed her book was a dream and not a project, but that wasn't a reason for her to lose it all. I wondered if she'd misplaced it.

"You looked everywhere?"

She sliced me with a look.

"I haven't lost my mind yet, Mr. Darrow. And I'm disappointed you would think that way."

Then she dropped the bit of data than pulled it all together.

"And my port decanter is four inches low." She blushed. "I mark it so I don't drink too much at one time."

"You think Henri broke in?"

This was a more malignant act that peeking through the keyhole. Had Henri finally crossed the bar to senility?

"I pay you a good rent, you know." Her washed-out blue eyes sparked at me. "A little personal security isn't too much to ask."

"Of course it isn't," I said, realizing that somehow she'd found out I owned the building.

"I do appreciate what you do, but do you think Mr. Voisin is all there?"

Everything other than his mental capacity to play backgammon was in question, as far as I was concerned, but I didn't want to alarm her.

"I honestly don't know, Mrs. Rinaldi."

"Dorothea. Please."

"Dorothea. I guess I'm going to have to find out where his family is and talk with them."

"I'm not so sure he has any family left." She looked down at the scarred pine tabletop. "He certainly never speaks of anyone."

The lease papers filed with my lawyer listed a next of kin for every tenant. I knew Dorothea, for example, had a son who was a fishing guide on Florida's Nature Coast. I'd have to check Henri's lease.

"I'll look into it," I said, trying not to sigh. I hated talking to lawyers. They made everything more complicated, and expensive, than it had to be.

"And I'll change the lock first thing in the morning. Will you be all right until then?"

"You know," she said. "I can't be completely sure I didn't leave my front door unlocked."

I looked around her kitchen—the plastic crucifix over the

stove, the single knife, fork, plate, and tumbler in the dish strainer—and felt unspeakably sad. She was trying to make up for her crack about the rent, God love her. If she hadn't been such a buttoned-up woman, I might have hugged her.

"I'll be by about ten or ten-thirty."

The snap of her deadbolt mocked me as I climbed the stairs, wondering if I was going to have to evict Henri. Not that it mattered—I was still going to have to talk to the lawyers about him. Fucking lawyers. Regardless.

Against all expectations, I slept like an innocent man, from the time I went to bed until eight-thirty the following morning. It was a sleep, restful and dreamless, that I woke up wishing I knew how to repeat infinitely. The sun in my southeast window was rounder and warmer than even a week ago, proof the earth still turned. I wondered idly if I'd have time to see any Red Sox games this year.

It took me ten minutes to run to Ace Hardware for a new lock, and as I fitted it to Mrs. Rinaldi's door, I mulled over why the police hadn't put more effort into Alison's death in the first place. If they'd found the pills and the money back then, they wouldn't be starting a murder investigation from so far back. Because I knew if I passed the two bags off to Burton, he would push until the case was reopened. The police had to work within a system, but that discipline didn't do much for corner cases, mysterious deaths that weren't classified as murders.

Friday was the busiest night we'd had in months. Since Eric had packed the place the first time he played, I had made a deal with him to play every other Friday night until school got out in June. And I paid him a percentage of the receipts on top of his minimum, so if he continued to bring people in, he'd make more money. I also decided, without saying anything to Eric about why, that I'd pay him the money directly. I didn't think

Cy deserved a cut off this deal.

He started out the evening playing light bouncy tunes, some Rodgers and Hart and toned-down rock. Though they weren't my favorite things, I did have confidence in his musical sense and his ability to guide the Esposito's audience to the vibe I'd been after, an energetic and respectful attention to the music. People were eating and drinking and listening, and I never stopped moving.

We closed the kitchen at nine-thirty and Marina started helping me bus the tables. People started ordering drinks from her as if she were a waitress, which she didn't like, but most of them were polite, and a couple even tipped her. I laughed when I caught her counting out her money on the bar.

"We split the tips here, you know."

She curled her upper lip, an expression so much like Carmen that I laughed again. Her bruises were faded, the swellings down, and Carlos hadn't been around since he was arrested. I hoped it was a trend.

Cy dropped in around ten-thirty, dressed in baggy charcoal slacks, a white turtleneck, and a short black leather jacket. He dwarfed the two-top that he sat down at, and a steady trail of youngsters from the music school dropped by to say hello to him. He shook hands two-handed and smiled a lot, though he didn't invite anyone to sit down with him. At the break, he left his jacket on the chair, something no one could have done in the Esposito a couple of months ago, and walked to the bar.

"Boy's made some leaps," he said.

Eric eased into a chair next to the eternally pouting Lorelei, his girlfriend. The bop princess was stunning tonight, her face fresh as Sunday, her long chestnut hair shimmering in the blue-gray air. A cashmere sweater the color of clean cotton sheets did her upper body all kinds of justice. I felt a swift flash of pain for Alison, lost, and for all the time I'd wasted too.

"I believe I can read your mind," Cy said.

"I don't think so." I arranged four highball glasses on a tray. "But you're right. Eric is improving. How's your guitar player doing?"

Someone yelled for music, and I slipped in a Dave Frishberg CD.

Cy knit his brows together as if he didn't know what I was talking about, then pushed his glass across the bar.

"Much better," he said. "Her daddy came into town. It is scary how fast everybody else gets old."

"Couldn't tell you."

Sober, I had decided I wasn't going to worry about how long I'd live. I subscribed to Raymond Carver's theory, that every day after you survived that kind of headlong drinking was gravy.

The between-sets rush quickly backed up at the bar, five and six deep.

"Help me out back here for a while?" I said.

"I suppose I could."

Big as he was, Cy was agile. You wouldn't have thought there was room for two of us, especially one at six-foot six and three hundred pounds, but we managed not to run into each other until the hordes subsided.

I was breathing hard. Cy's only sign of effort was the darker ring of fabric around the edge of his turtleneck. I poured him a belt of Babancourt and pointed him toward his table.

"Check is in the mail," I said.

He wasn't ready to leave the bar, though Eric was making his way to the stage.

"I could certainly use the money," he said. "You know I've got a family the size of a small African country down there in Florida."

It felt like he was apologizing for something, maybe taking Eric's money the last time.

"And you still owe me ten bucks from Starbucks the other day," I said.

He sipped some of the rum.

"You decide to look into this Alison thing on your own?"

The question made me uneasy—why should he care?

"I'm making my peace with it. It's still hard for me to believe she did it to herself, but there's no proof otherwise."

"And the cops looked into it."

"Not that hard," I said. "They saw it as suicide and left it there. Why? You know something?"

"No reason," he said. "It's just that there's a time to move on from everything like that. Not let it eat at you."

The sentiment was too ordinary for the weight he was giving it. His dark brown eyes looked sad, as if he foresaw a future he didn't love. But before I could probe, he carried his rum back to the table.

Almost before he'd sat down, Lorelei ran up to him. Looping her hair back over her ears, she seemed to be posing as she asked something.

Cy shook his head. Her body language looked more like begging then, shifting from one black-slippered foot to the other as if she were offering to dance for what she wanted. But his answer stayed no, until she stuck out her lower lip and stalked back to her own table.

The piano meandered into a long formless intro as Eric stared worriedly down at her from the stage in the corner. The girl looked as brittle as frozen leaves and I would have been worrying about her every minute if she was mine, too.

The drink orders quit and people settled back in their seats and modulated their conversations. Eric's piano led us up a trail of classic Cole Porter tunes, though embellished with the spiky style that Eric was developing. I heard in his selection how he tried to build on the earlier stages of his act, carrying the audience to progressively more challenging places, musically speaking, but in a comfortable way. And like an idiot, I got engrossed in what he was doing and forgot that I owned the place.

All of us were balanced on the pinpoint of attention to what he was doing with "Night and Day," and there wasn't a whisper, even in the rests between the notes. That made it all the more jarring when he crashed to a stop.

Then a glass smashed on the floor. I looked over to where Lorelei sat and movement there flurried, but everyone was standing so I had to get up on tiptoes, then push myself up on the bar to see.

Lorelei was trying to twist free of Tommy Cormier's hand, which gripped her wrist tightly. I hadn't even seen the Indian come in.

"Cocksucker!" she shrieked.

He sat immobile, like a fisherman waiting for his catch to stop flopping so he could club it.

Eric jumped down off the stage and started to push his way between the tables and the spectators. I vaulted down from the bar, amazed that my knees didn't collapse, and arrived at the table one instant before him.

Tommy released Lorelei, who slumped back in her chair and rubbed her wrist. He stood up, staring at Eric, and balanced his weight on the balls of his feet. Flexing his fingers, he slipped off a chunky turquoise and silver ring and dropped it in his pants pocket.

"Eric. Stay there." I stepped between them.

It was the natural hesitation of the chronic noncombatant that saved Eric from serious damage. Cormier acted like a man who enjoyed a good fistfight and I didn't think Eric or I was a match for someone who'd fight for the pleasure in it. And Eric needed his hands.

Tommy rode an insolent look up and down Lorelei's body,

trying to provoke something. Eric grunted. The chest-beating would have been comical if it wasn't so clear to me how dangerous Cormier was.

"I've been looking for you," I said. "Let me buy you a drink."

"You're Darrow," Cormier said.

"At the bar." I pointed.

"You got any old Scotch?"

"Sure."

I started back across the floor, looking back to make sure he was following. I caught a glimpse of Cy heading up the stairs toward the street, which disappointed me. I would have had more backup from Delford Woodley.

I walked around the bar this time instead of climbing over it. People separated quickly to give Cormier space. I wished Eric would get back up on stage and start playing again, but he was lecturing Lorelei about something. Suddenly, she shook her head, whipping her hair back and forth, then bolted, the long staircase turning her escape into a drama no one could avoid.

Eric walked dejectedly back to the stage.

Tommy, who'd watched the drama in the mirror, smiled.

"Isn't she a little on the young side for you?" I reached down the Macallan bottle and poured him a shot, stifling the reflex to give myself one too.

His smile tightened. "And what would you know about my tastes?"

He picked up the glass and sipped the whiskey, not pounding it back as I would have expected. He appeared to be in his late thirties, with white even teeth against the sunlamp tan and a right-angled jaw. His skin was smooth as calfskin, except for a cluster of small straight scars high on the right cheek. He wore an ivory silk jacket over black pants and a denim shirt. If you ignored the deadness in his eyes, you might have thought he was handsome.

I tilted the bottle again and he pushed the glass underneath it.

"This stuff is ten bucks a shot, you know." I didn't want him to think I was buying him drinks.

"She's strictly business, Elder," he said. "But she is my business. *Comprende?*"

I didn't like the way my name sounded in his mouth. I pointed to the glass.

"You going to pay for those or not?"

He pulled a fifty out of his wallet, crumpled it on top of the bar. Eric had gotten partway back into his groove, though he was playing the blues now.

"Keep 'em coming. What was it you wanted to talk to me about?"

I left some headroom in the shot glass, not the way I would have poured them for myself.

"How well did you know Alison Somers?"

He didn't seem like Alison's type, what I knew of it, but who knew how she might have changed? For the most part, she avoided the macho poseurs, the violent type, and anyone in love with his own good looks, which would have knocked Cormier out on all three counts.

"The singer."

I nodded.

He squinted at me. "Fucked her once or twice. She was a much better singer."

I was still holding the Macallan bottle and my immediate impulse was to crack it across that aquiline nose. I breathed.

"She cut you loose, then."

I was gratified to see that anger him.

"We had a thing." He shrugged. "Small, but fun while it lasted."

And I saw from the way he tried to downplay it that he was

lying, that she had affected him. I didn't like having that in common with him.

"Was she depressed the last time you saw her? Down enough that she'd kill herself?"

"Because she cut me loose, you mean?" He grinned.

"Tell me about it."

"The last time I saw her. Three weeks ago? She was fine. She always transcended her moods, you know."

Was I the only one who knew the moods she couldn't transcend, then? DesRosiers hadn't seemed to think she was vulnerable, either.

I leaned the bottle again, but this time, he put his hand over the glass.

"She seemed as normal as anyone," he said. "What else can I tell you?"

Something in his self-satisfied way provoked me.

"You can tell me why you think you can come into my bar and cause trouble."

He smoothed out the crumpled bill on the bar top precisely.

"I don't generally let people give me too much shit," he said. "Especially bartenders. I'd say you're close to your limit."

"Lorelei's a baby. Where's the fun there?"

The hard smile returned. "Old enough to sit at the table, old enough to eat."

"Sounds like poor white trash talk."

He tapped the edge of the bill on the bar, let it fall.

"Stay cool, Elder. It's a mean old world out there."

As Cormier started up the stairs, Eric switched gears out of the blues into an old pop number, the Eagles' "Desperado." I wasn't sure Cormier would get the joke, but halfway up, he pointed his finger at Eric, grinned one final time, and made his exit.

I exhaled hard through my nose, feeling as if I had dodged a nasty wreck through no doing of my own. I didn't like the vulnerable sense Cormier left behind.

Finally, I cleared everyone out and got the lights turned up all the way. Eric sat at the bar, staring down into his glass and not saying anything. I could see it was bothering him that Lorelei hadn't come back.

I handed him his money. "You doing OK?"

He dragged on a cigarette and shrugged, tucking the folded bills into his shirt pocket.

I hoped for his sake he hadn't gotten too fixed on the idea that Lorelei was going to hang around with him forever. Certain women—the ones Cy liked to call the rabble-dabblers—always liked hanging around with artists and musicians for excitement, the night life. But a rabble-dabbler always knew that when push came to shove, she was going to commit herself to the doctor or the lawyer, that stable fellow who would buy her a six-bedroom house in Wellesley, father her healthy single-race children, and lease her a big old Chevy Suburban to protect her beauteous ass in the rush-hour traffic on the Southeast Expressway.

To me, Lorelei looked like the classic rabble-dabbler, and even if I couldn't keep Eric from being hurt, I felt as if I ought to warn him, if I could keep from coming off like his uncle. But when I looked up from the dishwasher, all that remained of Eric in the Esposito was a balled-up napkin and an empty glass.

I counted out the change bag for tomorrow, zipped it into a vinyl envelope, and locked the rest of the money in the big safe in back, next to the bags of pills and bills. I was going to have to call Burton about them pretty soon. Just holding all that contraband was making me nervous.

Marina sorted and counted her tips on the bar yet again, her lime green tank top flecked with drips and spills. Then she pushed a stack of bills and coins down the bar toward me.

"I was kidding," I said. "You earned them—keep it."

She frowned. I pointed to the mason jar on the bar.

"I have my own supply, remember? Besides, if that kind of night happens very often, I'll have to hire a waitress. Enjoy it while it's happening."

Her chin lifted and she fixed her stare on me, but it wasn't to argue.

"Can you give me a ride home?" she said.

"Sure." I was happy to have more evidence of Carlos's absence.

The last thing I did was double-check the chain around the fire-door handles and make sure the fryer and grill were turned off. As I clicked off the front-of-the-house lights, Marina stood at the top of the stairs by the door. Then the familiar diesel horn bleated, out in Mercy Street.

She started to open the door.

"Forget it," I called. "We'll go out the back."

She whirled, shame reddening her face in the glow from the Exit sign.

"He thinks it's all going to be the same." She touched her cheek. "Like he's going to walk right back in and everything's the same. He needs to understand."

"Then let me talk to him."

"It won't penetrate," she said. "You know what he's like. He'll just pretend he doesn't understand you."

"Marina. He beat you up once already."

"He hit me, once. And I'm not getting that close to him again. But he's not going to believe we're all done until I tell him face to face."

"You're not going to change who he is," I said.

I had a deep fear she was talking herself into giving him one more chance—I'd seen stupider things happen.

The horn blatted again. Her face was grave as midnight.

115

"Make sure he knows I'm driving you home," I said.

She opened the door and stepped out into the street. The engine stopped.

I shut off the rest of the lights and climbed the staircase, stood inside the door with a ball of worry lodged in my throat. I could hear Carlos's voice hiss, her sharp replies echoing in the empty street.

As she threw out a long phrase in Spanish, the truck restarted. Its door slammed and it rumbled off.

I counted sixty more seconds in my head, and when Marina didn't come back inside, I zipped up my coat, keyed the alarm, and stepped out on the sidewalk. As I'd feared, she wasn't there.

Light rain, not much more than mist, drifted through the air sparkling in the faint orange streetlights. The asphalt mottled with shiny patches as it fell.

I turned up the corduroy collar of my jacket and walked around the corner of the building, down the alley, depressed enough to wish that I had stuck my nose in, even if it meant getting it bent. The bulb over the door of the warehouse next door was burned out again.

Under the yellow security light at the Esposito's loading dock, Marina leaned against the Cougar, tears mixing with rain on her cheeks. The pressure in my throat eased slightly.

She looked up at me, her face wrenched.

"I am such an idiot," she said.

I opened my arms and she came inside and hugged me as if I were her only possible comfort.

"Not such an idiot you went with him," I said.

I drove her over to the South End. As we pulled up in front of the three-decker, Carmen opened the downstairs door and peered out. Apparently she was keeping a closer eye on her daughter after last weekend.

"I don't think I'll come in," I said. "You be OK?"

She glanced through the windshield at her mother framed in the yellow light, then pecked me on the cheek. That would double Carmen's questions. She climbed out of the Cougar.

"Thanks," she said. "I'll have to talk my way out of this one all on my own."

The smell of her—mint gum, garlic, the trace of old tobacco—hung in the car as I drove to my apartment. Out of the frying pan and into the fire. But at least it was her mother's fire. She'd made the only smart decision about Carlos.

CHAPTER 15

Tommy wished he had sprung for the matte black finish on the Navigator, or at least hadn't had the vehicle waxed and detailed this morning. Even three blocks back of Carlos's pickup, the Navigator reflected the street lights like tracers. He balanced his binoculars on top of the steering wheel and focused on the door to the Esposito.

That ugly broad that Carlos used to hang around with was standing there giving him hell. She must have been special in the rack because her face looked like a bad batch of bread dough, but it didn't look like sex was very high on Carlos's list of wishes right now. She looked mad enough to cut off his dick and stick it in his ear.

Then she screamed something at him and ran around the corner, up an alley. Carlos squealed his tires getting away from the curb and roared away, straight down the middle of the street. Tommy gave him a second, then put the Navigator in gear and followed.

He stayed a couple blocks back, wishing Carlos would get in his own lane and slow down. He'd always been a hothead, which was going to make it that much easier for Tommy to convince Ricky that Carlos had stolen the pills.

Carlos bounced one of the dualie tires off the curb and that slowed him down.

All of it had to happen tonight, though. Ricky and his pacemaker came home from the hospital tomorrow, and if

Tommy didn't have his story bulletproofed by then, he might as well shoot himself as kill Carlos.

He tracked the truck by the distinctive cut-out covers over the taillights. The two of them went left on Huntington Ave., then down toward the Museum of Fine Arts. He hung far enough back in the thinned-out traffic that Carlos wouldn't see the Navigator, though Tommy doubted the kid was thinking that clearly. When Carlos turned right beyond the Museum, Tommy guessed he might be heading to the Muddy River, down behind the Fenway, which was one of his favorite places to go and smoke pot.

Tommy pulled into a dead-end street and parked the Navigator with the nose pointed out and the tires cocked away from the curb—anticipation being the key to any kind of success. He closed the door and used the key to lock up instead of the electronic remote. As he started toward the Jersey barriers that sealed off the end of the street from the back of the Fenway, he racked the slide on his Glock as quietly as it could be done.

He'd known as soon as Carlos opened his mouth at Alison's apartment that he was going to have to take him out—the only alternative was to kill Ricky, and Tommy wasn't taking that road, regardless. Ricky had done things for him over the years, and you had to give loyalty where you could. Besides, he thought as he climbed over the concrete, Spengler and Tesar would hunt him down like a dog if he killed the fat fuck.

No, this was optimal, blaming the theft on an unfortunately dead Carlos. Tommy knew that it would be a difficult conversation with Ricky, but he knew he could convince the fat man that Carlos had died before giving up the location of the pills. That would give Tommy the time he needed to sell them quietly and pull his stake together before he hit the trail.

He stepped around a length of chain-link fence that just stood there, separating nothing from nothing. To his left was a broad expanse of undeveloped swampy land that fell away in a gentle slope to the road that ran along the bank of the river. The slick black water reflected the yellow lights from the apartment buildings on the farther shore.

As Tommy stood and watched, Carlos's truck pulled into one of the MDC's rest areas: a paved parking space, a streetlamp, and a trash can—all the comforts of home. He backed the big Dodge around and shut off the engine. The big blue-white headlights went out a few seconds later.

As if the darkness made them more comfortable, a clutch of bullfrogs started croaking, off to Tommy's right. He leaned against the side of the building, passing the time with his affirmations. He particularly focused on the one about being a rich man in a warm climate. He wanted Carlos to be as high as possible before he popped him—he'd be easier to deal with and it might soothe the kid's pain a little.

Then he had to pull back into the shadow as he heard a car moving fast down the access road Carlos had just used—a beige Taurus with a whip antenna that pulled in next to Carlos's truck.

Tommy frowned. Nobody but a cop drove something like that. He focused his binoculars, but the angle of the Taurus's window reflected the streetlight, making the glass opaque.

"Fuck."

He couldn't clip Carlos now, after he'd talked to a cop—it would narrow the time window for his alibi too much. He thought for a minute, then started to ease down the slope toward the shadowy line of trees along the edge of the rest area. Maybe Carlos was meeting with the cops because he was a snitch. That would make a better story for Ricky, especially if Tommy did pop him.

Be patient and observe, he said to himself as he found a big pine within twenty feet, close enough to hear the driver's-side door of the Taurus open. A familiar thick-shouldered man got out, and Tommy didn't need the binoculars to see it was that cop who hung out in Darrow's bar, standing under the orange-yellow light.

He frowned again. What the hell did this guy have to do with Carlos?

The cop yelled at Carlos's window, but he didn't pull a gun or flash his badge. This was clearly not an official visit.

Carlos flung open the truck door and jumped down, startling the cop back on his heels. Then he punched the cop three times in the face: bam, bam, bam. Cop fell flat on his ass.

Tommy chuckled. Carlos had flyweight speed—good to remember.

The cop scrambled to his feet, but Carlos already had a snubby .38 out and pointed at the cop's right eye. Good to know that Carlos carried, too.

"Ech," Tommy said. "Don't shoot him, you asshole. You're fucking up my plan."

The cop raised his palms, not so much in surrender as in acceptance of the situation. He didn't believe Carlos would shoot him. Either that or he was braver than he was smart.

Carlos spit on the ground near the cop's shoe and said something not quite intelligible. The cop scrambled to his feet, took the Taurus out of there.

Carlos mounted back up in the truck, and a match flared behind the smoked windows. He was going to huff on that pipe for a while before his adrenaline came down, and Tommy didn't have that much time to kill, especially if the cop came back with reinforcements.

But he uncocked the Glock and stuck it back in the holster, slipped off the big silver ring and put it in his pocket. Blaming it on the cop would make it a better story for Ricky, one he would be able to verify independently. All Tommy would have to do is get the first punch in, and watch out for the little shit's hands.

His loafers squished in the grass and his breathing concentrated. He'd always been lucky, though he liked to believe it had more to do with having a well-prepared mind. The next time he saw the cop, he'd have to thank him for sticking his nose in. He'd make Tommy's life a whole lot easier and the path out of Boston a whole lot quicker. Ricky would have no reason not to believe him now.

CHAPTER 16

I was late getting to the bar on Saturday morning, and when I didn't see Marina waiting outside, I started to worry. Someone had taped an eight-by-ten envelope to the door, and I took it down as I unlocked. Maybe she'd left a note.

As I walked down the stairs, I admired the order of my place, the chair legs all sticking up in the air, the clean sharp smell of the disinfectant. Assuming I could convince myself to spend any of Alison's money, the first thing I might buy was some new linoleum.

I brewed a pot of coffee and slipped Paul Desmond's "Skylark" into the CD player, just loud enough to hear. Then I stripped the cellophane off a fresh pack of cigarettes and looked at the envelope lying on the bar.

My name was block-lettered across the front, like something out of a kidnap movie, so I assumed Marina had not left it. The flap was sealed with a double layer of packing tape and I fished an old knife out of the junk drawer and slit it open, turned it over, and shook out a single photograph.

I turned it over and ice crawled up my spine. It was a grainy black and white enlargement of an original taken with a very long lens. Alison was walking out through the glass door in a brick storefront, carrying a small white bag that was folded over and stapled at the top. The gold script on the window past her shoulder read "Fenway Pharmacy," but I would have recognized the strange decrepit drugstore near her apartment without it. I used to buy the Sunday papers at the newsstand next door. She was smiling in a way that made my throat hurt.

And that was the extent of the secret message in the envelope—no cryptic note, no arrow inked at the location of the buried treasure, no secret microdot. If it was supposed to make me jump up out of my bathtub and run naked down Commonwealth Ave. shouting Eureka!, it wasn't doing its job. I wondered who'd taped it up on the door, and why.

I slipped it into the junk drawer, supposing I could use it to convince Burton there was something funky about the whole thing, but I couldn't see him getting too excited about it either.

Marina never did show up for work, which after the other night made me worry about her all over again. I hoped she hadn't run into Carlos one more time.

At three o'clock on a Saturday afternoon, the bar was as dead as the Sargasso Sea, a low-pressure zone before the Saturday night storm broke. I hoped I wasn't going to have to call Carmen again and get her all upset.

Thelonious Monk was zigzagging his way through "Salt Peanuts" when the street door swung open and a dark man stalked down the stairs. His arms looked too short for his torso, though that may have been because his massive biceps bowed them out to the sides. My two remaining midafternoon drinkers glanced up, then returned to the engrossing spectacle of golf on the tube.

I knew he was a cop before he opened his mouth. He was about five-eight, one-fifty, but the belligerent air he pushed in front of him like a pressure wave suggested it wouldn't be smart to judge him on size. He might not be big, but he would for damn sure wear you out.

His gray tweed jacket, old enough to have belonged to his father, pulled across his chest. He wore it over an expensive pair of charcoal wool slacks, a white shirt, and a yellow knit tie. His oversized feet were shod in black ankle boots, and he walked as if he were still breaking them in.

"I'm looking for Dan Burton," he said as he walked up to the bar.

It offended me somehow that he thought he could walk into the Esposito as a stranger and get information just like that.

"One of the reasons people like a neighborhood place," I said. "It gives them a little privacy."

He twitched his pale reddish mustache and then stretched out the fingers of both hands like a pianist warming up. The gesture made me think of Tommy Cormier. Cops and crooks—nobody else exudes that much self-confidence at the same time they expected to be hated.

"Are we alone here? Where's your cook?"

I guessed he didn't think the two golf fans at the bar counted. When he mentioned Marina, my head came up.

"Why? Did something happen to her?"

"Interesting reaction," he said. "Maybe even guilty."

I'd been tired of his bullshit before he even spoke. I pointed at the sign over the kitchen doorway.

"This is a bar, not an information center. I can serve you a drink or I can ask you to leave."

I was pushing a little to see if he wanted to identify himself as a cop or if he were flying low. He brought out a trucker's oversized wallet from his back pocket and removed a ten-dollar bill.

"Tonic and lime."

I filled a glass with ice, charged it from the gun, and added a slice of lime.

"Maybe I should start over," he said, reaching his hand over the bar. I took it briefly.

"I'm Thomas Costain, with the Boston Police."

He'd only half-surprised me.

"Elder Darrow, though I assume you knew that."

"You're a friend of Burton's, which is why I'm here."

"I have met the man."

Costain pulled the lime off its plastic sword and squeezed. "I need to talk to him. He hasn't been in to work in a while."

I wondered if that had anything to do with Marina not being in to work for a while, either.

"Doesn't he work for you?" I said.

He sipped the drink as if he wished it were gin, but I had to be careful with my assumptions. Sometimes I thought I saw problem drinkers everywhere.

"How about we quit the bullshit?" Costain said. "This is a murder case. I could haul your ass right out of here and the ACLU itself wouldn't give me any shit."

I frowned. Had he somehow decided on his own that Alison had been murdered? I didn't think Burton had floated that idea explicitly with his superiors.

"Murder?" I said.

Costain flipped open a black leather notebook. "Your cook's name is Spinelli?"

All of a sudden I couldn't get enough air in my lungs. Burton would do more than freak if Carlos had killed Marina—he'd go nuclear.

The street door swung open and banged against the inside wall. I looked up and my knees almost gave—the woman in question was running down the stairs.

"Elder. I'm so sorry. I tried to call you. Carmen had a stroke last night—we've been at the hospital."

She came in around behind the bar and took off her coat. I grabbed her hands, which were icy.

"You don't have to be here," I said. "Is she OK?"

"Too soon to tell. We've been at the hospital since two."

Costain cleared his throat.

"Ms. Spinelli? I'm Captain Tom Costain, of the police department? Were you acquainted with a Carlos Tinto?"

She leaned an arm on the bar—the verb tense told us everything.

"Yes."

"When did you see him last?"

"This morning. Around one."

"The two of you were dating?"

"He was my fiancé," she said. "Two years. We were going to get married."

I wondered if the plan held after their conversation last night or whether she was being cagey.

" 'Were'?" Costain had picked up on it too.

"Until a few days ago."

I didn't want her telling Costain that Carlos had beaten her.

"Don't you have to warn someone before you interrogate them?"

"A barroom lawyer?" He shot me a sour look. "Mr. Tinto was found over in the Fens this morning. Beaten to a pulp."

Marina gagged, then walked toward the restroom.

"Very slick," I said. If I ever had the chance, he'd pay for that.

"So you can see why I'm looking for Burton," Costain said.

"Not exactly."

He hunched forward on the bar, forearms crawling out of the tweed jacket's sleeves.

"I know the two of them had a history," he said. "Burton asked one of his Narco buddies yesterday where this Tinto hung out."

"Really."

"I need to hear his story," Costain said. "I can't afford to lose him."

I shrugged.

"Darrow—I'm trying to help here. Unofficially. I'm not sup-posed to be out on the street."

But Burton hadn't trusted him, which was good enough for me.

"Wish I could help," I said.

"He's a good cop."

"He is a good cop," I said. "Maybe all the more reason to let him do his job."

Costain's color beefed up.

"Is that why you're being a prick? He told me you had problems with the Somers woman's case. This is something big-ger. Huge, in fact."

Burton didn't consider any crime more serious than life-taking. And Costain was management, an administrator. He'd mean huge in the bureaucrat's way: public busts, splashy headlines, lots of career juice.

"Haven't seen him in weeks," I said.

Marina walked out of the ladies' room, dabbing at a spot on her red blouse with a paper towel. Marina had clearly been otherwise occupied when Carlos died, though I wouldn't have been human if I hadn't thought Carmen's stroke was well timed. None of which meant Burton couldn't have done it.

Costain slid a business card on the bar.

"When you see him, have him call me. It's critical I talk to him. I'm trying to help."

I wondered how Costain had risen so high in the ranks of the PD without learning to lie any better than that. Maybe he didn't think he needed to use his best stuff on civilians.

The door at the top of the stairs sighed shut behind him. I tore the card in two and dropped the pieces in the trash.

Even after Costain had gone, Marina only came out of the kitchen once all night, to hang up the chalkboard with the night's specials on it. Her face was drawn and stony, and I hoped she wasn't feeling responsible for Carlos's death. Just because she'd dumped him didn't mean she had anything to do with his getting killed. His own decisions had done that.

There was only about an hour or so until closing and there were a few parties left drinking, but they were mellow and not so numerous that we wouldn't be able to close up on time. I was hanging clean wineglasses upside down in the rack above the bar and bobbing my head to Doc Severinsen's big band as they blasted through "St. Louis Blues." The Doc's cool quotient would be forever impaired by his long-term gig with *The Tonight Show,* but you could not dismiss his chops as a trumpeter or as a bandleader. It would be like saying Stephen King was a lousy writer because he was so popular.

As I wiped up the bar, Susan Voisine appeared in the upstairs doorway wearing a white ribbed turtleneck and a black leather miniskirt with a matching blazer draped over her shoulders. Her legs were so short she had to make a little hop to get down from one stair to the next, but somehow she made it look graceful.

A soft sigh seemed to emanate from the males along the bar as she safely reached bottom. She carried a red-handled Bean's bag with three or four boxes inside. Her makeup was on the pale side except for her lipstick, which was red as a valentine.

Her proportions were so perfect, you forgot how small she was until she stood right next to someone. Maybe that was why she didn't like to go out too much. She climbed primly onto a bar stool, ignoring the pasty-faced beer drinker in the crushable tweed hat who was staring at her legs, and set a small blue evening purse covered with glass beads on the bar.

"Susan," I said, as if she came in here every night. "What can I get you?"

She pulled the leather blazer around her shoulders, though

the air conditioning wasn't on that high.

"Can you make a Cape Codder?"

Pouring cranberry juice into vodka didn't tax my mixological skills. I set the drink in front of her on a coaster.

She tasted, needing both hands to hold the glass, then set it down to open her evening bag and remove a French-blue pack of cigarettes.

"I'm sorry," I said. "You can't smoke in here. Anywhere in public anymore."

The ordinance was a year-and-a-half old—could it really be that long since she'd been out to a bar or a restaurant?

She pouted. "I thought you owned the place."

"Majority rules."

"Well isn't that precious?" She held the pack. "I guess you can tell I haven't been out much."

She snapped the evening bag shut. "Janis Joplin once owned this bag."

"Very elegant," I said.

"Not Janis."

"I wouldn't call her elegant, no. But she had a voice."

"Like Alison."

I hoped we weren't getting into the same loopy kind of conversation we'd been having at her house.

"It's the last major piece I own," she said. "I've decided to get out of that business."

"I'm sure you'll do fine," I said. "Whatever you do."

"I'm leaving Boston, too. For Oregon."

I was surprised to feel a wisp of disappointment.

"Long way," I said. "Business problems?"

"Just time for a change. I'm not leaving for a month or so, though."

And then I thought I realized why she'd come to the bar, although it was always possible my ego was ahead of my reason.

"And that will give us a little time to get to know each other," I said.

She beckoned me closer, close enough that I could smell her scent, ginger and cloves.

"Thinking small can be a virtue," she said.

Something about her saying that seemed contrived, but I took the promise at face value. The rest of the hour until closing went about as fast as a high school calculus class. Once everyone was up and out the door, I told Marina I'd finish cleaning up and kicked her out the door so she could take a cab down to Mass General. I wanted to say something to comfort her, over Carmen and over Carlos, but the words weren't there for me, at least none that didn't sound lame.

I finished up in the kitchen, yanked on the fire doors to be sure they were secure, and when I turned around, Susan was right in my way, her face turned up, her blue-green eyes staring at me, the parted red lips an open target.

I bent over to kiss her and her mouth pushed up into mine, soft and labile, hot. The sensations spun me toward oblivion, and by the time I broke the contact to breathe, my neck was cramping.

I stretched my head to the left and right to make the cartilage pop. She grinned at me, her breathing noticeable, and pushed me back toward the counter with her small but solid body.

"Can I assume that there's something softer than a butcher block at your place?" she said. "Or do we just go crazy here?"

I nodded, not sure which question I was answering, but ready to leave.

"Let's go."

I followed her up the stairs, watching the leather miniskirt, and bolted the door behind me. But when we turned down the alley toward where I kept my car, all my fine anticipation just evaporated.

Burton leaned against the brick wall, just beyond the range of the streetlight, a square white bandage pasted to his forehead.

"Whoa . . ." I pushed past Susan, who stood there unmoving like a parking meter, her hand over her mouth.

Burton tried to stand up straight, then stumbled and caught himself on the wall. His face was the color of wet concrete, his freckles a sickly tangerine against the skin. Blood had seeped from under the gauze and dried to a crusty edge in his eyebrow.

"What the hell?" I looked around. "Susan?" She'd disappeared.

I got a shoulder under Burton's armpit and stagger-danced him down the alley to where the Cougar was parked. He was heavy as a bag of wet sand, and about as much help walking.

Once I unlocked the car, he sat in the passenger's seat, breathing hard. The knees of his khaki slacks were shredded and the blue cotton pinpoint shirt was sweated through and stained with oily black dirt and blood. The cleanest thing on him was the bandage and that was grimy, too.

"Where we going?" he said, trying to sit up straight and clutching his ribs.

"I'm thinking the emergency room," I said.

"Been there, done that."

"What happened?"

"I got one lick in, at least, then he sucker-punched me. Intern said to stay awake, in case there's a concussion." He pressed the bandage lightly against his forehead. "But it's dry now—I'm not going to bleed to death."

I wasn't going to press him on who he'd been fighting with, but if it was who I thought it was, he was going to have some problems.

We crossed Tremont Street, heading for the Expressway.

"You want me to take you home?"

Something dark flashed across Burton's face. Fear?

"Can I stay at your place?"

"Sure. I don't know how long I can stay awake, though."

I parked the Cougar in front of my building, in the space I reserved with my personal no-parking sign. When I opened the passenger door, Burton started to fall out sideways, as if he'd passed out. I reached down to brace him, and his eyes rolled wide and white. He shook himself awake, pinching my hand in the door frame.

"Jesus, Burton!" I yanked my wrist free and shook it.

It was dark in the foyer. Mrs. Rinaldi must have been at the light bulbs here, too. I half-shoved Burton up the stairs from behind, the banister creaking under our combined weight. Susan's scent rose up off my shirt and I wondered again why she had run away so quickly.

Burton fell into a chair by the window, sweating and puffing. I brought him a wet washcloth.

"Whiskey," he mumbled as he wiped his face.

"For concussion? I don't think so."

"I don't want to die sober," he said, without an ounce of humor.

"I don't own any booze. And you're not going to die."

He took a deep breath and gestured at the bandage.

"I ran into Carlos Tinto last night."

"While he was still alive?"

That stopped him in his tracks. He stood up and wavered, grabbed the back of the chair.

"You're shitting me. Are you sure you don't have anything to drink? Maybe we could have a toast."

"Don't even joke about that," I said. "What about Carlos?"

"He suckered me. Almost broke his hand on my head, the stupid fuck. I did hit him one good shot, though."

"He was alive when you left?"

"Kneeling next to a trash can, calling my mother names in

Spanish. I didn't kill him, though."

I believed that. Burton ran hot, but he didn't burn long.

"I know you didn't," I said. "I'll get you a blanket. I've got to get some sleep."

"You're not going to stay up and keep me from falling asleep? I might die from a concussion."

"I'll make you a pot of coffee."

I headed for the kitchen. If Burton had survived this much of the night, he'd make it through. I wasn't going to ruin my back and deprive myself of sleep out of some misguided sense of solidarity.

Somewhere around five in the morning, I awoke with a black sense of doom. When I looked out into the living room, though, Burton was fine. He was listening to music through headphones and reading an old copy of *Downbeat*. I almost said something, then saw that his cheeks were wet with tears.

When I crawled out of bed later on in the morning, he was gone. A sticky note taped to the dirty coffee mug on the counter said: "Thanks." A man of few words and a slob to boot.

I wished he'd told me where he was going and what he was going to do. If he got into trouble over Carlos, he wouldn't be able to help with an idea I had, about looking into Alison's death a little more closely. And I hadn't had a chance to tell him about the pills and the money, or about the fact that Costain was looking for him.

I ground some French roast and waited for the water to boil, wondering why Susan had come to the Esposito only to run off so quickly. The second she'd seen it was Burton, she'd bolted.

I fitted the plunger onto the top of the French press. And why would she quit her business if it had been profitable for her up to now? And move to Oregon? Was she under some kind of threat?

Watching the traffic ebb and flow on Commonwealth Ave., I

sipped my coffee. The ugly leaden sky did nothing to help clear up my confusion, and as morning unspooled into a long slow Sunday afternoon, I chewed over all the questions I couldn't answer.

Finally, around seven, I went out to get some dinner. I knew if I didn't let go for a while, I might be tempted to start answering my questions with Scotch.

CHAPTER 17

The heel of Tommy's cowboy boot skidded in a patch of dogshit as he turned the corner toward Ricky's luncheonette. He scraped it off on the curb, expecting to see the "Closed for Family Illness" sign taped in the front window. But the glass door was propped open with a wooden wedge and Tesar, skinny as a greyhound, a black stocking cap pulled down over his ears, was sweeping dirt out across the sidewalk into the street.

Tommy's gut twisted. He hadn't finished his second cup of tea this morning, but he didn't know what was cause and what was effect. As nervous as he was suddenly, he knew it was better to confront the situation than let things drag. Especially around Ricky, avoiding challenges didn't get you any closer to your goals.

He pinched Tesar playfully on the bicep, right above the scrolled tattoo that read "Mona."

Tesar bared his gray-green teeth and pretended to swat at him with the broom. He was queer as a grape and lusted mightily for Tommy, and more than once Tommy had thought that if it all went to shit, Tesar might cut him a break. Spengler, for sure, would not. In a million years.

"Ricky!"

He opened his arms wide as he walked into the restaurant, as if he might ever actually touch the fat bastard.

"I have to say you look a hell of a lot better than you did last week."

Which was purest bullshit. Old Icky Ricky looked older and ickier than ever. He'd dropped at least fifteen pounds, and the folds in his face and neck made him look like one of those Chinese dogs. His cheeks were rose-colored, as if he had been trying out coffin makeup, and the bags under his eyes were like baby eggplants.

"Stupid fucking Comanche," he growled back at Tommy.

Tommy wasn't picky about which tribe people connected him to, but the fact that Ricky knew full well he was an Apache made it more of an insult. He stopped next to the four-top by the door. Six customers were eating breakfast at a table in the far back corner, too involved in their eggs and whatever to pay any attention to what was going on.

"I'm an Apache, Rick. You know that." Tommy looked around. "Where's Spengs?"

Ricky gestured him in toward the counter with a pudgy hand and came around to sit next to him on a stool. Tommy nodded at the new kid at the grille, who wore an apron down to his shoe tops, like an old Italian waiter.

"Don't fuck with me, Tommy. I'm a very sick man. And now I find out, and not from you, I might add, that you've gone and lost my pills."

Tommy found himself hoping they'd put a bombproof pacemaker in Ricky's chest, because it was about to get a workout.

"I can tell you the story," he said. "But not if you've already made up your mind."

Ricky measured four sugars into his coffee mug, the chink of the spoon a slow sad bell. He withdrew it and pointed the bowl at Tommy.

"What?"

Tommy took a breath.

"Carlos Tinto. Carlos ripped them off."

"Carlos wasn't smart enough for that. How did he know you even had them?"

"He must have followed me to where I stashed them." Half-true, since he'd been at Alison's. Ricky wouldn't require forensic evidence, though.

"I do not believe that you are stupid enough for Carlos fucking Tinto to get over on you, Thomas." Ricky shook his head sadly. "I just do not believe it."

Tommy, who hated to be called by his full Christian name, controlled his urge to hit Ricky. After warming up on Carlos last night, he had realized the physical aspect of his work was something he missed. Management wasn't everything it was supposed to be.

But it was too late to change the story. You couldn't ride two horses with one ass, as his grandfather used to say. He circled his mug on the countertop.

"Rick. What can I say to you? I thought he was part of your family. One of us. You know?"

Ricky stared at him. Panic flashed through Tommy, which he tried to quell with a quick visualization: Hawaii, palm trees, monk seals sleeping on a white sand beach.

"And Carlos just happens to be dead," Ricky said. "Which makes him unable to confirm or deny your story."

"Ricky. He was beating up hapless niggers—that guy who sold bennies to a truck driver? Carlos was a liability."

Ricky stared at the vintage Coca-Cola sign over the commercial-sized toaster.

"You did him?"

Tommy shook his head.

"They think one of the cops, actually. Carlos was apparently popping his girlfriend."

Close enough, if not entirely accurate. As Ricky had so astutely pointed out, Carlos wasn't around to contradict it.

Ricky rolled his egg head from side to side.

"You're saying this was a coincidence? Carlos steals my pills from you, then conveniently gets himself killed before you can get them back? That kind of shit makes my ass itch."

Tommy spread his hands.

"Ricky. I'm here, right? I'm taking full responsibility. I'll get them back for you."

"How you going to do that?"

"You told me about this big deal you have going. What is it?"

Ricky jumped off his stool with a butter knife in his fist, pointed at Tommy's balls.

"Where'd you hear that?" His eyes were wide and white and Tommy hoped Ricky's heart would hold out a little longer. "Tell me what the fuck you're talking about."

Ricky clearly didn't remember what he'd said in the hospital.

"You told me in the hospital, Rick. We shut down the street because you had this big deal going, you didn't want the cops watching you." Tommy took a small push to see which way Ricky would go. "Don't you need me to work it for you? That's what you said."

Ricky sat back down and put the knife on the counter.

"I'm not a fucking invalid," he said.

"Whatever. You seem a little under the weather to me, but I'll do whatever you want."

"Goddamn right."

Ricky nodded at the kid, who topped up his mug and Tommy's too, spilling coffee on the counter.

Tommy tossed a napkin over the puddle and the kid stared at him—no fear at all. Was Tommy looking at his replacement?

"Sorry," Ricky said. "He doesn't know you don't like my coffee."

Maybe the kid was the answer to whether Ricky trusted him anymore. One horse, he reminded himself.

Ricky laughed and slapped him on the back.

"OK. This thing with Carlos, it's unfortunate. You didn't use the best of judgment. But maybe it's my fault—I haven't given you that many chances to step up. You make this deal work for me, and maybe I'll take my retirement, move down to Miami Beach, and leave you the guys. What do you think?"

Tommy held in his smile. It was far too late to tempt him with running the organization, but Ricky didn't know that. And he'd be happy to take Ricky's money. He manufactured the enthusiasm he knew his boss was looking for.

"Aces, Rick. You know I'll do the right thing by you."

"One comment?" Ricky swiveled on the stool so Tommy had to face him, smell his musty breath. "This 'nigger' stuff? You want to lose it. We have to work with all kinds, and everybody has prejudices. Don't make it so easy for people to know what yours are."

Tommy shrugged. For once, he was right.

"No problem, Rick."

"For example, I better not hear you've been calling me a guinea behind my back."

Challenge flavored the words and Tommy intuited this was a time to show strength.

"Is it all right if I call you one to your face?" he said. "A fat fucking guinea?"

Ricky looked stunned, then roared with laughter. Tommy stood up.

"I've got to go, Rick. If we're done?"

Ricky nodded, a smile still wrinkling his cheeks.

"Be good."

Tommy headed for the door, his exultation building. He'd achieved ninety percent of his goal here—a tad more patience on Ricky's part, a little more luck, and he was home free.

Donnie Spengler turned into the doorway. Tommy side-stepped him and smiled.

"Top of the morning, Spengs."

He was feeling good enough to pinch Spengler's bicep, too, the way he had Tesar's, but there was no sense in pressing his luck that way.

CHAPTER 18

Apparently taping envelopes to the front door of my bar was easier than using the telephone. When I arrived at work on Monday morning, I found another note in an unfamiliar script that said Marina wouldn't be back to work until Wednesday. She was arranging the funeral, since all of Carlos's family lived in Puerto Rico. I considered chipping in some money, but decided I wasn't that big a hypocrite.

I was eating an almond croissant and drinking my cappuccino, all by myself, when Susan appeared at the top of the stairs. I hadn't noticed the door open, but in the corner of my eye, I picked up on her hippety-hop movement down the stairs. She'd left the glamour at home this morning—she wore loose black Levis with the cuffs rolled up, white Keds, a black T-shirt and a red fleece jacket.

I'd spent a good part of a long slow Sunday afternoon thinking about her and whether I wanted to pursue the possibility she offered. It had been a while since any woman interested me and at first I'd thought it was only novelty, her size and the delicate beauty. But underneath those I saw intelligence and humor, and an ability to take care of herself, which made her more attractive. I just wasn't sure how honest she was.

She walked up to the bar with her hands stuck in the back pockets of her jeans like a farmer.

"Morning."

"Get you something?" I looked out over her head.

"Oh, poo."

She yanked the newspaper off the bar, almost spilling my coffee. I suppressed an immature reaction to grab it right back.

"Are you truly angry?" she demanded. "Or just trying to punish me for taking off?"

"I like to be able to count on my friends."

"So we are friends?"

"I thought we were headed in that direction."

"The only thing you and I were headed for on Saturday night was fucking each other's brains out. Correct? So how about a drink?"

It was barely eleven in the morning, but I wasn't her father. She didn't seem like someone who took advice well anyway. I mixed her a Cape Codder, wincing at the urinous smell of the cranberry juice so early in the morning.

"Three and a quarter," I said. "So, we were going to fuck our brains out? What happened?"

She removed the red plastic straw and sipped from the glass, two-handed.

"What happened was I recognized your friend."

"And?"

"The last time I saw him, he was frothing at the mouth and threatening to arrest me. Forgive me for not wanting to hang around for more of that."

Could she have missed the fact that Burton had been beaten or was she just being disingenuous?

"I didn't think you scared that easily," I said.

"Well, I do."

Irritated, I walked down the bar and changed the music over to Mel Tormé.

"At Alison's apartment," she called. "When I was looking for things to sell? That scared the crap out of me, that I'd steal from a dead person."

"That's not Burton's fault."

"I know that. But I was scared and he just scared me more."

"He wasn't in any condition to scare anyone the other night."

"Some of it was left over," she said. "He's very convincing."

"You could quit stealing from people."

"Didn't I just say I had?"

I put my hands on the bar in front of her and raised my eyebrows.

She placed her glass down on the coaster precisely.

"Did you ever collect anything?" she said.

"Stamps. I gave it up in junior high."

"You liked it, though. Maybe owning something no one else in the world had?"

"Tell me again where you know Cy Nance from."

The question didn't divert her at all.

"Around. I used to bar-hop a lot more than I do now. I knew a lot of people in the scene back then."

I got the distinct impression the question made her uneasy.

"The jazz scene," I said.

"Cy did me some favors."

I pointed at her empty glass, not sure I wanted to know if the favors were personal or professional.

She shook her head.

"I have an appointment. I just wanted to make sure you weren't too angry."

"I was. I mean, I am. Still."

"Not terminally, though." She smiled. "Because you did promise me something you didn't quite deliver."

The possibility of a rematch didn't bring me to an immediate boil, but I wasn't indifferent to the idea.

"We could go out on an actual date," I said. "I could close the bar for a night."

"I don't play games," she said. "Next Sunday is the first time

I have free."

She slid off the stool, her chin barely clearing the bar top as she looked back. She strolled across the black-and-white linoleum as if she knew I were watching. Which, of course, I was.

I felt like I was balanced on the edge before a free fall, a sensation I remembered from ski-jumping in prep school. I'd also feel the same way just before I downed my next drink, the one that would sail me all the way out of sobriety.

She turned at the top of the stairs and leaned on the railing. "What about it?"

"I don't know," I said. "Can you cook?"

Her laughter silvered down through the shadows, then she left me alone to wrestle with my anticipation. She still owed me for her drink, but I thought I'd let that go, in the interest of future relations. One kind or another. As I cleared away her glass and wiped the bar down, though, I did wonder what it was she didn't want me to know about her and Cy Nance.

Burton was suspended from duty while the BPD's version of Internal Affairs investigated whether he had beaten Carlos Tinto to death. At first, the break in routine seemed to do him good—he spent a lot of time in the Esposito, reading the newspapers, listening to music, and dreaming up obscure bits of jazz trivia to stump me with. He drank only beer, and then only in the late afternoons.

But all his open murder cases were put on hold while the bureaucracy ground itself fine, and I knew it bothered him that no progress was being made. Too, it must have felt insulting to be treated like one of the criminals he'd spent his professional life calling to account. By Friday afternoon of that week, he was as ugly-tempered as I'd seen him, and he was sinking a shot of rye whiskey with every second or third beer.

The drinking and the bad temper didn't do his relationship with Marina any good, either—she seemed to have accepted the BPD's notion that he might have killed Carlos. They went out of their way to keep from speaking with each other, which made me about as comfortable as a cat on a hotplate. But I didn't think business was so good yet that I could afford to fire a paying customer.

Burton knocked the bottom of his empty shot glass on the bar, a sound I was coming to loathe. I was starting to feel like I was his priest, not that he was confessing anything to me.

As I poured him one more shot of Jameson, I considered cutting him off. He'd been sitting on the same stool since lunch and it was almost five p.m. Eric would be coming in soon to set up for the band, and once we got into the evening crowd, I didn't think I wanted a sodden cop in a nasty mood taking up a seat in my nice civilized jazz bar.

He pointed at the niche up behind the bar, where the whiskey in Alison's glass had evaporated some more. I topped it off from the Macallan bottle.

"Waste of good hooch," he said. "Let me take another look at that journal of hers."

"Give it a rest, will you?"

Over the past couple days, we had chewed over every possible fact, fancy, and combination of theory about Carlos Tinto's murder, Alison's death, Tommy Cormier, Delford Woodley's mugging, everything even slightly odd that had happened in the last week. We still couldn't find a thread that bound them together.

And I didn't want to bring the drugs and pills I'd found in Alison's apartment into it yet, to protect him. The Internal Affairs cops would likely grasp any club they could find to ding him with, and having any knowledge of illicit pills and large untraceable amounts of cash wouldn't help his situation at all.

"You're giving up on that idea?" he said. "You were pretty sure about the fact she was killed for a while there."

I hadn't given up on the idea, but I couldn't explain a motive without the evidence I wasn't talking about.

"Believe me," I said. "I've been through the journal a dozen times. There's nothing there."

His brain seemed to spin like the Tasmanian Devil in the cartoon—I wondered if some of his craziness wasn't a function of the fact that he had no place to use all of his considerable energy.

"Gimmee," he demanded.

"What the hell do you think you'll see that I didn't?"

"You said you got that picture in the mail, right?"

"I showed it to you already. We have to go through this whole thing again?"

"Understand," he said. "The process is a pain in the ass. It's like reading the same book a hundred times, wondering what you missed. But maybe on the next time through, you see something you didn't see before. I got an idea."

I dug the manila envelope out of the junk drawer. Burton slid the picture out, then popped his forefinger on the surface.

"There. See it?"

I didn't. "What? The turkey?"

"Means it was right before Thanksgiving."

"I think your concussion just kicked in," I said.

"This drugstore is two blocks up the street from Ricky Maldonado's coffee shop and late November is right about the time the FBI ran that phony buy that one of his guys screwed up."

I didn't know any more about Icky Ricky than what I read in the newspapers. Maldonado was supposed to be a minor crime boss, unaffiliated with any of the established families, though they apparently had some kind of agreement that let him operate. One of his more endearing habits was apparently to insult unsuspecting customers at his lunch counter. The place, which was only open for breakfast, averaged one messy fistfight a week. A *Globe* columnist once opined in print that Ricky couldn't be a mobster since he acted like such a crazy man, but Burton must have told me a hundred stories that proved real crooks were stupider than the average of the population.

"What's he, a drug dealer?"

I wondered if there was a connection.

"Wholesaler, maybe," Burton said. "The Feds claimed he ripped off their task force for four hundred grand in marked money, not that that got them any sympathy. They supposedly had Ricky trapped in the old Washington Irving School in Roslindale, but when the smoke cleared, the FBI was holding a bag full of sand-filled capsules and the buy money was gone."

"Not a bad payday." I was thinking of the money in my safe—had it come from that escapade? But if so, how was Alison connected?

Burton shook his head.

"Money's marked, remember? First time someone spends dollar one, the Feds are on him like white on rice."

"So Maldonado owns the drugstore?" I tapped the photo.

"Wouldn't that be neat?" Burton said. "There might not be any connection at all, but it's easy enough to find out."

"Don't do it on my account."

I didn't want him to get himself in more trouble while he was supposed to be sitting behind a desk.

He sipped whiskey.

"There always has been something I didn't like about this case."

"That's not what you said two weeks ago. You're telling me I was right all along?"

"Don't get hot about it. Suspicion don't mean shit without

some evidence." He picked up the picture. "This could be evidence."

"You're supposed to be on leave," I said. "And your buddy Costain is probably looking for an excuse to bag you."

Burton shrugged and finished the shot.

"If he can put me in the bag, I deserve to be there."

"You do know what John Maynard Keynes said before he died?"

"Who he?" He stood up, wavered.

"The economist. On his deathbed, he said, 'I should have drunk more champagne.' "

"Fuck are you talking about?" Burton closed one eye, then opened it.

"Just be smart," I said. "You're already in enough trouble for one man."

"If that's what you meant, why didn't you just say it?"

Eric wandered into the bar around six-thirty, carrying a leather folio under his arm. It looked like he was playing solo tonight.

"I didn't think the pros had to use sheet music," I teased him.

He tilted the brim of his porkpie hat and gave me the expert-to-novice glare down his nose. It would have gotten him a job immediately at the John Alden Hotel.

He tapped the folio.

"Work in progress, man. I don't know if I'm ready to play it in public or not."

Some of the joy had leaked out of his life and I wondered how much of that was down to Lorelei.

"Want to eat?" I laid out a napkin and silverware without waiting for an answer, poured him a glass of water. "Where's the Bop Princess tonight?"

"Who? Lorelei? Rehab."

I stopped and looked at him closely.

"She's OK?"

Anguish spread over his face.

"Shit. I don't know. They don't let her talk to anyone outside for the first month."

Hardcore rehab, then, one that ripped you completely out of your normal life on the theory that life was what had gotten you into trouble in the first place.

"Rough," I said. "She check herself in?"

He nodded. Which meant she could check herself out.

I served him a plate with a thick slice of meatloaf, mashed potatoes, gravy, and peas. He scarfed two quick bites, then looked up.

"Cy said you used to be an alcoholic."

The music faded out of my hearing for a second.

"Prevailing theory, I always will be."

Eric shook his head once impatiently.

"I don't understand the mechanism," he said. "She's taking all these little pills, and other shit, even though she knows it makes her crazy and bad. It's like she can't control herself. Physically, I mean."

Could he really be that naive, or was he just looking for a way to talk it out with someone?

"You never stayed up all night playing the piano? Practiced till your fingers cramped?"

"I get it," he said. "Intellectually. But she knows it's hurting her. Why would you keep doing bad things to yourself?"

If Eric had made it this far in life without ever hating himself once, I envied him. But you couldn't make anyone who hadn't had to carry that ugly sack of self-hatred around understand addiction, because then you weren't talking about anything but symptoms. Root causes would always be a mystery to people like him, the extremely well adjusted.

"There's no one answer," I said. "You probably want to leave it to the professionals."

On top of it all, it annoyed me a little that he thought his twenty-one years of life experience meant he could understand and solve all Lorelei's problems. I sensed that he wanted to pick at the subject some more, but it was making me itchy. When he opened his mouth again, I pointed to the plate.

"Eat your dinner."

Then I walked down the bar to serve a couple who'd just come in, wearing matching leather motorcycle jackets and raspberry berets. On the way past the stereo, I changed out Susannah McCorkle for Dr. John, something loud and raucous. Something without so much memory associated with it.

CHAPTER 19

Ricky hated his fucking pacemaker, hated the whole idea that something in his body that wasn't part of his body had control over him. He hated the itchy patch on his chest where the hair was growing back—mostly gray and white—the pull of the stitches inside the incision, but most of all, he hated that tiny internal slam signaling the instant when his heart wasn't keeping up the beat on his own and needed a jolt. Ever since he'd left the hospital, he felt as if he were waiting for death to show up and claim his body. Just having thoughts like that depressed him. Worst of all, he couldn't get any more fun out of torqueing the tourists—they'd come to expect it.

"What's the matter with you two?" he said. "Didn't your mama ever make you eat your vegetables?"

Sitting at the counter was a thirtyish pair, German from the sound of them, pierced with so many studs and rings that Ricky wondered how they'd made it through security at Logan. Not only weren't they angry at his insults, they were fucking laughing at him. The bigger of the two—Ricky couldn't tell which one was the boy and which one the girl—dropped a twenty on the check. They left and Ricky was so demoralized he didn't even flip them off.

This problem with Tommy was a pain in the ass. He didn't remember telling the Indian all the stuff he'd supposedly said in the hospital, and that worried him. On top of that, he didn't trust Tommy as far as a horse could throw him and sure as shit didn't believe the bullshit about Carlos stealing the pills before he was snuffed. Any more than he believed some little round battery in his chest was going to keep him alive. He couldn't afford to get rid of Tommy until he and desRosiers got the deal done, though. And he needed the bag of pills Tommy had stolen to do it—that was the sample case.

The luncheonette door opened and he looked up hopefully. If only he could find a tourist who'd get into the spirit, give him back as much shit as he dished out, maybe he wouldn't feel so depressed.

He tensed. This guy looked like nothing so much as a mid-career cop, too young to retire, too old to bullshit. He was in his forties, middle-sized, with pale sandy hair, freckles, and a reddish mustache. He sported a couple of fading bruises and a cut healing up on his forehead. A nicely tailored green gabardine suit covered his starched white shirt and a plain bronze silk tie. Detective, probably.

He took a stool at the counter, leaving several seats as a buffer between him and Tesar and Spengler, who were poring over the racing form and giggling like the Bobbsey Twins.

"Coffee?" Ricky turned a mug right side up in front of him.

"Absolutely."

As Ricky was pouring, the cop slid a photograph out of an envelope. When he saw it was that singer Tommy used to fuck walking out of Vindalia's drug store, his hand jerked up. He sloshed coffee on the counter.

"Recognize someone, Rick?" the cop said.

"I know you?"

The cop stuck out his hand. Ricky automatically shifted the pot and shook.

"Dan Burton. BPD Homicide."

Ricky pulled his hand back as if he'd burned it, hamming it up a little.

"I didn't kill no one."

"Anyone." Burton pushed the picture forward. "You know her."

This must be Tommy's cop, the one who'd supposedly beaten Carlos to death? He didn't look tough enough or quick enough. Ricky pretended to inspect the photo.

"Pretty woman," he said. "If you like the artsy type. Don't believe I've met her, though."

"How about the drug store? Is that one of your many criminal enterprises?"

Ricky donned his best Mickey-the-dunce face as he set the Pyrex pot back on the burner.

"You've bought what the papers are selling about me, then," he said. "The lone wolf of mobsters, independent scourge of the underworld? You law enforcement guys need to get a clue, Mr. Burton. I don't have any so-called enterprises, unless you count this place here."

He swept his hand around the luncheonette, less confident than he acted. Burton had connected him with Vindalia way too fast, even if he was only fishing. It might crimp the deal with desRosiers if his nervous partner found out. Ever since he'd gotten out of the hospital, he was determined to get down to Miami—he wasn't going to let bullshit like this get in his way.

"Mr. Burton, do you have some identification?"

"Sure," Burton said. "If you want to make this more official than it is at the moment."

Ricky hesitated. He could be bluffing. If the cops really thought this guy had killed Carlos, he'd be on administrative leave, which meant he couldn't be here officially. He decided to roll with it.

"Not necessary." He bent over, pretending to look at the photo again.

"I know the drug store," he said. "I get my prescriptions

filled there. It's kind of crummy, but it's right on the way home. I don't know the young lady, though. I'm sorry."

Burton sipped his coffee and made a face.

"Isn't there a law against coffee this bad?"

Ricky brightened.

"Look, Burton. This isn't one of your frappa-dappa-ccino joints. Hey, if you're in Homicide, maybe you can answer a question for me. A cousin of mine was killed in the Fens the other night—they think a mugging. Would you know if they're making any progress? I'd like to tell my sister some good news."

Burton's neck swelled against his collar. Ricky wondered if he'd made a mistake.

"You'd have to speak with the investigating officers," Burton said.

"Supposedly he'd been arguing with this other guy. I wondered if anyone had told them that."

Burton's eyebrows went up.

"This other fellow's name?"

Ricky looked at the ceiling as if he were trying to remember. Burton had jumped on this like a frog on a fly, which implied a more personal interest. Maybe this would lead him away from Vindalia and the drugs for a while.

"Cormier, I think my sister said. Tommy Cormier?"

Burton's jaw clenched. Ricky felt better than he had all morning.

"You know anything else about him? Address, who he hangs out with?"

"Sorry," Ricky said. "It was just a rumor she heard. I probably shouldn't even repeat it."

Burton tasted the coffee once more, gave up, and backed off the stool.

"You know, Rick. They've got your reputation all wrong here. This isn't an unfriendly place at all. I kind of like it."

The glass door closed behind him. Ricky's heart bumped as the pacemaker kicked him. Until Burton had made that last remark, Ricky thought he was in control of the situation, but maybe he had overplayed it a little. He shrugged. Too late to worry about that.

But if the cop focused on Tommy, Ricky would have one fewer decision to make. Ricky couldn't let Tommy get away with jerking him around over the pills, but he hated the idea of having to kill Tommy himself. Up until now anyway, Tommy had been a pretty good Indian.

CHAPTER 20

Carlos's family returned to Puerto Rico soon after the funeral and by the next Saturday night, Marina was back in my kitchen turning out some terrific meals. Tonight she'd invented a one-pot dish with olives, tomatoes, and duck that had impressed even my less adventurous customers, the ones who wouldn't normally touch anything stranger than Swiss cheese. I never asked her how the funeral had gone and she didn't volunteer.

Eric, looking to make a little extra money, talked me into letting him bring in a bass player and a drummer, so we had a completely different sound and a little different crowd that night, more into the music. Lorelei seemed to have dropped out of his world or at least he didn't mention her to me.

Around eleven-thirty, some smart-ass ordered a pousse-café, that bartender's nightmare of seven layers of liqueur. The street door opened and I looked up to see Susan Voisine start her hip-hop down the stairs. I'd almost forgotten we had a date, of sorts.

Tonight's look was classier than the jeans and sweatshirt, though not as outrageous as the leather mini she'd worn the first night she visited the Esposito. A pair of tailored mushroom-colored slacks covered her high-heeled black boots, and the black silk blouse showed her collarbone, though not any cleavage. She wore a gold-embroidered maroon vest, something out of the Arabian nights, over the blouse, the sparkly thread picked up by a simple gold chain around her neck.

157

"Mademoiselle," I said, as she reached the bar. It felt like everyone in the place was watching us. "What's in the satchel?"

She was swinging the same canvas bag she'd been carrying the last time.

"A few little things." She winked. "A toothbrush."

I dribbled in the last layer, green, and carried it to the waiting student at the bar, who eyed it critically before handing me a twenty. Fortunately for him, I was in too much of a hurry to stop and teach him some manners.

"Cape Codder?" I asked, and she nodded.

"Be right back."

One of my daytime drinkers, the regular with the Irish tweed hat, ordered a shot on my way by. Eric's trio was bouncing through the intro to "My Funny Valentine." I set the drink down in front of her.

"You couldn't hold out until Sunday?" I said.

She nodded at the clock over the door to the kitchen. "Twenty more minutes and I would have."

Her voice sounded gravelly.

"You getting a cold?"

Then I saw the bruise, about the width of a finger and almost concealed by her makeup, darkening her neck.

"I'm fine," she said. "What time did you say you closed?"

"Another hour and a half. You want something to eat?"

She stroked her throat, as if making sure I looked at it.

"It's hard to swallow."

"Some soup?"

"No, little mother," she said. "I'm good."

Her energy level seemed low. I hoped she hadn't shown up just because she'd promised to. That wouldn't be any fun.

"I've got to work."

She waved her crimson-tipped fingers at me. The music ended.

I went down and poured more wine for a lesbian couple who'd been trying to get my attention, then dealt with the last rush for drinks.

Eric and his band worked through a last set, a little more ragged than they'd been at the start, as if they hadn't rehearsed the material together. Last call came and went, and the last drinkers finished up their potions, about as quickly as the Ice Age departed. While Susan went off to the ladies' room, I paid off Eric and slid the last clean rack of glasses out of the dishwasher to cool.

Marina walked out of the kitchen buttoning her coat.

"You need a ride?" I hoped not.

She tied a gauzy red and blue scarf over her curly hair.

"Burton's picking me up."

"Good for you."

"See you Monday," she said. "You going to be on time for a change?"

I stuck out my tongue, glad her attitude was back to normal.

The two women passed each other on the floor without acknowledgment. A married friend once told me to beware of a woman other women didn't like, but Marina was normally shy around strangers and I put it down to that.

"Ready?" I said.

Susan came to the bar, picked up her bag, and we started for the stairs. Did I imagine a chill coming off her, or was it just my nerves?

"You sure you're feeling all right?" I said. "I can drive you home if you'd rather, take a rain check."

She turned and reached up behind my head and yanked it down, rammed her tongue into my mouth and mashed her lips against me. I tasted blood, mine, and her desperation.

"I'd say I'm feeling fine." She tilted back her head to look up at me. "How do you feel about how I feel?"

I straightened up. "You feel fine to me."

Actually, it felt as if she'd made a commitment to herself and nothing was going to keep her from meeting it. Not the most romantic feeling in the world, but we could always talk about it later.

I started the Cougar, and as we exited the alley, Delford Woodley stumbled into our path. Susan gasped. I rolled my eyes. Déjà vu all over again.

Delford slapped his hands down on the hood as I braked, but he was only drunk, not hurt. The cast on his wrist now matched the color of his sweatshirt.

"Elder!" he yelled, though the car window was open. "Got a drink?"

He grinned at Susan like a feral cat.

"We're closed, Delford."

"Oh-kay, then, buddy. Catch you tomorrow."

I didn't have the heart to point out that tomorrow was Sunday and the Esposito would be closed.

"You're all right?" I said out the window.

He lifted the thumb that stuck out the end of his cast. "Just like the rain, bro'."

"Where you sleeping tonight?"

His smile disappeared and he tottered off down Mercy Street. Susan sniffed, as if I'd invited him home with us.

"You can't take care of everyone, you know."

"He's a customer," I said. "I can't afford to lose one."

But she didn't smile and as I turned at the blinking red light at the end of the street, I wondered where her mood had gone.

She seemed to curl farther in on herself as we drove through the city, though when I stopped in front of my building to move the orange plastic cones out of my parking space, she gave a little laugh.

"Your neighbors let you get away with that?" she said. "In my

160

part of town, they'd throw them through your window."

"I've been to your part of town," I said. "It's not that tough."

As we walked up the sidewalk, she laced her fingers with mine. Her mood had lightened, for no clear reason.

"Drink?" I had bought a bottle of chardonnay, which was about as safe a form of alcohol as I could have around. Every white wine I'd ever drunk had tasted like mouthwash to me.

"Come sit beside me for a minute," she said, perching on the couch.

I came and sat next to her, as tentative as if we were in high school and her parents were in the next room.

"Why does this feel so strange?" I said.

"I don't know, but I don't really mind." She unzipped her long black boots and pulled them off, flexed her very small toes. "I like things a little slower and quieter the first time."

I thought back to the kiss she'd laid on me at the bar, and wondered what she really meant.

"If it helps clear things," I said. "I don't want to complicate your life or mine. But this doesn't feel trivial to me."

"You could be right," she said. "But there's only one way to find out."

I leaned across the space between us. This kiss was the polar opposite of the Esposito one. Her lips were soft and hesitant and her tongue brushed at my lips until I opened them. She dropped her small hand to the front of my trousers, which I took as encouragement to help her up off the couch.

In the bedroom, I toed off my shoes and started to unlatch my belt.

"Would you hang that up, please?" she said, handing me the gold vest. "It used to belong to Cher."

I hung it over the doorknob, and when I turned back, she was skimming the blouse off over her head. She laid it over the rocking chair and used both hands to fluff out her hair.

Her brassiere was a diaphanous peach lace, and when she reached behind herself in that quintessentially feminine move, I couldn't look away. Her breasts were large for her height, proportioned like a teenage boy's dream and tipped with nipples the color of coffee. She smiled as she walked across the carpet until she was within reach.

I didn't have to raise my hands to touch her. She shivered, tugged my shirt free of my belt, unbuttoning as she went. I stepped out of my pants as they fell to the floor.

When both of us were naked, she closed her eyes.

"Pick me up," she said, and looped her arms around my neck.

I slipped my hands under her tiny behind and fitted her onto me with the faintest resistance, easily passed through. Our bare chests sealed together, the hard points of her nipples punctuating our heat. Sweat slicked our skins and the hunger between us manifested in the slow tidal rocking of her body against mine, a fierce wetness of mouths.

The rest was as good as the beginning. I felt balanced on a point between knowing my own sensations and giving her pleasure and that acute attention built into a mutual movement and finally into a series of mindless and muscular collisions. As I returned to full rationality, I felt how small she was in my hands, how that made me want to protect her.

"Cigarette?" We laughed at the same time.

I lit one and picked up a china saucer. She turned it over and looked at the bottom before letting me drop in the match.

"Meissen," she said. "You use your good dishes for ashtrays?"

I'd picked up a box of assorted plates from the cellar when I left home twenty years ago. It hadn't occurred to me that they'd be worth anything.

"I suppose."

"I'm still moving to Oregon," she said, as if I'd asked her not to.

I got up and put on some sweatpants, not sure that I cared. I walked out into the living room and put on some music.

Sitting beside her on the bed, I found the Sinatra schmaltzy, but when he started into "September Song," she closed her eyes and took my hand, hummed along.

"One of my daddy's favorites," she said.

"You have to be numb not to love the Chairman."

She stubbed out her cigarette and handed me the saucer, pulling up the coverlet to cover her breasts.

"Do you mind if I stay?"

I thought she would want to, but I was touched that she hadn't assumed it. Not waking up alone did break one of my rules for sobriety.

"Of course not. I might even have a new toothbrush somewhere."

"I brought my own," she said. "Remember?"

She wriggled down next to me, pulling the pillow over near mine so her mouth was within kissing distance. Slowly, her breathing deepened, and with an ease I hadn't felt in a very long while, I found myself matching the rhythm of her breath, until I fell away into the blackness.

CHAPTER 21

Even just two days in the hospital had reminded Ricky how much he hated doctors. But since he was counting on the doctor sitting across the table from him to make him rich enough to move to Miami Beach and drink margaritas all day, he was doing his best not to give in and strangle the insufferable preppy fuck.

Besides, he needed to be careful of his stress level. Every time the fucking pacemaker went off, it stopped him in his tracks, and the more wound up he got, the more often it blipped. He'd read about beta-blockers on the Internet and how they could smooth out your heart rate. He was going to get Vindalia to give him some—the side effects couldn't be any worse than the pacemaker.

"We need to call off this transaction for now," desRosiers said. "Things are too dicey. I'll pay you for the samples, of course. That will keep us going for a few months. But the main shipment is just going to have to wait."

Ricky shook his head, ignoring the stutter in his chest.

"We had a deal, doc. You know I had to make commitments to other people based on our agreement. This is not something you can just say no to."

He was goddamned if he was going to tell desRosiers that he didn't have the samples to sell him, and that he didn't really know where they were.

"Now, you want another coffee?" Ricky got up to go to the

counter. "Maybe it will relax you a little bit."

Ricky decided he was impressed with Starbucks. They'd come up with far more subtle and ingenious ways of insulting their customers than he had. There were no waiters to take your order, the counter help looked down their ringed noses at everyone without exception, and the baristas—you had to practically kiss their asses to get your drink. God forbid you ordered anything complicated, unless you loved being sighed at and seeing eyes roll. Ricky was disappointed about one thing—it was probably too late for him to get a franchise.

"I don't want any more coffee," desRosiers said.

The doc had been one step behind all morning, and Ricky had to wonder if he might be sampling his own meds. Not that Ricky cared much. He was focused on the deal, then Miami. Or maybe Tampa—great food, great cigars.

"Darrow—that bartender?—was poking around Alison's apartment," desRosiers said. "He's connecting the dots. He could ruin the whole experiment without even realizing it."

DesRosiers was a whack job. Ricky couldn't care less what he wanted the pills for, as long as he paid for them. He headed for the counter, where he ordered two coffees from a tall Oriental guy with four studs—two ear, two nose—and a six-inch goatee with a blue stripe down the center.

"You want room?" the guy said.

"What's this?" Ricky said. "A hotel?"

The server gave him a look of studied patience then a smirk Ricky wanted to slap off his face.

"Room for cream?"

One more reason to retire, Ricky thought. Nobody understood a joke anymore. He grabbed a stainless steel pitcher of milk and sat down at the table, short of breath.

"You've got nothing to worry about, doc." He diluted his coffee. "Besides, the samples are going to take a little longer to get together than I thought."

DesRosiers jumped as if someone had put a Taser in his ass.

"Then let's cancel the whole thing," he said. "I can't be vulnerable like that."

Ricky cautioned himself. He didn't want to freak the doc out so far that he'd quit, at least until he'd paid for the pills.

"Look," he said. "I'll ask around about Darrow, what he might know. I think you'll find it's just a coincidence. Tommy— you remember my man Tommy Cormier?—told me that Darrow used to date her. It's probably just some weird nostalgia trip."

Of course desRosiers would remember Tommy, Ricky thought. He'd taken the Alison chick right out from under Tommy's nose, and the doc didn't understand how long Tommy could hold a grudge. In fact, Ricky hoped that Tommy would decide to even that score. He was a little tired of the doc himself.

"He's the executor of her estate, Maldonado. How much of a coincidence can that be?"

Ricky sipped his coffee. It was good, but he liked his own better, even if it didn't come from the Ganges Delta.

"She was a singer, doc, right? An *artiste*? How much would she know about our business, unless you said anything to her."

Which actually was an important point. These preppy assholes were always trying to impress the women, and he had to wonder if the doc was one of them.

"Alison was a very intelligent person," desRosiers said. "She might have inferred a good deal on her own."

More intelligent than the doc thought, for dumping Tommy in favor of him. Every chick's dream, Ricky thought—a doctor, even a limp-dick asshole, beat a thug every time.

"And now she's dead," Ricky said.

Suicide, supposedly, though he suspected that Tommy might have offed her. He'd been pretty pissed off by her going with desRosiers, and Tommy was the kind of idiot who threw out the whole pie rather than share.

DesRosiers sighed, as if talking to a retard, and Ricky spilled coffee on the doc's fawn linen pants.

"Oh," he said. "Sorry about that."

Sometimes the doc forgot he was dealing with a man who didn't settle his disagreements in a courtroom. Ricky watched him do that slow-breathing thing to calm himself down and wondered if it worked.

"Look," Ricky said. "I can see you're concerned. I'll have Tommy talk to the guy directly. Will that help?"

DesRosiers nodded, all his certainty gone.

"But gently," he said. "All right? Let's not create any more palaver than we have to."

Ricky nodded. "Very gently. No palaver at all."

And he smiled, because he had just figured out how to tell if Tommy had stolen his samples. He picked up the half-full cardboard cup and toasted the doc.

"We OK, then?" he said.

DesRosiers was dabbing at the stain spreading on his pants leg.

"I suppose."

What a negative prick.

"Wonderful, then. Everything's fine."

CHAPTER 22

I slept so heavily that when I woke, I was completely disoriented. Memories of the night flooded in and made me feel loose and warm, as if I were coming out of an ice cave after a long winter. I smile, then realized Susan wasn't in bed beside me.

It must have been the noise of her entering the bedroom that woke me. She was fully dressed except for her boots, and her face was blank and white as typing paper.

"You better come downstairs," she said. "I think one of your tenants has had a heart attack."

Some logical bolt closed inside my head and I knew which tenant she was talking about and how she happened to be there when it happened. I pulled on my sweatpants and a shirt and followed her out the door, my pleasant mood chilled.

Mrs. Rinaldi's door was wide open, my keychain hanging from the lock I'd installed last week. I gave Susan a disgusted look, letting her know I understood now why she'd wanted to come home with me so much.

She pushed the door open without meeting my look.

"Let's keep our priorities straight, Elder. She's in the living room."

I followed her inside.

"Dorothea," I said. "Are you all right?"

The old woman was crumpled on the floor beside the couch on a rucked-up throw rug. Susan's red-handled tote bag sat next to the bookcase with one of the manuscript boxes inside it open, full of theater programs, "Boston Opera Company" printed across the top of the one I could see.

"Oh, bother," Dorothea said. "I'm fine. I just . . . ohhhh."

The relief I'd felt at the sound of her voice evaporated. Her pulse was thready and shallow.

"Did you call 911?" I said to Susan, pulling down the hem of Dorothea's nightgown to cover her blue-veined legs. A spot ached at my center, like decay in a tooth. "Susan!"

"They're coming." Susan stood with the telephone in her hand, staring down at us.

Dorothea gasped again.

"You'll be fine," I said, taking her hand.

But fear overwhelmed my sense of hope and I was angry at myself. All this was my responsibility—bringing a thief into Dorothea's life. It was unconscionably stupid.

Susan held out her hand, which I ignored.

"It wasn't enough to steal her memories?" I said to her. "You had to scare her to death, too?"

"She was lying on the floor when I came in," Susan said. "If I hadn't been here . . ."

The rest of her reply was cut off by the EMTs' arrival. I thought about how much prompter they were than when I called them for Delford Woodley.

"Forget it," I said. "I don't want to hear it."

There were two paramedics, a muscular black-haired woman and a twenty-year-old kid with a surfer's haircut and a terminally laid-back attitude. They set the gurney on the hardwood floor and the woman politely elbowed me aside.

"We'll take over now, sir."

I squeezed Dorothea's hand once more and stood up. Her eyes were closed, her breathing ragged.

"I was putting them back," Susan said.

I was so angry I couldn't look at her.

"I don't care, Susan. Really."

Outside Dorothea's window at Commonwealth Ave., the headlights from passing cars painted the asphalt and I wanted to cry.

Susan knelt by the bookcase and replaced stacks of papers, as if that would help anything.

After what seemed like hours in which the EMTs discussed Dorothea's condition by radio with the hospital, they settled her on the stretcher with an IV poking from the back of her bony hand. Her eyes were still shut. Surfer boy covered her tenderly with a blanket.

"Where are you taking her?" I said.

"Mass General, most likely." He slapped me lightly on the shoulder. "She should be fine. We got here in plenty of time and it looks like a minor one."

I wanted to punch him in the mouth, though it wasn't his fault that "fine" had been what the world was before I'd woken up, before I'd learned how Susan had used me.

"OK," I said. "I'll follow you—you're going to need insurance information and all that, right?"

"You can do that over the phone," he said. "But don't tell Admitting I told you that."

He grinned, gave me a thumbs-up, and rolled the gurney out the door. Metal clashed as they retracted the legs to carry her downstairs.

"Jesus Christ," Susan said. "Don't look at me like that."

"Like what? Like you . . ."

"Like I killed the woman. I was returning her stuff when I heard her groan."

"Returning it?" I said. "It wasn't worth anything?"

"I didn't steal it," she said. "I told you I was getting out of the business, didn't I?"

I closed my eyes. Maybe that would keep me from having to

listen to her lies.

"The same way you weren't stealing anything from Alison's apartment."

"I told you what happened at Alison's apartment. I don't want to go to jail." Her voice softened. "And I didn't want any lies between you and me."

"Please. You think retracting a lie is like taking out a splinter? Once it's gone, it's gone?"

"Fuck," she said. "You never made a mistake?"

I was exhausted suddenly. All the pleasure fled, leaving an ashy taste in my mouth.

"Just leave," I said. "You've done enough good work for one night."

She straightened up and pulled her shoulders back.

"You think you have it all figured out, Elder, don't you? You can't even see that I'm not your problem."

"The fuck is that supposed to mean?"

The skin over my temples felt tight and hot. There were footsteps in the hall and then Henri stepped into the doorway. The noise must have woken him.

"What is it?" I snapped. I didn't need his bullshit on top of everything else.

"I won't have you abusing my daughter," he said.

Susan walked over to him and he put his arms around her, patted the top of her head awkwardly. I felt stupid I hadn't made the connection.

"I'm sorry, Henri. I certainly didn't mean to abuse her."

I glared at her so she'd know I was only taking it easy for his sake. The old man looked like a sleepy rabbit in his white hooded terrycloth robe and black leather slippers.

"Don't take it out on him," she said. "This is all my fault."

In the morning, I knew, I was going to start eviction proceedings and I knew Susan wouldn't fight them, either. I could have her prosecuted for breaking and entering. Henri couldn't live alongside Mrs. Rinaldi.

"I'm taking Dorothea's side on this one," I said.

Henri stared down at the throw rug as if he'd peed on it.

I could tell Susan wanted to argue, but I herded the two of them out of Dorothea's apartment and started to pick up the bandage wrappings and tissues the paramedics had left behind. As the two of them walked downstairs together, Susan said something sharp to her father before the door to the ground-floor apartment cut off her voice.

Only then did I leave, relocking Dorothea's door and trudging upstairs to my own. I felt as if I'd dropped and broken something valuable, something I'd never even gotten a firm grip on. I folded up Susan's coat and her long black boots, piled them out on the landing, and dead-bolted the door behind me.

CHAPTER 23

It was the nicest morning of the spring so far, but Tommy barely noticed the singing birds and the warm smell of grass as he crossed the corner of the Common toward Copley Square. For some reason, Ricky had wanted to meet upstairs in the bar at the Ritz. Tommy wondered if the pudgy little prick had lost his mind—the two of them were going to stick out like turds in a bag of beer nuts. What was worse, Tommy was sure the conversation was going to be about Carlos again. He was wondering now if killing Carlos might not have been a bad decision.

On top of that, the Ritz required ties and jackets, and Tommy hated ties almost as much as he hated the soapy-water enemas his aunt used to give him to try and straighten out his attitude. If he hadn't hated ties so much, he thought, he might have made a legitimate businessman, a force in the corporate world.

He climbed the narrow stairs, the heels of his boots banging on the risers, and stepped into an upstairs room that looked like a very large parlor, full of couches and stuffed chairs, those round tables with the lamp sticking up out of the middle. Even though it was only eleven in the morning, the place was half-full of skinny old men in dusty suits and seersucker blazers, tanned younger women in summer dresses—lots of white belts and shoes and wide-brimmed straw hats.

Ricky was propped like a hard-boiled egg on top of a green and white striped chaise lounge in the farthest corner of the

173

room. He wore one of his short-sleeved khaki jumpsuits with the zipper halfway down, exposing a grubby white T-shirt. A blue knit tie hung loosely knotted, tucked under the jumpsuit's collar.

He waved wildly to get Tommy's attention, which warned Tommy he was in a ball-busting mood. He'd said on the phone that he wanted to give Tommy some details on the big deal, but Tommy didn't believe him. The only thing he was sure of was that Ricky wouldn't shoot him here.

"Rick." Tommy sat down in a maroon paisley wing chair on the far side of a fragile-looking coffee table, probably worth a fortune.

Ricky toasted him with a peach-colored drink, cloudy with fruit pulp and crushed ice.

"Aren't you supposed to be on the wagon with this heart thing?" Not that he cared if Ricky popped his cork. Tommy only needed him alive until he found out what Ricky's big deal was.

Ricky slurped through the red plastic straw.

"Nah. A little bit's supposed to be good for you, reduce the stress. You want one? It's a Fuzzy Navel."

Tommy shook his head, trying not to shudder. One of the reasons Ricky hadn't succeeded was that he never learned to blend into his surroundings. A Fuzzy Navel—the bartender must have had fun looking up that in his Old Mr. Boston book.

"Thanks, Rick. A little early."

A male waiter wafted up beside him.

"Green tea," Tommy said.

The waiter's lip twitched, as if Ricky wasn't already amusing enough.

"Something wrong?"

"Oh, no sir."

Ricky watched the waiter glide away.

"I have to say this, Tommy. You're slicker than gooseshit on linoleum."

Slick enough that he wanted to get this over with. Ricky praising anyone was enough to make Tommy nervous. Ricky praising Tommy was downright frightening.

"Rick, I don't want to be rude here, right? But the Ritz is a little off my normal track. Yours, too, for that matter."

Ricky shook his head.

"I like it here. I'm thinking of making it my local. You know, like in England?"

That would thrill the Ritz.

"Great, Rick. Can we get on with it?"

Ricky sat up straight with difficulty, trying to look serious.

"I wanted us to meet here so we could keep Spengler and Tesar out of it. They're good boys, but unsophisticated. This deal is huge, Tommy. Two to three million, if it plays all the way out."

Even allowing for Ricky's native tendency to bullshit, that was big money. Tommy reminded himself to stay on track. He didn't want to run Ricky's half-assed organization and he wasn't going to tie himself up in some convoluted deal that might take years to pay off. If he'd wanted to be a banker, he would have worked a little harder at the necktie thing.

Ricky pulled out a business card and a snapshot of a familiar-looking man in a Burberry raincoat. Cameron desRosiers, that scheming prick.

"You're in bed with this guy?" Tommy said.

Ricky frowned at Tommy's tone.

"He's our main contact. We're selling him large quantities of semi-legal medications for his research."

Ricky set the picture face down on the table as the waiter poured his tea. Tommy felt as if he were breathing pure oxygen—a chance to fuck this guy over? A gift. He calmed himself.

"You know I know this guy, Rick. But what do you have against him?"

"Nothing," Ricky said. "I'm not out to get him. I just want to be sure I get all the money I'm entitled to. And have him take the risk."

Tommy relaxed. Ricky's agenda would become clear before too long.

"So what's the deal?"

"It's really too bad Carlos got that bag." Ricky sucked up some Fuzzy Navel. "Those were supposed to be the samples. DesRosiers was going to pay two hundred large for them."

Tommy felt a thick weight in his gut.

"Bullshit," he said. "That's practically retail."

"Street retail, maybe. Not pharmacy."

"What? He's going to sell them through a drug store?"

"But that's all right, the Carlos thing," Ricky said. "Water under the bridge. But you and desRosiers need to organize the first shipment, a couple of weeks from now. DesRosiers supplies us with empty cartons, we send them, uh, down there, get them filled, and ship them back."

Tommy hardly heard. He was trying to judge if he could retrieve the pills from Alison's, sell them to desRosiers, and get out of town before Ricky found out. Another two hundred K would be plenty of fuck-you money and he could probably figure out a way to blame the whole thing on desRosiers, which would be a bonus. Assuming he didn't decide to kill him for taking Alison away.

"Tommy. You listening to me?"

"Yeah, yeah."

"So when can you meet with him?"

"Anytime, Rick. Sooner the better."

Ricky finished his drink.

"Excellent. Let's get it done, then. Just let me know if you need anything from my end."

Tommy smiled as he poured more tea from the white pot into his fine china cup. He looked around at the Ritz, the blue blazers and tea dresses, the faint odor of old money—even when he was rich, this wouldn't be his scene. He thought about des-Rosiers and Alison and felt the rush of pleasure he'd feel in screwing him over.

"You wouldn't mind too much if I fucked him up a little, would you, Rick? After you get your money, I mean."

CHAPTER 24

As I threw the dead bolt on my apartment door, I wondered whether Susan was going to stay the night with Henri, and whether I could use that in an eviction proceeding. I would have remembered if I'd seen her visit him, so I had to wonder if they were estranged somehow. Or maybe she stole from him too. I hadn't craved a drink so badly in all the months I'd been sober, but somehow it seemed appropriate it was a woman who triggered the desire, that and a reminder of my inability to read other people.

I walked into the kitchen and removed the bottle of white wine I'd bought for Susan, a Pinot Gris from Oregon that the wine snob at the liquor store recommended. I twisted off the top and sniffed the inside of the cap, inhaling its must, and my body went up on point, every fiber drawn like metal filings to the pole of a magnet, clamoring for more effect than the scent would give. I took a pint glass down from the cabinet and filled it.

Dorothea had been trying to tell me something the day I drove her to church, maybe even asking for help in her oblique and fiercely independent way. Had I missed her message completely? Could I have helped her avoid this, if I'd been listening better?

My panic faded, and as much as I would have like to deny it, it was because I had a drink in my hand. I dipped my nose into the glass, the bright acidic fumes dizzying. Despite the depth of my addiction, I knew I wasn't going to swallow it. Breaking a year and a half of sobriety on a bottle of wine I'd bought for Susan Voisine was a little ironic for my mood. I drained the glass down the sink, then tipped the rest of the bottle over, too.

But I couldn't sit still. I slipped the blues and sorrow CD, my collection of female singers, into the pocket of my jacket. When I went out the door, Susan's boots and coat were gone, but as I passed Henri's door, I heard laughing. It might have been them or some late-night TV show.

Outside the air was dry and steely, the temperatures of March crowding back in. I climbed into the Cougar and drove.

Stopped at the light by the Museum of Fine Arts, I felt the first wave of despair crash over me. If Dorothea died, I'd be guilty of negligence, moral if not legal. I accepted responsibility for the care of my tenants, people like Henri who weren't completely independent anymore, and in Dorothea's case, I'd failed. It gave me some idea why Alison's death wouldn't let me go—despite my need for independence, I had to take responsibility for someone else, something beside myself.

I pulled a U-turn over the trolley tracks on Huntington Avenue and returned past the statue of the Indian on the horse in front of the museum. Two more blocks and I realized I was headed for the Esposito.

All my worries about Alison's death, I saw now, were selfish, rooted in my own guilt rather than a care for her. She had always needed me more than I needed her, and I'd used my drinking as an excuse to pull away. I'd quit on her and somehow I believed that, murder or suicide, she would never have died if I'd stuck it out with her.

The finest part of the drive was the anticipation of the bar, cruising the blank streets, parking the Cougar out front, opening up and turning off the alarm. I made every step of that trip deliberately.

As I descended into the blackness, I looked at my watch. It was quarter to three. I flicked on the thermostat as I stepped behind the bar, though I knew the cold I felt was not the kind more heat would help.

Savoring my slowness, I turned on the radio and found an all-night station out of BU. The college kids who hosted these shows had far more interesting taste than the commercial FM stations, especially Public Radio, and they weren't constrained by commercial play lists. The show was on a Sinatra jag, though, and I could not hear the Chairman's voice that night without my gut twisting up.

I sat down on a bar stool, away from the bottles, and thought about how selfishness had ruled my life, drunk and sober, everything it had cost me, and the people I cared about. I'd always been too self-centered to pick up the hints people were sending.

I'd failed Alison the same way I had Dorothea, by not listening closely enough. When I left Alison, the truth was I had been strong enough to quit my drinking and stay with her—I only feared the effort it would take, the potential for failure. If I had stayed, was there any assurance she wouldn't have started down the black road that ended in her death? I didn't know, but I knew all I was doing now was trying to soothe my conscience. The effort now cost me nothing, and threatened nothing I cared about.

I stood up and walked behind the bar. I would not be able to plead ignorance or some momentary loss of attention later, or an imperfect self-control. I was clear-headed and I knew exactly what I was doing. The whiskey would give me a few hours' relief from the pain of my failures, and if I didn't take a drink right now, I might go find a gun and blow my brains out.

I reached for the glass of Macallan in the niche by Alison's journal and tossed the liquid down my neck so fast I barely tasted it. Electricity grabbed at my throat, then eased. The whiskey's solo warmth spread through my chest like life and love and happiness dissolved in one potion. Whatever I did after that first sweet drink, I would not remember, nor did I intend to. My last conscious thought was whether I had locked the door of the Esposito behind me. After all the time it had taken me to get to this point, I did not want to be interrupted.

The earthquake began as a low rumble of rocks rolling downhill and increased in period and intensity until it sounded as if someone was hammering a new set of laws into my front door. As I swam up through the bruised muck of my unconscious, returning from a place I'd hoped I was never going to visit again, I was only half-relieved to find out I had survived the night.

The sun had been rising when I left the Esposito, I remembered now, but I could not remember how much I had drunk, whether I'd played that sad sad music I'd carried to my bar, or even if I'd remembered to lock up when I left. In fact, I had not even a vague memory of how I'd made it home.

"Elder Darrow!"

My eyes were glued shut with night substance and the pain in my head stabbed repeatedly, exquisitely, as if someone were shoving a sharpened piece of piano wire in through my eyeball. I wasn't dead yet, but I was afraid that the first time I moved my head that would change.

And who was calling my name, sounding panicked and noisy? I closed my eyes.

But the memory of last night, before I got drunk, slipped back in: what had happened to Dorothea, how Susan had betrayed me, what I'd done to myself afterward. If my life was a three-legged stool, one leg had collapsed.

"God damn it, Elder." Marina shouted in the hallway. "Open

this fucking door."

The cursing was what forced me up out of my wallow. My tenants didn't need to hear that kind of language.

I rolled off the couch onto my hands and knees, tangled in the afghan. My stomach lurched like a tsunami and the gray-green bottle of Macallan fell over, a couple of tablespoons of whiskey still sloshing in the bottom. I couldn't believe I'd left a drop undrunk, and I didn't know whether to attribute it to diminished capacity or a newfound self-control. I know what I'd bet on, though.

I achieved something approaching vertical by climbing the arm of the couch like a chimp. The pain concentrated itself into two burning disks behind my eyes.

"Coming," I croaked, but I didn't think she could hear me over the pounding of her fist.

Crabbing along the wall, I made it to the door in about an hour. When I turned the bolt, she stopped pounding and my ears quit ringing.

Marina hadn't known me when I was a drunk before, but there was no question she'd know what I'd been doing last night. I was still partially drunk, if a compelling desire to shut my eyes and let the world spin me away was any guide. I tried to pull it together. I didn't know how she was going to react, but I did care.

I opened the door finally. Even my smile felt ghostly.

"Good morning."

She frowned, standing there like a tree. Now that she had seen I was alive, she didn't seem to know what to do. She was wearing a long brown leather trench coat and I wondered if Carlos had given it to her.

The clock on the top of the bookcase said twelve-thirty. The sun through the windows meant that was daytime.

"What's all the noise for?" I said.

She glared at me. "I've been pounding on your door the last twenty minutes. You didn't show up at the bar. You didn't call."

I wished she would yell at me or slap me, do anything but give me that sad-eyed put-upon look.

I turned and limped into the kitchen, the inside of my skull a carpet of spikes, my brain swollen tight against them. I welcomed the pain, I'd earned every bit of it, and given the myriad ways in which I'd fucked things up in the last few weeks, I deserved it too. Coffee wasn't going to do anything but wake me up enough to feel the pain more clearly, but I was going to have to outrun my remorse if I were going to get anything done. Getting conscious would be a start.

"If you just gave me a set of keys," she said, "you could take a day off and get drunk anytime you want. You know you don't have to worry about Carlos drinking up all your profits anymore."

The sarcasm suggested she thought my profits might be in more danger from me than from anyone else. I would have liked to be able to assure her this was a one-time thing, but that's what every backsliding alcoholic ever said. A year and a half of day-to-day discipline had been wiped out by one impulsive swallow, then another. And another. The quaint idea I might someday be able to call myself a social drinker burned in the back of my throat.

"I had a little bit of a rough night," I said.

"No kidding."

"One of my tenants had a heart attack." For an instant, I thought she might let me get away with that as an excuse, even if I couldn't.

"How is she?"

"I don't know. How do you find out?"

She frowned again, and then I felt ashamed for using Dorothea as an excuse. I had drunk the whiskey all on my own. At least I could own up to that.

Marina pulled the Yellow Pages off the shelf by my phone.

"What hospital?"

I tried to pick through the wreckage in my mind.

"Mass General? Her name is Rinaldi. Dorothea Rinaldi."

Marina banged the phone book down on the table, which made me flinch. She punched a number into the phone.

"You have a patient named Rinaldi? I don't know what room she's in."

I watched dumbly. Was it really such a simple process if you weren't afraid of what you'd find out?

"ICU. Thank you. Yes."

Marina stared out at Commonwealth Ave., probably so she didn't have to look at me.

"Andrea?" She ran off a burst of Italian. The only word I caught was Dorothea's last name. *"Grazie."*

She hung up and turned back, but she wouldn't meet my eyes.

"The lady is resting. She had a small heart attack. You think you can make it in to work now?"

"Thank you for doing that. You want some coffee?"

"Not your kind," she said. "But I'll make it."

I followed her into the kitchen like a sick dog and sat down at the table, resisting the urge to lay my head down on the Formica.

"Something else happened," she said.

Her concern, which I didn't deserve, only added to my self-disgust.

"Susan," I said.

Marina set a mug down in front of me. The first sip of coffee scalded my tongue and then my stomach lurched. I thought I might have to sprint for the bathroom.

"Beating yourself up won't make you feel any better," she said.

Fuelled by small sips of the coffee, I told her how Susan had stolen Mrs. Rinaldi's opera memorabilia, then used the opportunity of sleeping with me to return them. Marina listened without offering a solution and I realized how much I missed having someone sane to talk to. Burton didn't really count as sane.

"You didn't like her," I said. "I should have paid attention."

Marina shook her head.

"I was jealous of her, not you. Her looks."

I stood up and handed her the key ring.

"Go ahead and open up. And get yourself another set made. I'll grab a shower and be down there in an hour."

I was angry rather than guilty, which I took as a good sign. She didn't look at me, but she made no move to leave, either.

"Please," I said. "I'm not going back to that place."

She separated the Esposito's door key and the round-headed alarm key with a dexterity I wouldn't have had, and tossed the rest of them back on the table. The crash split my skull.

"If you're not there by one o'clock, I'm sending Burton," she said.

She was smart. The last thing I wanted was for him to see me like this.

"Was he waiting for me to open up?"

"He has something to tell you," she said.

A jolt parted the fog. "What?"

"I don't know. You are coming in, right? Because I am not running the place by myself."

"Shower and breakfast," I said. "I'll be there."

"You have any liquor here?" she said.

"There's about an inch in the bottom of a bottle in the living room," I told her. "But I have no desire to drink it."

Knowing I was saying something true raised my self-esteem, if only by a whisker. Never in the past had I left a bit of anything undrunk.

"I'll pour it out," she said. "One hour."

I looked at the clock, feeling better.

"I'll try for forty-five," I said. "Sometimes we have that early lunch rush on Mondays."

She gave me a look, entirely justified, that said she'd believe it when she saw me.

Once she was gone, I stood at the sink and drank the rest of the coffee as quickly as I could, then tried another with a little milk in it. The vomiting came on so quickly that I didn't make it to the bathroom, but that was positive too; my body was rejecting the alcohol.

I ran cold water and splashed my face. My headache was fading already, which was a miracle, and from experience I knew the stretched muscles in my neck from throwing up would ease in a while. I climbed into the very hot shower, scraped the stubble off my face, and dressed in black pants and a starched white shirt, as if I were going to work at Starbucks.

The Cougar was parked in front of the apartment house, slightly askew but legal. I marveled at how instinct could furrow so deeply that you could perform complex and dangerous tasks like driving while you were under the influence. God protected all fools and drunks, but most especially those who were both. I started the engine and drove off toward the Esposito, undoubtedly qualified.

The Esposito was humming like the proverbial machine when I rolled in about quarter past one, but my headache returned as soon as I saw Burton behind the bar. He was too comfortable playing publican, drawing a draft beer and chatting sociably with a young woman in tight white shorts and a yellow halter

186

top who looked as if she had indigestion. He must have been trying to cheer her up.

"Glad you could make it," he cracked as I walked behind the bar. "I wouldn't want the cops to think I was starting a new career."

Marina walked out of the kitchen with her hands full of plates and smiled as if he'd said something hilarious. I wondered if they had finally gotten together. It wouldn't be a relationship destined for eternal happiness, but then whose was?

Burton inspected me with a connoisseur's eye.

"You tied one on?"

"Can't fool you," I said. "Come back here a minute."

On the way in, I'd been thinking about what was in my safe. I had no legitimate reason to possess the marked money or the pills. Claiming I was Alison's executor and that they belonged to her estate, while technically correct, wasn't going to buy me any mercy from Costain or the rest of the cops.

Back in my office, I sat in the lumpy black leather chair.

"I need your professional advice," I said. "I have in my possession a bag full of hundred-dollar bills and another one full of assorted pills, pharmacy medications they look like. I found them in Alison's apartment. Unless your evidence technicians missed them completely, which I doubt, someone hid them there in the last week."

"There were no techs," Burton said. "But I would have noticed the money if it had been there."

"Under a pile of shoes in the bedroom closet?"

He went quiet. "Didn't look there."

My hopes fell. If the bags had definitely not been in the apartment when Alison died, there was a chance she hadn't been dealing.

"So what should I do with them?"

"Who gives a fuck?" he said.

"Are you serious?"

He sighed, the barman's bonhomie evaporated.

"I've got bigger problems. Sharon found out I was suspended. Now she wants a lump-sum payoff instead of alimony checks."

His almost ex-wife.

"What good does that do her?"

"Her lawyer's trying to scare her. He told her that if I keep getting suspended, I'll probably get fired, which will mean she'll never see her half of my pension."

"Your pension? She's got the right to money you haven't even earned yet?"

Burton snorted. "They'd attach my unborn sperm if they thought I had any to spare."

"You're not retiring anytime soon, though."

"I'm not even eligible. But she wants the payoff before she'll sign the decree."

"And that's all that's holding it up?"

I had an idea, but I didn't know if Burton would be insulted by it.

"Sharon's a cash-on-the-table girl," he said. "If it's anything more than a hundred bucks, I ain't got it."

I dialed open my safe, pulled out the bags, and unzipped the pill bag.

"Holy shit." He grabbed a handful of the packages. "You were serious."

"They're worth something," I said.

"On the street. You should flush them, though. There's no reasonable explanation for you to have this much dope in your possession. I don't care how you got hold of it."

"What about the cash?" I lifted the other duffel.

"Give it to the nuns. It's marked."

Out front, the sound system started playing reggae, which startled me. I suppose if I asked Marina to run the place for me, she should get to play her own music.

"I want to hire you," I said.

"I have a job," Burton said.

"I want to know what Alison's story was, whether she was dealing, why the pills and money were in her apartment. Just get all the questions answered."

"Do I look like a private eye to you?" Burton said. "I'm a police officer."

"What would it cost you to buy Sharon off your back?"

"I don't know," he said. "Fifty?"

It was worth that amount to me, especially since I'd be paying him with money I didn't have a week ago.

"Done. Call her lawyer."

Hope rippled across Burton's face.

"I'm not taking drug money," he said. "Or FBI-marked, either."

"I'm Alison's executor," I said. "Plus she left me some money."

He bulled on as if he hadn't heard.

"And I'm still on suspension. I don't want to get caught moonlighting." He looked at the duffel bags. "Let me think about it."

I was flipping through the folder the lawyer had given me, when the agent's name on the contract with Alison stopped me cold.

"You think too hard," I said. "You'll just find a way not to do it. Yes or no."

Burton shrugged.

"OK. But only if it's enough to get Sharon off my ass for good."

I nodded.

"And only until the suspension is lifted. I might only wind up working on it a day or two."

I doubted the department would reinstate him that quickly, but I agreed.

"If there's anything left over, I'll apply it to your bar tab."

"Do I owe you money?" he said innocently. "So. Why the toot?"

"Different problem altogether," I said. "Thanks for asking, though."

"You back to drinking full time?"

"Nope. Total noncombatant." I wished he hadn't brought it up. "What happened when you talked to Icky Ricky?"

"He doesn't own the pharmacy. But he definitely reacted when I showed him her picture. I talked to a friend of mine in OC."

"Ricky counts as organized?"

Burton was serious now that we were talking business.

"They think he's funneling stolen stuff through the store. Medical supplies, prescription drugs. None of it shows up on the books, but they don't know where it comes from, either."

"Laundry?"

"Some kind, maybe. Not cash."

"So the interesting question," I said. "What's the Ick got on the owner?"

"And what does any of this have to do with Alison?"

"The photograph was supposed to draw a line from her to the drug store?"

"You weigh the bag of pills?" Burton said.

"Thirty pounds?"

He ciphered on a napkin.

"Hundred and fifty thousand assorted pills. Twenty bucks a pop on the street. You do the math."

I liked that he was assuming Alison wasn't the dealer.

"Take a long time, though. Who hid them in her apartment?"

"You know someone named Cormier? Ricky tried real hard

to drop him in my lap."

"He dated Alison. He works for Maldonado?"

"We need some evidence," Burton said. "And don't talk to me about the hair on the back of your neck."

"I'll hold onto the pills until we find out whose they are."

"The owner can't find them, he's going to come looking for you. How many people know you're the executor?"

"A few."

"If you're worried about them, I'll take them with me," he said.

"You'd be off the force in a heartbeat if they caught you with a half a million dollars' worth of pills. Not to mention the FBI's money." I tossed the bags back in the safe. "I'll give them up the minute someone asks me for them. At least we'll know whose they are."

Burton headed for the front of the bar as I followed.

"Things are moving now," he said. "Feel that?"

I hadn't seen him this positive in weeks, though it wouldn't last long if he lost his job.

"Don't get cocky," I said. "Remember what Cousy used to say when the Celtics got ahead? 'Momentum is twansitowy.' "

CHAPTER 25

Thinking about his meeting with Tommy, Ricky decided he would make the Ritz his headquarters while he was still in Boston. The atmosphere had intimidated the Indian and given Ricky an advantage in the conversation. There was no reason that wouldn't work with other people. Sure, the help was rude, but they were rude everywhere these days, and he favored the leisurely pace at which things moved in the hotel. After all these years of running his ass off, he liked the idea of a world where people weren't striving, there wasn't any sour-milk or bacon-grease smells, and fewer people yelled at him through the short-order window.

"Berto." He called from his corner table to the kid behind the counter.

Berto wore his apron down to his shoes, like one of the eighty-year-old waiters at Jacob Wirth's. Ricky's New York references said the kid was colder than dry ice, even if he looked like an altar boy afraid of getting caught skipping school. Ricky's main worry was that if he didn't find Berto someone to kill pretty soon, he might abandon Ricky's organization or turn on him.

"Get one of the boys to wash this floor tonight, will you? It smells like a baby's diaper in here."

Berto nodded with the flat black look they all learned from television these days and went back into the kitchen.

Before Ricky screwed off to Miami, he had to figure out how to take care of his guys, except Tommy, of course. Tesar and

Spengler weren't going to make it on their own. Tesar was halfway down the black well of speed addiction and Spengler wasn't smart enough to know there were nonviolent solutions to problems. But both of them had been loyal, unlike people he could name, and he wished there was a way to set up a trust fund of some kind, to protect them when he finally stepped down. It would be a disaster for either of them to try and run the organization—they'd get eaten alive.

He rubbed his chest, right over the pacemaker. It had quieted in the last few days, which he hoped meant his body was adjusting, that this work wasn't going to kill him before he got what he wanted. The rotary phone on the wall by the pass-through rang and he answered.

"I thought you told me the samples were lost," desRosiers said, without any greeting.

Ricky felt depression sink in on him. DesRosiers was bringing him the news about Tommy that he'd dreaded. The urge to kill the messenger was almost overwhelming.

"They were, the last I knew," Ricky said.

His chest thumped and that unwanted warmth spread out through his pectoral muscles.

"You better get a handle on your crew, then, Maldonado. I just got a telephone call from your man, the dark fellow?"

"And?"

"He said he can deliver half of them."

Interesting. Tommy was going to keep half of the pills for himself? He was definitely planning to bail, then.

"So what's the problem?" Ricky massaged his abdomen.

"I've shelved all my experiments, given the subjects full dosages."

"So unshelve them." Ricky shrugged. Maybe mental rigor mortis was a requirement for passing medical school. "Go with the flow, doc. Looks to me like we're back in business."

He wasn't happy, though. He and Tommy had worked together a long time and even if he didn't like the son of a bitch much, they'd made some money together. But the time for sentiment was past. Tommy was going to have to go.

"I hope the rest of your organization isn't this disorganized," desRosiers said. "I might have to rethink."

"You need me for anything else right now, doc?" Ricky was exhausted. Maybe he ought to go upstairs and lie down.

"No."

"Pay the man what you owe me when he shows up. We'll discuss the rest of the transaction later."

Ricky hung up first, the only pleasure he'd felt all day, chased by knowing he was going to have to have Tommy taken out.

"Berto!"

But not until Tommy took the payment from desRosiers. Ricky could trust Berto to follow Tommy, pick up the cash, then tap him. Berto only cared about taking life, not money.

The kid slouched in, but brightened when he saw Ricky's grave mood.

"Berto. You know Tommy, right?"

Berto flushed, then nodded. Ricky wondered if Tommy had been giving the kid shit—not a wise move, if he had.

"I need you to keep an eye on him for me." Ricky hardened his tone. "And that's all I want you to do for now. You remember the discussion we had about discipline?"

Berto looked at his shoe tops and nodded.

"If things go the way I expect, you'll get the chance to exercise your talents. But only when I say it's OK."

The kid was untying his apron.

"Starting now?" he asked.

Ricky nodded. The apron flew into the corner, and Berto was gone.

Ricky sat at the counter with his coffee and thought about

whether he ought to have desRosiers done, too. It would be bad for business, but he was going to be out of the business soon, and he didn't trust the doc not to fold under pressure. If Ricky were going to have a successful retirement, he didn't want des-Rosiers somewhere cluttering up the picture, maybe attracting cops long after their deal was done.

But these particular pills were useless to anyone but desRosiers, not that Tommy knew that. As pleasant as it would be never to hear the doctor's Beacon Hill tones again, Ricky didn't think he could afford to kill him. Tommy's disappearance wouldn't generate much heat, but the murder of a society doctor, no matter how bent, would bring down a species of shit that Ricky didn't want to deal with, now or ever.

Maybe later on, he thought. In the meantime, the least he could do was fuck up desRosiers's practice somehow or smother him in some quasi-legal bullshit. What he was doing with these low-dosage pills couldn't be legal or ethical.

He grimaced at the rest of the cold coffee. That was probably the way to go, fuck up the doc in a way that would annoy him most, by ruining his experiments. There wouldn't be any trouble making that happen—there might even be a way to have some fun with it, if he set his mind to it.

CHAPTER 26

During the midafternoon lull, Marina bullied me into eating a bowl of Tuscan white bean soup, and though the first few sips were touch and go, eventually I ate it all, along with a rosemary ciabatta from the new bakery up the block. I belched as I walked back out front, tasting the garlic and spices. Aside from a thirst for club soda that I couldn't quench, I was close to the man I'd been at this time yesterday, physically at least. Mentally, who knew?

When Cy opened the street door and started down the stairs, I thought about Burton's comment about the owner of the pills coming to see me eventually. The heels of his eelskin cowboy boots rang on the metal risers.

I tried to get focused.

"I've been trying to call you," I said.

He looked annoyed.

"Is this still a bar? Can a person get a drink?"

I poured some Babancourt in a glass and set it in front of him. He unbuttoned his black leather blazer and unwound the yellow scarf from around his neck, inspecting me with a knowing eye.

"You're back to following the drinking gourd."

I was tired of people noticing, not to mention assuming it was any of their business.

"You didn't tell me you were acting as Alison's agent." I set the file folder on the bar and he looked at it. Fearfully?

"You didn't tell me you were her executor, either."

"The difference is, I just found out."

The sight of the paperwork seemed to bother him more than the fact that he'd traded on our friendship. He sipped some rum.

"There didn't ever seem to be a good time," he said. "You were wrapped up tight right after she died. I didn't see any sense in troubling you."

"I can think of any number of conversations you might have slipped it into," I said.

He turned the heavy glass in his hand, staring into the bottom for an answer. I could have told him that whatever it was, it wasn't there. The whites of his eyes were tracked with capillaries.

"Alison had trouble with promoters," he said. "Especially those of the white persuasion. She ended up being too nice to them."

"Like Tommy Cormier?" I said.

He looked surprised I knew the name, though he didn't confirm or deny.

"After you, she wanted a brother in her corner. People used to try and intimidate her: she was a woman, she was black, and tender in the emotions. A couple of people she sang for even stiffed her, but she came back and performed for them anyway. I tried to help. Without a venue, she couldn't sing. Without the singing, she couldn't live."

I suspected his sincerity, especially since the accounting of the estate showed he owed it about thirty thousand dollars. Would he have been desperate enough to kill her for that kind of money?

"You became her agent out of humanitarian motives?" I was disappointed—I'd thought he was my friend, and Alison's too.

He dipped his head, showing the thin patches in his steel-wool hair.

"Well, she did pay me, Elder. I'm not so rich I can turn down compensation for the work I do."

"And all these gigs she did in the last six months? She got paid for all of them?"

He looked at the bar.

"I'd have to go back to my office, look at the records."

I pulled a list from the folder and slid it across.

"This is a copy. The checks were all mailed out, according to the people I talked to."

"I'll look into it," he said.

"Over thirty grand, Cy. Which needs to be paid before I can close the estate."

He looked startled.

"I don't have that kind of cash on hand."

"Is that why you didn't want me looking into her death? Because I'd find out you'd been cheating her?"

"I considered it a loan," he said. "Can't we just forget about it? Not like she needs the bread."

Anger tightened my throat.

"I'm the executor, Cy. If I don't account for everything, then I become liable. And you also have a bequest, which I can't disburse until everything else is settled."

I wasn't going to let him or anyone else get away with cheating Alison, even posthumously. He perked up a little when he heard he was in the will, but he wouldn't have if he'd seen the list of bequests.

"I could pay it back a little at a time maybe."

"You have until we read the will."

He pushed his glass forward and pulled out a twenty. I guess he understood he wasn't getting any more free drinks in my bar.

"I flat don't have it, Elder."

"So I'll go to the police. It gives you a motive."

"To kill her? Shit, man. I'm not that stupid. Or greedy."

I wanted to believe him, but couldn't quite.

He drank the rum until it was gone, then stood.

"You act like you're innocent," he said. "You know what goes on in this place. Always has."

In a flash, I saw what I hadn't before, mainly because I trusted him. I saw Lorelei begging the night he was in here, all those students he'd been shaking hands with.

"You were selling dope in here?"

Enraged, I stiff-armed him in the chest. It was like shoving a concrete pillar. He looked at my hands.

"You fucking used me that way?" I said.

Stupidly, I launched a fist at his head. With the bar between us, all he had to do was step to the side, but he grabbed my wrist and twisted. My face banged on the bar.

"No one beats on me," he said.

Then he started to sniffle and let me go. I rolled my eyes. He was sad because he'd been caught out, not because he'd developed a sense of shame.

A flat crack on the bar made me jump. I straightened up and shook out my arm.

Marina slapped the flat of her big chef's knife on the bar again, a noise like a small-caliber gunshot.

"Get out of here." Adrenaline made her voice a screech. *"Scuta."*

Cy tucked his hands in the pockets of his blazer and started toward the stairs, his shoulders hunched forward like a broken-down boxer.

"Friday," I called after him. "We're reading the will on Friday."

It took a few seconds for my heart to slow down. Marina was

back in the kitchen, stropping the knife.

"Thank you," I said from the doorway.

She looked up and made a face.

"What are you doing all this for?" she said. "You're not a cop. You don't even have the temperament."

It sounded like something Burton would say.

"Alison," I said. "I have to know what happened."

She shook her head. "You know you can't change it, no matter who did what. You're just looking for new ways to hurt yourself."

She might have been right, but I wasn't going to look at the assertion too closely.

The Esposito eased into the dinner hour, busy but not crazy. Some of the people who'd stopped in after work for a pop stayed on for lasagna and a glass of wine. The weather had turned cold and blustery again, and we were serving the right kind of comfort. At least I could be happy about the bar—it was starting to feel like a neighborhood fixture, which was what I'd hoped for all along.

Between orders, I leaned on the bar and thought about Cy's confession. If he'd embezzled that much money from Alison, could she have not known? She wasn't money-hungry, but she wasn't naive, either. If her death had been by violence, I would have suspected Cy, but the forensics didn't support anyone throwing her out the window. She'd definitely jumped, according to Burton.

As the dinner crowd cleared, I picked up tables and thought about my slip last night, wondering eventually if I shouldn't turn to another kind of business. Running a bar wasn't the most intelligent career for someone who wanted to stay sober, and assuming Burton didn't burn up all the money Alison had left me. I'd have a little left over to go in another direction. Maybe I could find something that would engage my thinking brain more than tending bar.

I piled dishes in the dishwasher and listened to Charlie Parker's headlong solo on "Cherokee." There was a man who sacrificed everything to his addiction, even though he had left something beautiful behind. I knew I didn't have that kind of talent, though. Anything I left behind would be of a totally different character.

Berklee was on spring break this week, so Eric wasn't going to be playing. Business was down that weekend because of the vacation, but I didn't mind so much. I was starting to recognize some of the faces in my nightly crowds and it pleased me to think the Esposito was developing regulars.

I wasn't too surprised when Susan Voisine strolled in the door about eight-thirty—I'd been expecting a play for sympathy for a while. She looked desirable hip-hopping down the stairs, but in the way a beautiful woman in crisis always looks good. Her hair was a touch greasy and she wore baggy black jeans and a lavender sweatshirt so old the collar was ragged, but the effect was to make her look more vulnerable, more in need of help. Images of the two of us in my bed flashed through my brain. I tried to ignore them, but I wasn't going to stop wanting her, apparently, betrayal or no.

She walked up to bar, trying and failing to hold my gaze.

"Just listen a minute," she said.

I placed my hands palm-down on the bar.

"Mrs. Rinaldi was already on the floor when I got there. She'd already had the heart attack when I went in. I didn't scare her into it."

I'd figured that much out on my own. My real problem was that I couldn't decide whether Susan had slept with me to gain access to Dorothea's apartment or because she'd wanted to. Whether she'd been stealing or replacing the opera memorabilia was immaterial in the face of that question.

"Ends up the same, doesn't it?"

"Does it have to?" she said. "Because actually the woman could be dead if I hadn't been there." She finally looked at me. I thought I saw shame. "Is there coffee?"

Grateful for an excuse to step away, I walked out to the kitchen and poured her a mug.

She took a long time with the cream and sugar, getting the color she wanted.

"I don't want you to take this out on Henri," she said.

"I can't keep a tenant who breaks into other people's apartments," I said.

"It's Alzheimer's," she said. "He thought he was doing me a favor."

"Diagnosed? Or are you just guessing?"

That added information I hadn't considered—was she saying Henri had stolen Mrs. Rinaldi's material? Then Susan really may have been trying to return it.

"He's going to have to go to assisted living soon," she said. "No more than six months, probably."

"And you want me to put up with him until then?"

"Do you want me to say I used him?" she said. "I used him. But he thought the whole thing was a lark, and he was fixated on the woman besides."

It felt like she was running me from one side of a squash court to the other.

"How do I know he won't force his nutty behavior on some other poor soul? I'm running an apartment building, not a loony bin."

She pulled a thin white envelope out of her back pocket. I backed away with my hands in the air.

"You think you can buy me off."

"This is Henri's rent for the next year," she said. "He's going to stay a lot stabler if he can stay somewhere familiar. I really don't want to uproot him. Will you consider it at least?"

I shook my head.

"Don't do the whole false pride thing," she said. "Think of it as a gift to an old man."

"That's it?" I said. "No more to the bribe?"

She frowned at my word choice.

"Let's call it what it is." I still hurt from the other night.

She tossed a square lavender envelope onto the bar, my first name scrawled in Alison's spiky handwriting.

"Your friend Burton was too polite to put his hand down my pants that night."

I started to reach for it. She put her small hand down on top.

"We have a deal?" she said.

"Henri stays. But only if you come running the minute I tell you it's time."

"One other thing."

"What?"

She looked at the empty shot glass up in Alison's niche.

"Nothing," she said. "Just don't yell at him anymore."

I slipped both the envelopes into the drawer behind the bar as she disappeared up the stairs and out the steel-clad door, leaving me with a rock in my stomach and the screaming need for a drink. I wondered if I would see her again, or if I wanted to.

The night dragged on mercilessly. I was aware from one minute to the next of relearning that frail discipline, the habit of not filling up a glass and emptying it down my throat every time I had the urge. It was more difficult now than the first time around, since I'd just had a reminder what was at stake. That nearly two years of not drinking was no more than a memory. I didn't get credit for it.

When we closed up, Marina asked me for a ride home. I

didn't ask her where Burton was.

"That's a very Catholic thing, the altar." She pointed at the empty shot glass as we walked out. "I thought you Episcopalians were all cold and rational."

I didn't have an answer for that, so it was a long quiet ride down to the South End.

After I dropped Marina off, I went home, a decision validated by finding an open parking space three doors down. As I climbed past Dorothea's empty apartment, I reminded myself to call Mass General in the morning and see if she needed anything. I doubted, the way hospitals were these days, they would keep her very long.

I turned on all the lamps in the living room, trying to chase the dark scraps of memory that roosted in the corners. I put on the water, ground some coffee beans, and slipped the lavender envelope out of my pocket. Alison had scribbled the date at the top of the note, two weeks before she died.

"Old Elder." She used her pet name for my overserious self. "I do wish I knew why I missed you so much these days. Even though you're only a mile or two away as the bird flies, you've gone beyond me, into the past with the rest of the ancestors.

"I suppose I should be happy. I have some love, the songs, my health—what I can't see is why if it looks so good from out there, I'm not any happier inside."

My sob surprised me. I walked out to the kitchen and brought back coffee.

"Somehow I thought all those drunk and thoughtless nights were going to keep us together," she wrote. "I used to think we could dry out together someday, but I guess we won't know that now.

"I'm giving it up, love, sad to say. I know how you hate the dramatics, and I know we had a deal, but I just cannot hold it together anymore. You know that blackness doesn't scare me at all—I've skated out on the thin ice so often, it might just be a relief to fall through.

"I don't know if I will follow through, but if I do, know you were the one who almost kept me on earth. I was always the woman with the hollow spots, the places you filled. One day, maybe, I'll run into you shuffling up Commonwealth Ave. You'll be shocked at how good I look, and I'll kiss that bristly cheek and whisper something dirty in your ear just to make you blush. I did love you, Elder. Don't you ever give that up."

My head dropped and tears splotched the paper. For the first time since Alison died, I let myself go, the grief fountaining out of the deep places I didn't know I had, and it went on and on, seemingly for days, until I was aware of a knocking out in the living room.

I wiped my face and blew my nose. When I saw Henri through the peephole, I undid the bolt. His face was screwed up like a baby's, and twin tracks wetted his cheeks.

"What is it?" I said.

He pushed his way into my apartment without asking, remarkable in itself for a man who was normally so polite. I could no more be angry with him than at a puppy.

"You're mourning her too," he said.

Grief rode him fresh and deep as my own. The tight wrinkles on his face were lined with shadowy flesh, the graininess of no sleep marred his skin, and the rims of his eyes were raw.

It took me a second to understand he meant Dorothea.

"Mrs. Rinaldi?"

"I knew something wasn't right," he said. "I care about her."

He thumped down in the armchair, his thin shoulders shaking as if he were standing in a hurricane.

"She's going to be fine," I said.

I sat down with him until the sobbing receded, and I thought about love and not declaring your love when you had the chance and how emotions grew contorted when they didn't have room to unfold.

I wondered if what crippled us was our inability to spend all our love, to give it all away without guarantee of return. It was as if we'd conditioned ourselves always to reserve some of it, against a future need.

He stood and walked over to my bookcase and pulled out the backgammon set.

"Could we play a game, Jackson?" he said. "It seems like a long time since we had a game."

CHAPTER 27

Early Friday afternoon was becoming my favorite part of the week. I'd checked in the deliveries of food and liquor to carry us through the weekend. I'd been to the bank and bought plenty of change. The beer coolers were rotated and filled and the spare bottle shelf was stocked so I wouldn't have to run out to the storeroom during a rush. Even all the garbage—the lemons and limes and oranges—were sliced up and packed into plastic containers. I loved the feeling of being prepared.

I was leaning on the bar with a cup of coffee and reading the sports page of the *Globe*, focused on the spring training stories out of Fort Myers. The place was deserted, since most of my Friday lunchtime drinkers skipped the noon hour entirely and came in at three or four to start their long slow slide into the weekend. It was about two when Tommy Cormier walked in, stepping very lightly down the metal stairs for someone of his size. Marina had run up to the bank to deposit her paycheck.

I'd returned the duffel bag full of money to Alison's apartment, then had the locksmith rekey the place, but I'd kept the pills at the Esposito, wanting to see who might come after them. I might have made a mistake believing they were Cy's.

"Mr. Darrow," Cormier said as he came up to the bar.

I reached down a bottle of Talisker I'd bought for a customer who'd asked for it once, then never come back. It was eighteen years old and smooth as a baby's bottom, or so I imagined. They'd only started importing the best single malts after I stopped drinking. The first time, that is.

But when I turned over a shot glass on the bar, Cormier surprised me by shaking his head.

"Business," he said.

I held onto the bottle in case I needed a weapon. Cormier looked amused.

He wore a pale blue denim jacket with a tapestry yoke in desert colors: rust, yellow, beige. An oval silver buckle the size of a fried egg held up his loose black jeans, the cuffs of which ended one perfect inch above the goat-roper heel of his boots. All he needed to look completely out of place was a black Stetson hat. He clasped his hands in front of him, displaying that big silver and turquoise ring.

"You're a businessman, Elder. Am I right?"

You could have greased a motorcycle chain with his smile.

"Trenchant observation, Tom."

I might have been afraid of the physical Tommy, but the verbal one didn't frighten me much.

"And business and emotions make a messy combination," he said. "So I would prefer that we keep our business on an unemotional plane if possible."

"Unless you want a drink," I said. "I don't believe we have any business to discuss at all."

His fingers curled slightly and I stepped a pace to the right, so at least he'd have to reach to hit me.

"I believe you're holding something that belongs to me," he said. "A couple of somethings, in fact."

The confirmation that Cy had talked to Tommy snapped my last strand of sympathy.

'This isn't baggage claim, Tom."

He pounced on my mistake.

"I don't think anyone said anything about baggage." He smiled. "Though oddly enough, that's exactly what I'm missing.

A couple of duffel bags."

He held his hands apart to estimate the dimensions. "About so."

"Haven't seen a thing," I said.

The door at the top of the stairs opened up again. I relaxed. Cormier wasn't going to get physical in the presence of witnesses.

But my relief reversed itself when I saw Lorelei, wearing a green wool duffle coat and a ratty stocking cap pulled down to her eyes. Her eyes were set deep in the shadowed hollows of her face, and she kept her right hand in the coat's pocket. At the bottom of the stairs, she stopped and leaned on the bottom railing.

Cormier rapped his ring against the bar.

"I am not fucking around here, Elder. Someone's changed the locks on Alison's apartment."

"I'm glad to see she's keeping herself occupied." I nodded at Lorelei.

The smile wrinkled the corners of Tommy's mouth again.

"She's just a regular Patty Hearst, isn't she?" He sounded proud. "Check out the coat pocket."

It might have been her finger or it might have been a gun barrel pushing out the fabric.

"I'd be the innocent customer who happened by," Cormier said. "Too late to save you from a deranged woman with a gun."

"Sounds a little baroque."

Tommy looked puzzled.

"Whatever. She's high enough to do whatever I tell her."

"Why don't you give me an idea what's in this bag, maybe help me identify it as yours?" I don't know why I was poking this snake with a stick, but I thought he might know more about Alison's death than he was saying. Maybe he'd trade me information for the pills. Plus the longer we talked, the sooner

Marina would return or some other customers would show up.

"Blue and white and pink?" he said. "A lot of little bits of altered states. Now. You through fucking around?"

I would have liked the chance to consult with Burton, but I couldn't think of a reason not to hand over the pills.

"Let me check my lost and found," I said. "Maybe someone left something that looks like that."

Tommy slid off the stool as if I'd invited him to follow me into the back. I poured him a shot of the Talisker, finding it interesting he wasn't pushing too hard for the bag of money. He must have known it was marked.

"Stay out here and make sure she doesn't shoot the customers, all right? I don't have so many I can afford to lose one."

When I came back with the bag, Lorelei was gone, and Tommy looked more relaxed. The shot glass was empty.

I slung the bag up on the counter.

"I want a couple answers first," I said.

He frowned. "Or I could just take it away from you."

"Was Alison your wholesaler?"

He laughed like a goose.

"Alison. You must not have known her very well," he said. "She hated drugs, all kinds of them. She didn't even like taking the antidepressants."

"Where did all her money come from, then?"

Cormier shrugged. "Didn't know she had any."

I believed him. His ego was too big to let him fake an ignorance. I pushed the bag across the bar.

He unzipped it far enough to look inside, then set it on the floor.

"Good place to hide it," I said. "You two must have been close if she gave you her keys."

He nodded. I was astonished to see his eyes get moist.

"Like that," I said. "I'm sorry for your loss."

"This," he kicked the bag, "has nothing to do with her."

I took a chance on his momentary weakness.

"You think she jumped out that window on her own?"

"No way." His pain was evident. "She was doing fine until she hooked up with that doctor. She was never strong, but she was working, taking her pills like she was supposed to."

I thought about the note she'd written me. She hadn't been doing fine when she wrote that.

"She wasn't taking her pills," I said.

"I lived with her up until the week before she died," Cormier said. "I watched her take them every morning."

"That's not what the autopsy said. She didn't have a thing in her system except a couple of glasses of wine."

"You're not bullshitting?" Cormier asked thoughtfully.

"Why would I?"

"She was acting down when I saw her, the week before. She said the new pills didn't seem to work as well."

"She'd changed her prescription?"

"Doctors. She was seeing a guy with a clinic up in the Back Bay. He must have been writing her scripts."

So desRosiers had lied about not prescribing for Alison—big surprise there.

The upstairs door opened and Marina appeared, breaking the frail connection between Tommy and me.

"We should discuss this a little more," I said.

Cormier gave me a cold brilliant smile. "I don't see why."

He knew something else I needed to know, but I couldn't think of a way to force it out of him.

"You say so."

Marina came behind the bar and stood next to me as Cormier climbed the stairs. She huffed.

"He didn't even recognize me," she said. "Carlos hated his guts, you know."

"Carlos worked for him?"

"Tropical Tommy," she said mockingly. "He used to give them all pep talks, like at a sales convention or something."

"He is a piece of work."

She shrugged and walked back into the kitchen.

I leaned on the bar again. The doctor had supposedly been in Norway when Alison died, and I had to assume Burton would have verified his whereabouts. And if someone else had killed her, how had they made it look like suicide?

I'd been hoping Burton would drop by and report, but instead I got his boss again. It was close to four in the afternoon when Costain swaggered downstairs into the Esposito, preceding a pale unhappy man in a blue wool suit. The captain wore jeans and tan construction boots, a puffy green down vest and a watch cap. I wondered if his partner was his administrative assistant—he had that pale and harried look.

"Darrow." Costain nodded.

I walked down the bar to change the music over to something a little mellower. When I came back, the man in the suit was smiling in a way that made me wonder how he was going to mug me.

"Linda Frisell," he said. "Outstanding guitar player. Better than her husband."

It couldn't have been a lucky guess—she was too obscure a musician—but that didn't mean I had to take him any seriously. He was very closely shaved, the knot of his solid red tie tight against the white shirt collar, and his steady eyes were the color of young bourbon. If it had been the eighties, I would have pegged him for an IBM salesman. Today, he had to be a Federal officer of some kind, and so definitely not Costain's subordinate.

"Dressed up for a stakeout, Captain Costain?" I said.

He sighed.

"I used to poke snakes with a stick when I was a kid too. We're here to do you a favor, Darrow. Let me introduce Agent Donald Manelli. With the FBI."

Costain registered my uneasiness.

"Yeah," he said. "We're pretty sure you're involved in something illegal here, just not what. But speaking personally, if you mess up Burton while you're doing it? I'll have your ass."

"Didn't know you went that way, Captain."

His vehemence seemed to embarrass Manelli, who spoke a word in his ear. Costain stalked to a table near the empty stage and sat.

Manelli stuck his hand out over the bar.

"Sorry to disturb you," he said. "Though better now than in the middle of the dinner rush, eh?"

"That sounds a little ominous. How can I help?"

He reached into an inside pocket of his suit, pulled out a fifty-dollar bill in a plastic sleeve, and laid it Grant-side up on the bar.

"Is that a tip?" I said.

"You don't have to prove to me how quick you are," Manelli said. "I wanted to know if you recognize it."

I laughed.

"I run a cash business. You want me to recognize a specific bill? Maybe if it had Dizzy Gillespie's face on it."

But my heart bumped. The money in the bag at Alison's was all fifties and hundreds. It was probably the cash the FBI lost trying to bust Ricky Maldonado.

"It came from your night deposit bag."

I picked up the plastic sleeve. "Is there something special about this one?"

"You serve coffee here?"

He was telling me he would stay as long as it took to get his answers.

213

"This is a bar," I said. "I wouldn't expect too much."

By the time I returned with his mug, I'd decided it would be smarter not to play games.

"If you say the bill must have come through my register, I believe you. But I must see a dozen fifties a night. There's no way for me to tell whose pocket it came out of."

Except for the fact that I had a memory of Tommy Cormier crumpling a fifty and tossing it on the bar, the night he and Eric almost fought.

"This bill is marked," Manelli said. "I can't tell you how. But it was part of a Federal drug buy a few months back."

I smiled.

"And you lost the money? I can see why you'd be trying to trace this."

Costain was yapping on his cell phone. I poured myself a glass of club soda and squeezed in a lime wedge.

"I think your friend Burton was involved in the theft," Manelli said, glancing at Costain. "He was liaised to the task force that was making the buy. Then this other thing happened."

I didn't believe there was such a verb as "liaise."

"Other thing," I said. Alison's death? Carlos's?

My first good-citizen reaction was to tell Manelli about the money in Alison's shoe closet. But that wouldn't do Burton any good if they already suspected him—in fact, since he'd had access to the apartment, it would look very bad. The tiny bureaucratic minds never believe in coincidence.

"Agent Manelli." I hoped I wasn't being too sincere. "I do a decent business here. You've been reading my night deposit slips, you know that much. If I have drug dealers coming in here to drink, it's not obvious to me."

Except for Cy Nance and Tommy Cormier, that is.

Manelli sipped the coffee, controlled a grimace.

"Talk to the local cops, if you like," I said. "For a long time, they were down here every night. I spent a lot of effort discouraging the undesirable element here. I don't want them."

Manelli shook his head.

"One of the things that drives the Bureau crazy," he said. "Cash businesses. So often they turn out to be fronts for other kinds of crime: drugs, even terrorism. When times are good, they can sneak under the radar, but with a recession on?"

"I wish I could help." Vague threats meant he had no evidence. I hoped.

Costain had gotten loud and animated on the phone, then stood and headed for the staircase.

"Tom," Manelli called.

"They just caught someone trying to break into the Mayflower Room."

Manelli extracted a business card from the back of his badge case and laid it on the bar.

"Call me if you decide you want to stay out of trouble, Mr. Darrow."

He jogged off up the stairs after Costain, the tails of his suit jacket flapping. I ripped the card in tiny pieces and tossed it in the trash. I didn't see anything in this situation, or any other one, that could be improved by knowing a Fed.

CHAPTER 28

Tommy turned off Gloucester Street and headed north into the tangle of dead-end alleys and one-way streets until he reached desRosiers's clinic. The building was low and flat, stucco and brick behind a high chain-link fence. Two curtained picture windows bracketed the front door and he wondered how the doctor kept people from throwing rocks through them. Technically, this was the Back Bay, but not the part the Chamber of Commerce bragged about.

As he turned off the Navigator's engine, Tommy throttled his anger down so he could concentrate on the business at hand. Talking to Darrow just now, he had connected up some things that Ricky had said with the fact that Alison hadn't had antidepressants in her blood. DesRosiers had been the one who killed her, probably by prescribing her off-brand pills like the ones Tommy carried in the bag. She'd either had a reaction or the pills hadn't had enough active ingredient to do what they were supposed to. It was as much murder as if the doctor had shot her with a gun.

He locked the truck and transferred the duffle to his left hand. He was warring with two desires: grabbing his fuck-you money and splitting or making desRosiers pay for Alison's death. They hadn't been a great couple, in love or any of that bullshit, but he loved listening to her sing and she'd treated him as well as any woman ever had. As long as it didn't interfere with his business, he thought, he should do something to avenge her.

Priorities straight, he walked up the cracked concrete path. Scraggly green daffodil shoots lined the walkway and close up, the picture windows showed the metallic sheen of safety glass, which answered his question about broken windows.

The pale blue blank steel door contained two brass locks and a hasp for a padlock, open right now. The doctor wasn't taking any chances up here, though how successful could his practice be if he worked in such a crappy location? Tommy had a hard time seeing the matrons from Louisburg Square wandering down to this neighborhood for their weekly confession and absolution. Maybe that was part of the thrill.

The door sighed open as he set his foot on the stoop. DesRosiers looked down his long thin nose, apparently ignoring the fact that Tommy could break him in half with one hand. And wanted to, badly.

"You're late," desRosiers said.

"You're not so easy to find down here in the slums, doc." Tommy controlled his anger by focusing on the money.

DesRosiers made a point of checking out the street over Tommy's shoulder, as if he might have been followed. Tommy breathed deeply, knowing desRosiers was going to pay for all the insults.

The waiting-room walls were covered in a beige sea grass, the carpet a medium white cheap flat-weave. A row of scarred wooden armchairs sat along the wall next to a reception area with a round metal grill. The glass panel was pulled shut, the area behind it deserted. The place looked like a methadone clinic or an unemployment office.

"Everybody off today?" Tommy said.

DesRosiers looked at him with contempt. Tommy added that to the payback list.

"I don't expose my regular staff to my experimental activities." He held out an imperious hand. "Let me see what you have."

As soon as he had the money in hand, Tommy was going to ace this asshole. There just wasn't any reason for someone with a shitty attitude to ruin everyone else's day. It wouldn't just be for Alison. He'd consider it a public service.

"Let's have the money up here first," Tommy said. "Just so I know I haven't wasted my time coming out to see you."

DesRosiers whirled, his lab coat flaring open to show a white-on-white shirt and a mauve-dotted tie, Now there was a tie Tommy could see himself in, assuming he could force himself to wear one.

"You people are unbelievable," desRosiers fumed. "You have the pills, you don't have the pills. You want to sell them, you don't want to sell them. I told your fat little boss and I'm telling you, you'd better get your act straight if you want to continue to do business with me."

Tommy froze. "You spoke with Mr. Maldonado?"

DesRosiers unlocked the office door. They walked into the bare square cubicle behind the sliding window.

"Of course I did," he said. "He's been my contact all along. Why would I change that now?"

Tommy forced himself to breathe. He wouldn't have time to sell the rest of the pills on the street, but he could still score enough off of desRosiers to get out of town. He'd have to leave today. Ricky wouldn't waste any time coming after him, now that he knew.

The doctor grabbed a package the size of four bricks wrapped in brown paper and duct tape from under the desk and thrust it at Tommy.

"Here," he said. "It's all there."

Tommy didn't have time to sit here and count it, but desRosiers would be too afraid of Ricky's revenge if he shorted him.

"It better be."

He set the money down and handed the bag over. When the doctor sat down in the swivel chair and bent over to unzip the bag, Tommy started to bend over him to snap his neck.

"I don't know why you're only selling the half." DesRosiers sounded sly, as if he thought he could put one over. Tommy stretched his fingers. "When you see Maldonado, tell him. If he can locate the rest, I'll take them."

Tommy stepped back.

"You have the money for them?"

The rest of the pills were in the back of his Navigator. He could double his money, keep the phony pills, and still kill the doctor. Win–win–win.

"I can have it in an hour." DesRosiers's eyes flashed.

Tommy wondered if he could stay out of Ricky's way for another hour. With that kind of money, he could afford Santa Fe.

"Four o'clock." He snapped his fingers. "I'll be back. And no excuses."

"There isn't any need to be unpleasant," desRosiers said in his pissy way.

Tommy changed his mind about how he would kill the doctor—quick wouldn't do at all.

He was walking very fast when he came out the door and caught a sudden movement across the street, a body ducking behind a rusted Chevy Tahoe. It was Ricky's new cook, recognizable even without the apron. What was his name? Bento? Berto.

Tommy unlocked the Navigator and tossed the package of money on the back seat. So Ricky knew where he was right now. So what? Another hour wasn't going to make that much difference, though it would be smart to slow down Berto's transmission of the news if he could.

He ran across the street, locking the Lincoln with the remote as he went. He didn't want to lose his money to some random thief while he was over there settling Berto's hash.

CHAPTER 29

I was leaning on the bar trying to decide if Manelli really believed Burton had stolen the FBI's buy money, when someone touched me on the arm. I almost jumped through the ceiling. Marina must have let Burton in through the fire door.

"Don't you have something a little more musical we could listen to?" He jerked his head at the speaker. "Maybe Quasimodo singing *Sweet Caroline* while gargling broken glass?"

I'd been a Blossom Dearie fan since I was in prep school, and only the fact that there were other people whose musical taste I respected who didn't like her voice kept me from smacking him.

"This from a guy who worships Sinead O'Connor."

"Better than Sandra Day," he said.

He stepped around me, outside the bar, and settled himself on a stool as if he planned to stay.

"Who was the suit with Costain? As if I didn't know."

"You were here the whole time?"

"I went around the back when I saw Costain's car. I don't need any grief from him about the company I'm keeping."

"Manelli."

"From Fart, Belch and Itch." He put his fingertips to his temples like Karnack the Magnificent. "Wait, wait. Don't tell me. The Maldonado drug-buy money."

I nodded. If he wasn't going to worry about it, I had nothing to say.

"Did Sharon's lawyer give you a number?"

"Fifty-six thousand, five hundred dollars. I can't imagine what the odd five hundred is for, except maybe press-on fingernails and artificial sweetener."

"That's in the budget," I said. "Just let me know how and when you want it."

I hurried on. I didn't want him to feel like he had to thank me.

"So what have I gotten for my money so far?"

He flipped some pages in his notebook.

"The drug store in the Fens. Ownership goes through shell corporations and various dodges. I'll trace it eventually, but just the fact that it's buried so deep is indicative."

"That's it."

He frowned.

"The rest is confirmation of things we already know. Alison was happy enough, she was working. You knew Nance was acting as her agent?"

I told him about the thirty thousand Cy owed the estate.

"It doesn't seem like enough to kill someone for, though."

"I've seen people kill over quarters," he said. "You know, I keep coming back to the fact that there's no physical evidence that she didn't jump out the window on her own."

I didn't think this was the time to tell him my theory. He didn't know how fragile she'd been, either.

"She had two boyfriends," Burton said. "A part-timer and a guy who spent a lot of nights at her place until a week or so before."

"That last would be Tommy Cormier. The other guy is probably Cameron desRosiers. Doctor. Tall, thin, balding? Walks like he's got a bottle brush up his ass?"

"If you already know everything, what am I supposed to be doing?"

"Good question," I said.

"Let me have a beer."

"Those pills turned out to belong to Cormier." I popped a Heineken. "He came by to claim them."

"You gave them up."

"Considering he threatened to break my face, I thought it was the right thing to do. He mentioned the money but he didn't press me for that."

"If he works for Icky Ricky, he was probably the guy who grabbed it from the FBI," Burton said. "He'd know it was marked."

The street door opened. Two men and three women in business clothes laughed their way down the stairs and took the big table.

"Would Alison have known Cormier was pushing?" Burton said. "Maybe he killed her when she found out. Or maybe she wanted to get into the business and the pills were going to be her capital."

I poured red wine and mixed some Manhattans. One of the women paid for the drinks and she and her companion carried them back to the table.

I shook my head, repeating Tommy's words, which I knew to be true.

"She hated pills, even the antidepressants. She used to say that drugs did more to ruin jazz than disco."

Burton grinned. "I liked her, that time we met."

"Strange days," I said. "So we're back to where we were, basically. Is it worth going to Icky Ricky again?"

Burton shook his head.

"He wasn't that impressed with me the last time. And I can't push him that hard if I'm on suspension."

"What about getting the FBI money back? Would that impress anyone? It's right there in Alison's apartment."

"Nah. Ricky knows it's marked." Burton started to get up off his stool. "And speaking of money."

"You want to take a check?"

"Sharon's lawyer wants a 'demonstration of serious intent.' "

"His boat payment must be due. Ten?"

"Five is fine," Burton said. "She's not getting another fucking cent until I get a signed decree."

I went in back and wrote out the check, waved it dry as I returned.

"Thanks," he said. "Maybe I'll mention the FBI money to Ricky, see if I get a bite."

"Only if you think it will get us anywhere," I said. "You are the trained professional, after all."

He tucked the check in his shirt pocket. "I'm glad somebody still thinks so."

Still in the doldrums of the afternoon, I spread the *Globe* out on the bar. The phone rang, and not for the first time I considered installing one that would only call out.

"Esposito."

"Elder? Eric O'Hanian."

"Piano man. What's the story?"

"Nothing."

His tone was too casual. It made me listen harder.

"We're still on for Friday night, then?" I said.

He'd called me a couple of days ago to say he'd found a bass player as good as the young Charles Mingus. Even allowing for the youngster's hyperbole, it would be worth a listen.

"Small problem." His voice cracked.

"Where are you, bud?"

"South Station. Getting the bus out of town."

School vacation was last week. Eric might miss a chance to perform in public if his mother died, but only if she had been very good to him. I wondered if this had something to do with Lorelei, who must have slipped out of rehab to be Tommy Cormier's moll.

"Hang on," I said. "I have some money for you. I can drop it off before you leave."

Silence on the line.

"Eric?"

"Mail it," he said. "You've got my address."

"I can be there in ten minutes. Wait." I hung up, counting on his innate good manners to do what I asked.

I stuck my head in the kitchen.

"I've got to run downtown," I told Marina.

She wrinkled her nose.

"Yes, it's important."

I tucked a blank check in my pocket, wondering what had bothered Eric enough to make him want to run away.

Ten minutes to South Station meant I was flying low, but the traffic gods were kind. I parked the Cougar on a yellow line on Atlantic Avenue and checked up and down the street. Mid-afternoon was shift-change for the meter maids. I probably had a half an hour's grace.

I walked up to the concrete island where the buses parked and checked the schedules. Nothing left for at least an hour and a half.

"Elder."

I turned around. Eric stood under the plexiglass shelter in a raggedy sheepskin coat and a red toque, a blue backpack slung over his shoulder. A bright white cast covered his right wrist, out to the tips of his fingers, and he looked scared.

"Hey. Thanks for waiting," I said. "Let's get some coffee."

I thought getting him away from the bus station might help. We sat in the uncomfortable black wire chairs outside of Starbucks. Besides being scared, he was very angry.

225

"It's like he's got her mesmerized," he said. "I had to try and do something."

I'd been right.

"Lorelei's an addict, Eric. It doesn't matter what substance she's taking, it's her personality. She's got a hole inside her nothing else is going to fill. It wasn't Tommy giving it to her, it'd be someone else."

"I couldn't let him drag her all the way down. We almost made it out of there."

Leaving her would have been a smarter move, but I didn't want to say that out loud.

"She's going to be a junkie. Whoever she's with."

"What the hell do you know?" He pouted.

"Only a little. But unless you're prepared to bring in the police—which probably wouldn't help her with her family?" He nodded. "You're better off letting it be."

He lifted the cup awkwardly with his casted hand.

"At least he didn't break it."

I was relieved to change the subject.

"Why the cast, then?"

"Stretched ligaments. The doctor said no playing for at least three weeks."

"Why leave, then? You've still got school. Right?"

His eyes started to fill.

"I can't stay around and watch her kill herself, man. She never would have started drugging if we hadn't started playing around with it."

Some people could handle social use, some weekend chipping, but a natural junkie like Lorelei wasn't ever going to leave it at that. I wish I knew a way to convince him that it wouldn't have mattered if they'd never tried anything stronger than root beer together. She'd still have gotten to where she was.

"All I can tell you is what I said before. She could have been hanging around with the Sisters of the Little Flower and the same thing would have happened, eventually. It's in her bones."

Eric sipped his coffee and stared at the traffic. I smoothed out the check on a magazine and filled it in for twice what I'd paid him in cash for the other night. He wouldn't take it.

"You're going to need a little extra until you can play again, yes? And I want to know you're not thinking about getting revenge on Tommy Cormier."

Eric shook his head, not convincingly. There was some steel in his anger.

"It'll just annoy him," I said. "And he might actually kill you."

"Sure. I got it."

I sighed. You couldn't force a kid to be smart.

"Listen. Get your ass back up to school and catch up on your classes. Three weeks?"

"Give or take."

"You should be a star student by then. Drop in for dinner some night." I stood up. "You want a ride uptown?"

He shook his head, but I didn't think he was leaving town now. He'd be all right as long as he didn't let the brooding get too deep.

"All right, then."

The Cougar bore no ticket, but the meter maid was six cars away and she gave me the look of a junkie denied her needle. My street-side rear quarter panel had a new narrow dent, as if a taller vehicle had sideswiped it. I shrugged. No one drove a pretty car in Boston unless it belonged to someone else.

I pulled out into traffic, waved at the meter maid, and laughed at myself playing daddy with Eric. I wouldn't have listened very hard when I was twenty, either, but I really hoped he didn't push on Tommy Cormier. There just wasn't a way for him to win that kind of argument.

★ ★ ★ ★ ★

I might as well have been selling snow shovels in Florida for all the good it did my bottom line but the last of winter had disappeared into an April afternoon so soft and warm I couldn't blame anyone for not wanting to sit in a bar. All across Massachusetts, hundreds of backyards were hosting the first barbecue of the season tonight.

There wasn't any dinner business to speak of, so I closed the kitchen early and sent Marina home. She didn't want to go, which made me wonder if she was fighting with Carmen again. Carmen seemed to like Burton even less than she had Carlos, which was saying a lot.

A couple who lived two streets over popped in for a beer with their German shorthair. I don't like dogs much but did my best to be the charming host. The people converting turn-of-the-century buildings on the fringes of the neighborhood were going to be key to my bar's survival.

When Cy came in wearing those big square Ray Charles sunglasses, the male owner of the shorthair was trying to untangle its leash from the chair so they could leave. The left side of Cy's face was swollen, but his hands were unmarked, as if he hadn't thrown any punches himself. I wondered how he squared that with what he'd told me about not letting himself get beaten on anymore. He walked to the bar, ignoring a friendly sniff from the pointer and a nod from the dog's owner, a beefy sixtyish man who looked a little thuggish for his custom-made linen jacket.

I tensed, until I saw Cy looked more defeated than angry.

"I need to get my money. Whatever she left me," he said. "I'm flat."

I poured him a rum.

"I told you what I need to have first."

"Blood from a stone, man."

"Then we don't have anything to talk about."

He sighed deeply and reached a long white envelope out of his inside pocket.

"You always were a tight-ass," he said. "Can we get this over with?"

I was so angry that he'd tried one more time to play me that I didn't bother warning him about Alison's strange bequests. Tommy Cormier was slated to receive fifty dollars and a note telling him to use it to buy a decent shirt. Dr. desRosiers's bequest was a small odd amount for a breakfast check that he hadn't wanted to split with her. Cy's was worse than that. She'd been evening up some scores.

"I'll be right back."

We traded envelopes over the bar. Mine contained a check for thirty thousand dollars from the account of the Mayflower Room, illegibly signed.

"What's this shit?" I said.

Cy tapped his envelope on the bar without opening it yet.

"I knew you'd bitch about it," he said. "Don't worry. It's good."

"You expect me to take your word for it?"

"Call the bank."

"At eleven at night."

"Look," Cy said. "I don't have the time to fuck around anymore. Whether you want to believe it or not, I'm an honest man. And I know if I floated an asshole like you a rubber check, you'd prosecute me. I can't afford to lose my job over something like that. The check is good."

"It better be." I'd pass it on to Attorney Markham in the morning, let him verify its soundness.

Cy slid a thick forefinger under the flap of his envelope, pulled out a single sheet of paper, and unfolded it. He groaned, then tossed it on the bar.

I turned it over, curious. I was pretty sure he wasn't going to be getting any money out of Alison, but the list of bequests had only spelled out "a sealed envelope" for Mr. Nance.

Years ago, I remembered, there had been a fad among office workers of sitting on top of the photocopy machine and making copies of their naked rear ends. Alison had bequeathed Cy just such an image, the copy sharp enough to show the outlines of her labia even, the black wires of pubic hair. A single line across the bottom read: "As close as you'll get, baby."

Oddly enough, it made me sad.

"She got into payback," I said. "You know she could be nasty if she thought she'd been wronged."

"She didn't like me much," Cy said. "The dealing, I think."

The need for a drink flashed through me like a heart attack, then faded.

"You dealt dope in the places where she sang?"

"That's the way Cormier got his hooks into me. I owed him so much I couldn't say no." Cy shook his head. "I didn't mind working the clubs. But I should never have gotten in with the kids."

"You shouldn't have been dealing in my bar, either."

"No choice, Elder. Everybody's always saying you have choices, but sooner or later you get to a point where you don't. Besides, it was pills. Nothing hard."

That sounded like saying to a drunk he could have as many beers as he wanted as long as he didn't drink whiskey. Tell that to the Loreleis of the world.

"You could give him to the cops, Cy."

I wasn't that big a fan of law and order, but Cormier had done a lot of damage in the world.

He grimaced.

"It's not that easy. You familiar with the name Maldonado?"

"Icky Ricky," I said.

"You understand, then. All I can try and do is save myself."

"He'd go to jail too."

Cy gave me a look that said I was a simpleton.

"Where he can catch up on his reading and wear out his old clothes. And his organization will roll right along."

"You're not selling pills anymore?"

"That's why I'm so tapped," he said. "That check I gave you is a loan I ain't going to live to pay back." He looked at me. "I heard you scored out of her will."

"Not that much," I said. "And I'd spend every bit of it to find out who killed her."

Cy snorted.

"Nobody killed her. She was about as depressed a human being as I've ever seen, no matter how many pills she took. If she didn't jump out that window, I'm Rush Limbaugh's black baby brother."

"Pills."

"The anti-Ds, man. She was doubling up, but they weren't helping. She flew because she chose to."

Cy believed it, that much was clear. I looked at the bar clock. "I'm closing."

He picked up his piece of copy paper and slipped it into the envelope.

"I don't condone that." I pointed. "That's a pretty harsh thing, payback from the grave."

"Yeah." Cy stood and buttoned his jacket. "I have a feeling that's how I'll be paying my debts too. Real soon now."

CHAPTER 30

Ricky pushed the nose of the pistol into the short hair on Berto's neck, guiding him through the back room to the walk-in cooler. They stopped at the bottom of a heavy wooden ramp scarred by dolly wheels and he handed Berto the key.

"Go ahead and open it up."

He wasn't afraid of turning his back on the kid, just being prudent. If the kid had disobeyed him, it was better to talk it out now, not risk him in a situation where the stakes were higher and have him fail.

Berto unlocked the padlock, which was the size of a coffee mug, and Ricky sensed him wondering whether he should smack Ricky in the head with it and run. Ricky took it as evidence of innocence that the kid did not obey the impulse. Berto hadn't killed Tommy. But Ricky knew he had to play the hand the way Berto expected it.

They stood in the cooler. Ricky leaned against a stack of boxes of frozen French fries, their breath mingling in clouds in the air.

"I did exactly what you said, Mr. Maldonado. Even when he came running across the street after me. I could have tapped him right there. I know I would have been wrong, but I would have been justified. Yeah?"

"It's justified when I say it's justified." Ricky's heart wasn't in the reprimand. He'd known pretty much from the moment he'd heard about it that it wasn't Berto's fault. Bombs were impersonal and Berto liked things up close.

He shoved the gun back in his waistband.

"I know you didn't kill him, Berto. Not quite your style, is it?"

Berto nodded emphatically.

"Like a man, I would have done it, Mr. Maldonado. Straight up, looking him in the face. Not sneaky-like."

Ricky rubbed his face. Down deep, he had a pretty good idea who'd killed Tommy but he didn't know why, and the not-knowing irked him as much as losing his own chance to punish the Indian.

"Plus the girl in there with him," Berto said. "I don't hold with killing women. Unless they do something bad. Or you tell me, of course."

"Let's get out of here," Ricky said. His fucking pacemaker was kicking over about every three seconds.

In the office, he pulled out a chair for Berto, a gesture of apology.

"Tell me the story, Berto. There's something I'm not seeing."

Berto sat and crossed his knees under the long apron.

"He runs out of the doctor's place like he heard something he didn't want to know."

"And he's carrying what?"

"Not the duffle bag. A brown paper package."

Ricky sighed. The bomb had not only scattered pieces of Tommy Cormier and his junkie girlfriend but the money from Cameron desRosiers.

"Go on," Ricky said.

"He comes straight across the street at me, like he's going to use some of that martial arts shit, so I show him the gun. I didn't shoot him, though. Like you said, I got the discipline."

"I know, Berto. I know. So you showed him the gun."

"He says some swear words. In English. I don't understand

them all. Then he goes back to his car and while I'm starting the Chevy, he takes off, real fast."

Berto slouched unhappily.

"That's when I lose him. But I figure he's going to his place, so I take the shortcut and get there before him. I'm out front, I see him pull in the parking lot around the back, then I hear this boom."

He shaped a mushroom cloud with his hands.

"And that's all she wrote?" Ricky said.

Berto gave him a level look.

"I know what dead people look like, Mr. M. He must have stopped to pick up the chick somewhere. Both of them were burning, like. Like hell."

Ricky leaned back in the swivel chair and rubbed at his chest. It had to be desRosiers who set the bomb. No one else had any reason to knock Tommy off, except maybe Ricky himself. The doc must have slipped it in with the money.

And that thought made Ricky sit up straight. DesRosiers was too greedy to blow up the money—he must still have it.

"No one else came near the car while Tommy was inside the doctor's office?"

Berto shook his head. "But remember, I didn't get there until after he went in. But there's nobody else living on that block—it's like, what, a ghetto."

Ricky took a deep breath.

"OK. Tommy got what he had coming. You did a good job, Berto. You were disciplined and you did what I asked. Thank you."

It would be almost suicidal not to praise the kid for holding back. Who knew how much or how little it would take for him to turn on him?

Berto beamed and Ricky wished he could combine his loyalty with Tommy's former intelligence and ambition.

He had a different problem now. Tommy had been killed while he was working for Ricky, which meant Ricky had to avenge him, despite the fact he'd been a traitor. If he didn't take out desRosiers, the rest of his organization—Tesar, Spengler, the street guys—would think he'd lost face.

He handed Berto a hundred-dollar bill.

"Take the day off. Go see a movie or something."

Berto stood uncertainly and untied his apron.

"It's OK," Ricky said. "I just have to think."

Once Berto was gone, Ricky rocked from side to side in the chair, thinking. Ruining desRosiers's practice, which would be simple, wasn't going to be enough. And giving him up to the cops only meant that Ricky wouldn't get a direct shot at him. He mulled it over for the better part of an hour, and only when Ricky realized that he was actually a little sad about Tommy did he come up with his best idea how to avenge Tommy's death. He leaned across the desk and picked up his phone.

CHAPTER 31

Susan called me at home on Wednesday morning.

"Henri's all right?" she said, the first thing out of her mouth.

"As far as I know. I haven't been checking on him."

"The assisted-living place is going to call me this afternoon. They might have an opening."

"Let me hear," I said, but the phone was dead.

I stared out my apartment window at Commonwealth Ave., wondering whether Alison had been getting the medications she thought she was taking. Maybe desRosiers had been prescribing experimental drugs, something with weird side effects.

I drove across town to the Fens, the sky gray and gloomy. The air carried that breath of humidity that spring and summer always brought to the Northeast. It might have been my least favorite part about living here.

I parked in the loading zone behind Alison's building, walked around front, and let myself in. The elevator was draped with moving pads and propped open on the ground floor with a piece of two-by-four. The call bell was ringing too. I ran up the stairs.

The apartment had a dead-air feeling that reminded me, as if I'd needed it, that Alison was truly gone. I didn't bother to check the closet—as soon as I'd realized the money was both marked and belonged to the Feds, I had no interest in it. I supposed at some point I was going to have to figure out how to get rid of it, but it wasn't why I was here.

In the bathroom, I opened the medicine chest and picked up an amber plastic bottle. The label claimed the pills were Zoloft, an antidepressant I'd heard of, and the prescribing physician was named as Cameron desRosiers. The prescription had been filled at the Fenway Pharmacy. None of this came as a surprise, but it had to have something to do with Alison's death.

I wrestled the childproof cap free and looked in at the dozen pills left, similar to ones I'd seen in Tommy Cormier's bag. I wasn't sure what Zoloft was supposed to look like, but a pharmacist ought to know. I tucked the bottle in my shirt pocket, relocked the apartment, and walked up the block.

The Fenway Pharmacy occupied a smoky yellow brick building, barely holding its own against the encroachment of urban renewal. A cracked green sunshade film covered the inside of the dusty plate-glass windows.

I pushed open the heavy glass door, which was obscured with stickers for about twenty different debit and credit cards. A hand-lettered sign on cardboard was also taped to the window. It read: "We accept cash also!"

As I walked up the aisle toward the high counter in back, a pale skinny man wearing a black toupee looked up. His narrow shoulders slumped forward to cup his chest and the two knots of jaw muscle below his wide ears made his face look lumpy.

"One minute, please," he said.

"Just looking."

Most of the goods on the shelves—jockstraps, Ace bandages, cold remedies, and contact lens solution—were filmed in dust, as if no potential customer had touched anything for years. I looked at a display of Trojan-Enz and wondered who would be desperate or horny enough to trust one of those crushed and broken-open boxes.

The pharmacist finally raised his head and pulled the glass

window to one side. A brass-plated plastic name tag read "Mr. Vindalia."

"What can we do for you today, my sir?" His smile was a little off, as if he'd learned it from TV.

I handed him the pill bottle from Alison's bathroom.

"Can you tell me if these pills are the same as what's on the label?"

Vindalia's throat worked and his shoulders pulled back. He twisted off the top, dumped the pills onto an empty plastic tray on the counter.

"They are."

Then he swept them into the trash with his hand.

"Hey."

He tossed the bottle and cap into the wastebasket too. I noticed that his eyes were watery gray and the pupils well dilated. It made me wonder if he was sampling from his own inventory.

"Sir." He smiled biliously. "These pills are by law controlled substances. Since I filled this prescription in the first place, I know it does not belong to you and therefore you have no legal right of possession. If I don't confiscate these medications from you, I am myself in trouble."

I wondered how stupid he thought I was.

"Mr. Vindalia."

His toupee glistened as I leaned into his space.

"I don't know where your attitude comes from. But you can give me back what I came in the door with or we can call the police."

Vindalia laughed weakly.

"I must say, Mr., uh—"

I waited until he'd stopped pretending to wipe his eyes.

"I think people may have died because of those pills, Mr. Vindalia. If you're part of a conspiracy, you'd be better off coming forward. It might save you from going to jail."

He stared at me with the fixity of a statue. I had to resist a sudden urge to run down the long rows of merchandise with my arms extended and scatter his goods all over the floor. The situation clearly required official attention, Burton's deft touch.

But as I turned my back and walked toward the door, a pill bottle arced through the air over my head and landed on the floor in front of me. I picked it up and felt pills clattering inside.

"You want to tell me what's going on?" I turned back toward the pharmacist, but Vindalia was disappearing through the back door behind the counter.

It was close to lunch time by the time I parked the Cougar behind the Esposito. Burton, for all the money I was paying him, hadn't come up with much. I felt as if I were doing all the work. My conversation with Vindalia was something he should have done.

I jogged up the alley from my parking space by the loading dock, wondering if Marina would think I'd gone off on another bender. She stood next to the Mercy Street sign with a big bag of groceries, a frown twisting her mouth. And when she started to speak, I interrupted.

"You're absolutely right," I said. "I've got so much other crap going on, I'm not taking care of business. You've got your own keys and you can be in charge for a while."

"You mean I could play some decent music sometimes?"

"You could even hire Carmen, if you want."

She grimaced and handed me the grocery bag, opened the door, and keyed off the alarm.

"How's Burton doing?" I hadn't seen him for days, and I was starting to wonder what he was doing.

She took the bag back and I followed her downstairs into the kitchen.

"Drinking too much," she said. "And I'm holding his head."

"I wondered why I was the only one coming up with any information."

"It's the private detective idea," she said. "It isn't him."

I set a mesh bag full of lemons on the counter.

"He could have told me that before I gave him the money."

"He doesn't know how to do it." She ignored the divorce allusion. "He's used to having an organization. The department. He's not someone who can do it all himself."

"So what am I supposed to do?"

"Cut him loose," she said. "Let him get back to work."

"I can't do that yet."

"All he knows how to do is be a cop," she said.

"They'll reinstate him." But I don't know where that certainty came from.

She started slicing a huge Portobello mushroom.

"If they decide to get rid of him, he's gone. And it will only be easier if he's moonlighting."

"You want me to fire him?"

She started dicing scallions. "You'd be doing him a favor. And me."

"You open?" A male voice called in from the bar.

"Be right there." I'd worry about Burton later. Right now I needed to follow up what I'd learned about the pills.

"How did Carlos get hold of Tommy Cormier when he needed to talk to him? Did he have a cell number?"

Our would-be customer knocked on the bar like it was a door. Marina hesitated.

"Come on," I said. "It's not like you can get Carlos in trouble now."

"There's a diner over by the Fens," she said. "Up above Houston Street. Tommy used to hang out there."

I'd bet a dollar it was Icky Ricky's place.

"Thanks," I said.

The man out front was a lawyer on his way to court. The lawyer part I figured out because he was dressed well and had shitty manners. His preparation for trial apparently consisted of three consecutive shots of twelve-year-old Scotch, which he drank without sitting or even unbuttoning his black cashmere top coat. I recognized a member of the brotherhood, no matter how much his suit cost, but when he left me a twenty-dollar tip I had to admit he occupied a different stratum than I'd ever been.

After he left, I pulled out the phone book and walked back into the kitchen. I wanted to ask Tommy Cormier about the pills he'd repossessed. Vindalia's tossing me the pill bottle implied something was wrong and though Burton could probably get the pills analyzed at the police lab, it would be quicker if I could get Tommy to tell me.

"You know the name of the place?" I asked Marina.

She shook her head. She was chopping onions with the big chef's knife she'd used to scare Cy off.

I frowned. The last thing I wanted was a chance to see Tommy in person again.

So I put it off until the next day. I'd planned to sleep in, but when I woke, I was feeling guilty about how much I'd been asking Marina to handle without me. She was so happy to be in charge that she hadn't even asked if I would pay her extra to run the place when I wasn't around. I didn't want her to feel as if I were using her.

When I walked into the Esposito, the music from the *Buena Vista Social Club* movie was playing and Burton was sitting at the bar drinking a cup of coffee, his face as rough as a night at the wrestling matches. As I walked down the stairs, he stepped around the bar, rinsed out his cup, and put it in the dishwasher. Marina had him trained, hungover or not.

His eyes were bloodshot and his hands shook, but he was clean, close-shaven, and back to his usual sartorial splendor. His white shirt looked soft and shone like silk and his dark green tie bore yellow L.L. Bean boots marching down the front. The tan wool suit fit him closely—an Italy-meets-backwoods-Maine look. The good suit meant he was still on suspension. He wouldn't take a chance on ruining it at a murder scene.

"You familiar with a kid named Eric O'Hanian?" he said.

I waved good morning into the kitchen. Marina jerked her head in Burton's direction, reminding me what I'd promised.

"He's a kid who plays music here on the weekends sometimes. Why?"

Burton exuded a seriousness of purpose I hadn't seen in weeks. "He's in the pokey."

"You can't be serious."

"Suspicion of murder."

"I saw him yesterday," I said. "He was sitting in South Station waiting for a bus back to Vermont. Scared out of his tree."

"He must have gotten over it," Burton said. "Tommy Cormier is all done scaring people. Took out his lady of the moment too."

"Lorelei? Shit."

Burton nodded.

"All the more reason Eric didn't do it," I said. "He was crazy about the woman. He have a lawyer?"

"You civil liberties types." Burton snorted. "They only picked him up an hour ago."

I reached for the phone. Daniel Markham wasn't in his office, but I left an urgent message for him to call me. Cormier had almost certainly died as a result of whatever drug-dealing he was doing. Eric wasn't a likely suspect, though they must have had some reason to pick him up. Then I remembered I was supposed to fire Burton today and wondered how I was going to work that into the conversation.

"You know him pretty well?" he said.

"He's a good piano player. He got upset when Cormier stole his girlfriend, but she's a junkie. And Cormier threatened to break his hands."

"That sounds like motive."

"How did it happen?"

"Car bomb. Right behind Cormier's apartment building."

"You're talking about a nineteen-year-old kid," I said. "His idea of a big night is a piano in tune and a glass of Seven and Seven."

"Actually," Burton said. "I think you're right. Not that my opinion's carrying much weight down there right now. But it makes me think your lady friend was killed, too."

"Why?"

He looked at me pityingly. "The link between her and Cormier. And Cormier's death could not be construed as an accident. In any way."

"Or suicide."

"Someone's nervous," he said.

"I went by Alison's apartment one more time." I told him about Vindalia's implicit acknowledgment the pills were defective.

"I know someone in the lab," Burton said. "Let me have them."

"Don't lose them. They're evidence, right?"

"You're watching too much *CSI*. Without a chain of possession, they don't mean a thing."

I heard a little wistfulness for the order and process of the force.

"Any news on your suspension?"

"Hearing was yesterday," he said. "They went pretty easy, but only because Costain fell in the shit with someone higher up the food chain. I should know what's going on in a few days."

The phone rang.

"I gave up criminal law just as soon as I could," Markham said without preliminaries. "But I know just the shark, assuming the young man can pay her freight. It'll only cost you a nominal referral fee."

"I'll cover the tariff if I have to." Though I hoped Eric's father would turn out to be a banker or a stockbroker.

"I'll call you as soon as I talk to her," Markham said.

The inactivity was getting to Burton. He bounced up on the balls of his feet.

"I'm going over to talk to your pharmacist right now. As soon as I drop the pills at the lab." He shook the bottle like a maraca.

"What makes you think you'll get any more out of him than I did?"

He flapped open his wallet and waggled his badge.

"He's not going to know I'm on hiatus," he said. "But if he has any sense, he'll know I can fuck him up. The War on Drugs left a lot of silly laws on the book, God bless it, and nobody knows them all."

"Just don't fuck up your reinstatement," I said to him, wondering if all this manic energy was coffee or booze. Or both.

"I'll call you when I know something." He stalked out through the kitchen.

I hoped the fluttery feeling in my stomach wasn't a prophecy of doom. It felt as if we were inching our way toward the something dark and slimy that might have killed Alison Somers. For a moment, I wished I could go back to being a hermit and not worry about what had happened to her.

I heard Burton saying goodbye to Marina, then the fire door from the kitchen to the alley creak open and shut. I shook my head, put on some Big Band music to jump myself up, and got back to work.

★ ★ ★ ★ ★

I half-expected a call to go downtown and bail Eric out, but the idea became moot when the Esposito filled up for lunch. It was mostly a burgers-and-fries crowd, and by the time two-thirty rolled around, I felt as if I had been spray-painted with a film of meat grease.

Since the place had emptied out, Marina and I took a break at one of the tables before we tackled the cleanup. She shook a cigarette out of my pack and lit up, not something I was used to seeing her do.

"How well do you know Burton?" she said.

Her tone was serious, that deep as death one I always avoid when I'm talking to women. I gave her an abbreviated version of my history with Burton, the guitar player who'd been stabbed to death on the Esposito's stage, Marina's predecessor in the kitchen.

"So, not so well?"

"What are you asking?" I wasn't following.

She tipped ash onto the waxed paper liner of a sandwich basket.

"He doesn't sleep very well. Nightmares, cold sweat."

"I'm not sure what you want me to do about that." Though if I could do anything, I would. Burton was as close to a friend as I had.

"Just listen." She dragged, blew out smoke. "He's a sweet guy, he cares about his work. He's thoughtful in bed . . ."

"Please."

"You're a prude, all of a sudden?" She frowned and stared at her cigarette. "I'm just afraid he's not going to make it. Something's dead inside there."

I stubbed out my cigarette and collected all the dirty silverware into a handful.

"What is it you want me to do?"

245

"I'm not going to dump him," she said. "I'm just trying to see how he and I are going to make this work."

The street door opened up and saved me from my congenital inadequacy at this type of conversation. Susan Voisine appeared at the top of the stairs.

"I thought there was a law against smoking in this town." She waved her hand in front of her face as she hopped down the stairs.

Marina went out to the kitchen. She brought back a can of orange air freshener, which she sprayed around until I coughed.

"Jesus," I said.

"It smells worse than the smoke," Susan said.

"You here to drink?" I said.

"No. I don't want to get plotzed before my interview."

I looked at her again. She was dressed in a severe navy skirt and jacket, corporate high style.

"Tea?"

She nodded.

I brought out a cup and a little steel pot full of hot water. "What's the interview?"

"Events coordinator at Hynes Auditorium. Organization, planning, booking rooms and talent for corporate events."

"Public contact?"

"Some. Why?" She looked vaguely insulted, then lifted the tea strainer out of the pot, poured herself.

"You decided not to go to Oregon?" I said.

I thought I was happy she was staying in Boston, but I wasn't sure how to let her know it.

"For the time being," she said. "The economy's starting to pick up and I've got to get something substantial on my resume. Nobody's impressed with self-employed people any more."

"You're still selling the house?"

She grimaced. "It's too big for me. And it's the only asset I've got."

"You might think about . . ."

She flared. "You're going to give me advice?"

"All I was going to say was that you've paid for Henri's apartment for a year. When he goes into assisted living, you could live there."

"You want me to move in with my father?" She rubbed the back of her spoon on the bar.

"After your father leaves."

"And I'd be closer to you."

I felt as if I were jumping off a high rock into a shallow pond.

"Just think about it," I said. "It might work out and surprise us both."

"I will." But she was looking at her watch. "I've got to go."

"Let me know how it comes out."

She grinned as she headed up the stairs, the flex in her calf muscles drawing my attention.

"Oh, yeah," she said over her shoulder.

As the door swung shut behind her, I thought about luck, good and bad, and what I might be able to do so I didn't scare away any good luck I was having. This time, at least.

CHAPTER 32

Marina stomped out of the kitchen and headed up the stairs.

"I'm going to the market," she snapped. "We need some asparagus."

I wondered if she was angry about Susan or just uncomfortable with her around. She hadn't responded to my offer to run the Esposito and I wondered if something had changed her mind. Maybe she was thinking about quitting. Or marrying Burton. That was the point where I stopped thinking and started emptying the dishwasher.

Cy walked down the stairs with an elephantine slowness. His dark brown skin showed ashy undertones and his shoulders drooped under the long leather coat. Much as he loved his rum, I'd never known him to start drinking until he finished work, and unless they'd changed the standard workday on me, two o'clock was still the middle of business. He sat and rested his elbows on top of the bar, cradling his head like it was heavy.

I fought back my feelings of sympathy—he'd earned everything that had happened to him.

"Drink?" I said.

The whites of his eyes were webbed red. "They fired me."

I winced. He'd loved the music school job.

"For dealing?"

"Anonymous tip," he said. "Did you do that?"

"Nope. Someone from Maldonado's crew?" Although if it had happened recently, it wasn't Tommy Cormier.

"I think it was this kid whose credit I shut off," he said. "They gave me fifteen minutes to pack my desk and get out of the building. Had a damn security guard escort me."

I shrugged. No sympathy here.

"I believe I will have some rum," he said. "I thought I was screwed before, but this is going to put me way out in the puckerbrush."

Cy had never, in my experience, lived like a man who spent more money than he made. I wondered how he'd gotten to a place where it meant so much.

"I didn't think of you as a gambler," I said.

He sighed as I poured him a drink.

"I've got a family the size of a small congregation down in Florida. I've been carrying every one of them for twenty years, and they're expecting me to send the beans. I'm the sole support for eighteen people."

I frowned. "And none of them's ever been able to find work?"

"You don't have family, do you?" He stared into the bar mirror. "Music school don't pay like football, but it was steady."

"You're going back to dealing?"

He shook his head, a baffled old rhino.

"I can't find Tommy and Ricky's out there pretending he was never in the drug business, the little prick."

Cy obviously hadn't heard about Tommy.

"Cormier recruited me, maybe six, seven years ago. He was expanding into schools and he didn't have the right kind of people. It was so low key, I thought it might help keep kids out of the crappy parts of town. Then every so often a Lorelei came along."

"Every generation has its junkies." I didn't know why I felt the need to ease his pain.

He looked down his nose.

"You say so. I was doing great until Ricky put this freeze

down, a month ago. Made no sense—everyone's making money, so let's shut it down?"

I guessed that Ricky had found something big enough to forego the short-term gain and I'd have bet it had something to do with desRosiers.

"Maybe he was moving into harder drugs."

Cy played with his glass, but didn't ask for a refill.

"I don't think so," he said. "I would have gotten out right away if he did. I don't sell heroin. Or blow."

As if that was something to be proud of.

"And you never got a hint of what else he was doing?"

"Nah." He sighed like the brakes on a semi. "So what do I do now, brother?"

His whining was starting to irritate me. I wished he would leave. He was a reminder of the days with Alison, but Alison was cold and didn't sing anymore and I needed to make some new memories now. I fumbled around in the junk drawer under the bar.

"You're definitely leaving town?" I slid one of the new keys to Alison's apartment off the ring. He nodded.

It was a selfish act—it would rid me of a useless bag of money and take some of the pressure off of Burton if Cy left town carrying the FBI's cash. Not incidentally, it would confuse Manelli wonderfully if someone in Florida started spending the money.

"I've got some cash for you," I said, wondering if I was setting him up with his own greed. "It's dirty money, though. Very dirty."

His chest expanded and he sat up straighter, as if he'd taken a hit from an oxygen tank. He made me feel guilty—I wouldn't ruin him myself, but his own greed would and I didn't mind the prospect half enough.

"It's in the closet of the bedroom in Alison's old apartment. You know where that is?"

He stiffened at my tone.

"The bills are marked and they belong to the Feds somehow. You spend it, you better be a long way from Boston, and moving to boot."

"What's in it for you?" But the question was pro forma. He was already figuring out how the cash was going to save him. And maybe it would, if he was patient enough.

"Peace," I said. "I don't want to see you in my club anymore. Or my city. Knowing the way you used people. Take the money or don't, but get the fuck out of my world."

He stood and buttoned his coat, his face brighter than when he'd come in.

"Thanks, Elder. I won't forget this."

"Please do. And remember what I said about the bills."

"I hope you find out what happened to Alison, man. I liked her."

I wished I could believe him, but in the face of his actions, I didn't have the luxury.

"I'm sure you did, man, I'm sure you did."

The next morning, I overslept, then dawdled an extra fifteen minutes with my coffee, watching the passing parade on Commonwealth Ave. The living room warmed up as I sat in my leather chair and smoked. Every morning, I was feeling a little less motivated to go to work, especially since Marina didn't seem to need much guidance from me.

In the light of day, my way of dealing with Cy made me feel hypocritical. Here I was, an alcoholic bar owner. Who was I to get prissy about someone pushing pills to college students? What bothered me most was how he'd used our friendship, but the more I thought about it, it didn't seem to be that important.

Someone knocked on the door, then started banging before I could get out of my chair. Burton. No one else I knew was that impatient. When I opened the door, his choirboy face was stuck in a grin as if he'd just won the Massachusetts State Lottery.

"Don't you go to work anymore?" he said.

I followed him to the kitchen. He sloshed the last of my coffee into a mug.

"Your girlfriend's covering for me," I said.

A ghost of pain flitted across his face and I wondered if Marina had dumped him, despite what she'd said.

"I've been reinstated," he said. "But the bad news is . . ."

"They don't want you moonlighting."

"I'm not telling them I already was. But I'll get you the money back, even if it takes a while."

I was glad he hadn't wanted to pay off Sharon's lawyer all at once.

"Don't sweat it. You get anything from Vindalia?"

"Cagey guy," Burton said. "But he hates Icky Ricky."

"The Ick has enemies," I said. "Imagine that."

"Vindy claims that Ricky hooked up with some guys in Mexico who supply him with cheap prescription drugs. Vindalia runs them through the pharmacy and splits the profits."

"Cheap and legal both?"

Burton shook his head.

"Foreign origin means no quality control or regulation in this case. Nonstandard dosages in a lot of cases."

He reached a sheet of paper from the inside pocket of his black-and-white checked sport coat.

"Those pills from Alison's really were Zoloft."

The paper was covered with graphs and tables of numbers.

"Give me the idiot version," I said.

"The pills were a twenty-milligram size. With a five-milligram dose."

A black cold flowed in under my heart.

"You noticed who prescribed the pills?" I said.

"Dr. desRosiers? Is that the boyfriend?"

"One of them. He had to know they were bogus."

"That we can do something about," Burton said. "I'll get a warrant. Vindalia allowed as how there had to be a physician involved but all his dealings were with Ricky."

"DesRosiers has a clinic in Back Bay."

"Is he stupid enough to leave evidence there?"

"Arrogant enough, maybe."

Burton buzzed with the energy of working where he was supposed to be, doing what he was supposed to do. It made me feel better. He slapped me on the arm.

"You did it, pally. You stuck to your story and it turned out you were right."

Even if he were correct, even if everything I hypothesized was true, it didn't give me as much satisfaction as I'd thought. Denying Alison the amount of medication she needed was as good as murder in my book, but I doubted the legal system would see it that way. DesRosiers would likely go free or just get slapped a little.

"Still have to nail his ass," I said.

"Oh, I will."

Burton, beaming, was out the door before I said anything else.

I hoped the system was as strong as his confidence in it, but I doubted it. I walked back into the kitchen and washed out the coffee pot, then got ready to go downtown to get to work.

When I opened my apartment door, Mrs. Rinaldi was standing in the foyer. I got the sense she'd been standing there for some time, getting up the courage to knock. Her color was better than it had been in months and she seemed less diffident, as if her time in the hospital had increased her self-confidence as well as her physical health. Her mild heart attack had been complicated by dehydration and poor nutrition. I planned to keep a closer eye on her.

"Good morning, Dorothea."

"Almost afternoon," she said. "If you have a moment, I'd like to discuss having a little more work space down in the basement."

Her "workshop" already occupied half the cellar, and two of the three storage cubicles were piled with the miniature opera sets she'd built. I wasn't ready to give up hope that I'd ever own anything I wanted to store, though there wasn't anything in my cube right now except boxes of records and old ski equipment.

"I'm not sure there's enough light at the far end of the basement for you to work in, is there?"

Then I kicked myself for giving her excuses to steal more light bulbs. I hadn't missed any since she came home from the hospital, now that I thought of it.

"I'd rather not have to move out of the building unless I have to," she said. "But I will."

"Whoa," I said. "What's going on?"

"I have a commission." I saw her trying not to smile.

"For a miniature."

"At first. If they like the model, the Boston Opera wants me to design the sets for *Der Rosenkavalier*. This season's production."

I took her hands. She blushed.

"That's terrific."

She shook her apricot curls. "I'm sure I can get you a ticket if you like. Without charge, I mean."

I'd go see Tiny Tim first, but it was sweet of her to offer.

"Let me call a contractor I know. Make up a wish list and we'll see what we can manage."

When she smiled, I had a glimpse of what a beautiful woman she once had been. I thought of Alison, never growing old in her art or her life.

"I am very grateful to you, Mr. Darrow."

I knew she meant for more than what we'd just been talking about, but I felt humbled anyway. I hadn't done that much.

Her good news floated me all the way to the Esposito, where Marina was handling the lively lunch crowd on her own.

"I'm sorry," I said. "I got hung up."

"I need to talk to you," she said.

Thinking she wanted to bitch about my being late, I shrugged her off.

"Go on back and get caught up. We can talk after the rush."

She stomped into the kitchen.

As I served the customers, I started to feel angry at myself. Sooner or later, I was going to have to decide whether I trusted her to run the place. And if I did, I'd have to let her do things her own way.

When the rush slowed down around one-thirty, I went into the kitchen. She was still angry—the muscles in her forearms writhed as she dried her hands on her apron.

"Sorry." I tried to forestall an argument. "I know I've gotten a little sloppy about the schedule."

"That's nothing," she said. "I'm worried about Burton."

"You talked to him?"

"Not a chance. Three hours after he was reinstated, he was stinking drunk. He showed up at three in the morning, banging on my door. I almost smacked him, I was so mad."

"Carmen must have loved that," I said.

"She did not."

Marina stared off into the corner at the stage. I wondered if she was thinking that maybe she'd only traded in one bad-bargain male for another, and what that said about her.

"It isn't you," I said.

"I know. I just don't want him to lose himself."

"He seemed all right this morning when he came by."

"That's the game that all you drunks play, though, isn't it? How drunk can you get and still function the next day?"

I concentrated on keeping my temper. She had every right to assume I was still a drunk.

"Tell him how you feel about it."

"If I put pressure on him," she said. "Then it's me or the booze and you know how that'll come out."

"Maybe not," I said. "You don't want me to talk to him—I couldn't even fire him for you."

"Give yourself credit," she said. "He listens to you."

Could I convince someone as proud as Burton that he needed help? Maybe. I just didn't have so many friends I was willing to risk losing one.

"How short is your patience?" I said.

"I'm not ready to dump him. But Carmen will eat us both alive, if he keeps it up."

"Let it be for now. Going back to work should help."

She sighed, underlining my uselessness.

A red-haired woman in a trench coat walked up to the bar and handed me her check and a Visa. She smiled in a way meant to encourage me, but I was too bound up in thinking about Burton to respond. I had no idea how to talk to anyone else about drinking or quitting. I could barely talk to myself. And any authority my dry years might have given me was long gone now.

She handed me back my pen and copy of the charge slip, a little disappointed.

"Well, you have a nice day," she said.

"I am having one," I said. "A terrific day."

CHAPTER 33

To make up for my being late, I'd told Marina to come in late the next day and before I opened, I did all her kitchen prep work, too. Making salads and chopping vegetables were the kind of mindless chores that always helped me think.

As I wiped down the bar out front, I realized I'd been missing Delford Woodley, and I wondered if he was ever coming in for his morning pop again. It was possible I'd gentrified the Esposito beyond his tolerance.

And I wondered if Burton was using Marina to cut himself loose from Sharon. Maybe his infatuation with Marina wasn't going to survive a definitive break with his wife, and he was staying drunk so he didn't have to face it. As so often happened when I was thinking about someone, Burton phoned.

"I got the warrant on desRosiers," he said. "The clinic."

"Excellent." My truer reaction was more complex: Why was he telling me, and what did he expect me to do about it?

"I need someone to cover me," he said.

"Isn't that what I pay my taxes to the Commonwealth for?"

Burton sighed, as if I were being stupid.

"As soon as I ask for backup, it'll get to Costain. I have to get this done before the Fibbies get involved."

"And you think they'll let Alison's death go?"

He snorted at my innocence.

"They only care about the drugs and the money. I'm the one who's talking for her now."

I owed him something for sticking with this. And seeing des-Rosiers pay was worth the small risk.

"I don't want to get in your way."

"All you have to do is watch my back," he said. "Call in the backup if we need it."

"The Back Bay address?"

"Half an hour. I'll be a block or two east, in a dark green van."

"Then."

I hung up, trying to convince myself he hadn't been drinking. But the energy in his voice sounded grandiose, as if he expected to redeem himself from all his problems with one bold arrest. I might have to protect him from his own emotions more than anything else.

When I walked back out to the kitchen, Marina was chopping more onions, weeping. She must have slipped in while I was talking to Burton.

"What?" I said.

She slapped the knife on the cutting board.

"I'm fine."

"OK. I've got to go out for a couple of hours. Can you handle things?"

"Haven't I been handling it all along?"

"Thanks," I said and turned away.

But when I stepped out of the kitchen, Captain Costain and Agent Manelli were standing on the other side of the bar.

"Burton here?"

I shook my head. Manelli, more patient, was also the more dangerous of the two. He shook his head.

"Don't tell us fairy stories, Darrow. Your friend could lose everything. Not just his career. Something serious is at stake here."

"Something more serious than catching a murderer? I

thought Burton was back on the job."

"I can suspend him all over again, if that's what he wants," Costain said. "Or have him shit-canned altogether, if that's what it takes to get his attention."

"Why don't we have some coffee?" Manelli said.

I had the sense they were running a bad-cop, half-bad-cop thing on me. Or maybe I was signifying my hurry to leave somehow. Burton would go ahead and arrest desRosiers by himself if I didn't get there and it would probably be fine, except that I'd said I'd be there, and I hated not doing what I'd promised. But I couldn't fob these two off without raising suspicions.

I filled two mugs with the oldest coffee and wrote out a check, which I slapped down between them.

"Your friend keeps stumbling through things that aren't his concern," Manelli said.

"That's exactly the kind of attitude that brought us Watergate," I said.

But Manelli wasn't even thirty, Vietnam was half a chapter in a history book, and he wouldn't remember a time when the press respected a sitting President.

"As I said, I thought he was a homicide cop. Isn't it his job to arrest people who kill other people?"

Costain was trying to hide a smile, which confused me.

"It's a jurisdictional thing," Manelli said.

Then I saw the light. Costain had been overplaying his anger for Manelli's benefit. The FBI had stomped into his world and bullied him into ignoring a homicide in favor of some ostensibly more important Federal crime. Drugs or terrorism were the two most likely.

"Jurisdictional," I said.

"Look," Costain said. "We're sorry as hell your girlfriend got killed. But the bigger issue here is breaking up the Maldonado gang."

I almost burst out laughing as the truth opened itself up. The FBI had lost its money in an aborted buy and now they were going to take it out on Ricky.

Costain's grin was back. I realized I'd misjudged which side he was on. Manelli made a face like Costain had farted and pulled the knot of his tie.

"I can't say anything more." Ignoring the fact he hadn't said much of anything anyway.

"I told you, I don't know where Burton is," I said.

"We've cancelled his warrant," Manelli said. "Anything he does will be unusable in court."

That might have been an issue for them, but I only cared about whether desRosiers had caused Alison's death. Punishment was the responsibility of the legal system.

"I still don't know where he is."

Manelli's face got dark. "I'm not threatening anything. I'm promising. He fucks up my case, he's toast."

I was reminded once again how much our government prefers its citizens obedient and compliant.

"You don't think I'd save him the grief if I could?"

But that didn't convince Manelli.

"By the way, we found who passed the drug money through your bar."

It was a little late to worry, but I wondered if Cy could implicate me.

"I told you about little cash businesses," Manelli mocked. "This clown had a drug store he was laundering money through."

Cy was more patient than I thought, then, though I didn't have any sympathy for Vindalia.

"Another case closed," I said. "Congratulations."

The darkness on his face deepened, until I worried for his health. Costain threw another business card on the table, his cell phone number scrawled on the back, and they left, Manelli first.

This time, I tucked the card in my pocket and watched them climb the stairs to the street.

It was after two p.m. by the time I got my Cougar up out of the alley and onto Mercy Street. I didn't think they would tail me, but I didn't want to be cocky about it, either. I ran three yellow lights in a row, watching my mirrors all the way, but that wasn't a remarkable act in Boston. By the time I pulled up behind the unmarked van on Hereford Street, I was sure I hadn't been followed.

Down the block, a router-carved wooden sign bolted to the wall by the front door proclaimed desRosier's Clinic—aside from the punctuation error, nothing too criminal seemed to be happening.

"You're late." Burton made me jump.

"They pulled your warrant."

"I don't give a flying fuck if they think this is a Federal case," he said. "Anyone kills someone in Boston, it belongs to me."

"They're going to bury you," I said. "You'll be doing crosswalk duty on Sunday mornings in downtown Roxbury."

"So maybe it's time I'm done with the cops," he said. "If so, I'll go hard. High note."

I didn't like the sound of that.

"It's not a high note if he walks, is it?"

"He's going to walk anyway." He picked up a chunk of asphalt and whipped it at the clinic's front window. "Can you say probable cause? I believe we have some probable cause."

The glass hadn't broken, but a klaxon started whooping inside the building.

"You're certifiable."

"My, my," he said. "A burglar alarm. I'd better investigate. You stay right here."

He slipped a pry bar out of the sleeve of his jacket, walked up the front walk, and wedged the claw into the door jamb. When he heaved, the alarm got ten times louder.

"Make it fast," I said. "He could be wired into an alarm company. Or a precinct."

He turned and Grouchoed his eyebrows at me, then disappeared through the door.

I knew he'd been looking out for me when he told me to stay out here, but it was a good idea anyway. If other cops showed up, maybe I could keep him from getting shot.

Ten seconds after he went in, the klaxon quit. I looked up and down the street, but no curious faces showed. The neighborhood was quiet as a cemetery on Christmas Eve.

When I heard a sharp pop inside, I straightened up fast. It didn't seem loud enough for a gunshot, but everything I knew about guns I'd learned from television. I reached inside my jacket, pulled out my cell phone, and punched in the number on Costain's card. It was past time for the pros to take over.

Costain answered after one ring.

"Yes? Darrow?"

I left the connection open without saying anything. Costain would be able to trace the call's location.

I slipped the phone into my pocket and started slowly up the front walk. Another pop, sharper and louder, sounded inside the building. I turned my body sideways so it would be a smaller target and stepped in through the open door.

In a deep threatening silence inside, I felt my heart thudding. The entryway was painted beige, with a white carpet that meant desRosiers wasn't a doctor with patients who bled. Wooden armchairs ranged along the wall next to a sliding glass window with a metal speaking grill in the middle. Beyond the glass was an office space, bookcases full of files, and a computer with a flat panel display.

The hardwood floor in the corridor squeaked as I passed the waiting room. I stepped through an open door toward the back of the building, passing four examination rooms off the hallway. A burnt acrid odor I assumed was gunpowder hung in the air.

The heavy steel door at the end of the corridor was ajar and wisps of blue-gray smoke drifted up toward the ceiling, backlit by a single unshaded light bulb. Cardboard cartons were piled high along three walls of the room, which was roughly a dozen feet square, and a red-handled fire door was set in the back wall, its handle chained shut.

Burton backed into the open doorway in front of me, a pistol in each hand. He looked unmarked, which relieved me.

"What happened?"

He gestured me into the storeroom. desRosiers sat on the concrete floor to his left, his back leaning against one of the stacks of cartons. A wide red stain spread across the right side of his chest and his chest shuddered with heaving breaths. His scanty blonde hair was pushed all over his head and his eyes were shut.

"Jesus," I said. "You had to kill him?"

"He called it." Burton handed me the gun in his left hand. "Pulled the trigger while I was taking it away from him. I never fired my own."

I weighed the oily cold steel. Holding it gave me a loose and airy feeling, as if that much power could make me faint.

"He's shot in the lung." Burton eyed desRosiers. "He'll survive, if they get here in time. I assume you called 911?"

"Help's on the way." I didn't specify what kind. I was absorbing a little of what it cost Burton to do his job. I might have fewer good reasons to drink than he did.

"I had the feeling you'd be a law-abiding citizen," he said.

I shook my head as I read the labels on the cartons, all misspellings of popular drugs: Porzac, Zoftol, Prisolec.

"They didn't have much imagination," I said. "And you'd better get your butt out of here or you're not going to have a job tomorrow morning."

"All the asshole could talk about was his mother," Burton said. "As if he did it all for her."

"I'm serious. Costain can't protect you from this, especially if desRosiers turns out to be connected."

"I can't leave the scene of a shooting," he said. "Costain's all right."

With the gun he'd given me, I fired a shot into the ceiling. There would have to be residue on my hands to convince them I'd shot desRosiers. Burton looked at me as if I'd lost my mind.

"I came here looking for information about Alison," I said. "desRosiers threatened me with a gun. I got it away from him, but in the process, tragically, he got shot. Now go home and wash your hands with Clorox."

Burton nodded slowly, as if what was at stake had finally penetrated. "I'll owe you."

The first siren sound drifted in through the open front door.

"We'll work it out. You could pay your bar tab."

desRosiers groaned and opened one eye. Burton hesitated.

"Go," I said. "He's so deep in shock I could tell him the Jolly Green Giant pulled the trigger."

"Thanks." Burton slipped out the back.

The first patrolman through the door handcuffed me to a chair, but I'd expected that. When Manelli came in and saw me, his complexion deepened back to that dark red he'd shown at the bar, the one that suggested incipient stroke. He strode across the waiting room toward me, his hands clenched and his shoulders up around his neck. I hoped there were too many witnesses for him to think about hitting me.

"You fucking amateur idiot." He breathed garlic and old coffee in my face.

Costain, on the other hand, was almost jolly. The setback to the Feds' case didn't bother him half as much as if the two agencies had actually been working together. I might have misjudged him earlier.

I watched the paramedics carry desRosiers out. From their chatter and the lack of haste, I gathered that the bullet had bounced off a couple ribs, making a gory but relatively unthreatening mess. The good doctor was raving in shock and pain, which meant my story was still the most believable.

"Where the fuck is your buddy?" Manelli said.

"Last I heard, he was back at work. Why don't you ask his boss?"

I nodded toward Costain, who was chatting with a female evidence tech. Manelli grabbed my ear and twisted.

"There something funny about that?"

"Except that you don't look like my third-grade teacher?" Tears sprang into my eyes and I considered kicking him in the nuts. He was close enough.

"Captain Costain?" I called.

Manelli let go as Costain wandered over, trying not to grin.

"You don't really think I'm going to bolt, do you?" I nodded at the handcuffs. "And I know you're not going to book me."

Manelli huffed under his breath. Costain keyed open the cuffs.

"Thanks." I stretched my shoulder muscles.

"What's with the boxes?" I said. I knew, but I wanted to make sure Costain had picked up on the phony pills thing. "Was desRosiers smuggling drugs?"

"Subdosage," Costain said. "Little or no active ingredient.

Looks like he was experimenting on his patients."

"Nice. He told you that?"

Costain shook his head.

"We found his lab notebooks. It's amazing the kind of shit people will write down."

"You know he was connected to Alison Somers."

"I get it, Darrow. I'm not as stupid as I look."

I decided not to say he couldn't be.

"I was just thinking that a murder charge, even if it couldn't stick . . ."

"It'll stick," Costain said. "Something will, anyway."

But I could tell he was thinking about how to bring Icky Ricky in using desRosiers.

Manelli still didn't get any of it.

"Your girl jumped out a window, Darrow. All by herself."

I shrugged.

"I'll leave all that up to you," I said. "The professionals."

"I'll mention your suggestion to Dan," Costain said. "It's still his case."

And he winked at me while Manelli was looking in another direction.

A few more perfunctory questions and some half-hearted hassle from Manelli later, they let me loose. As I climbed into the Cougar to drive back to the bar, I wiped the burnt residue of the gunpowder off onto my pants leg. It left streaks, but I didn't have time to go home and change my pants. My apron would cover it anyway. As I drove downtown, I thought about whether this was over now, whether it was enough to satisfy my desire for an explanation of Alison's death. Somehow, it still felt a little weak.

CHAPTER 34

Ricky leaned back and the wooden swivel chair squealed. The mahogany top of his old desk was scarred with black burns from the days when he smoked those fat brown Conestogas without any fear. He rubbed at his chest, realizing he was developing the mannerisms of a very old man, the overconcern for bodily health, the worry that every new twinge was the last thing he'd feel on earth. He was tired of feeling old and tired of being unhappy and he wasn't sure how to fix it.

Berto leaned against the cases of fruit cocktail and listened to him rave. Besides being an ice-water assassin, he was a very good listener.

"I hate that fucking Tommy Cormier," Ricky said. "He causes me no end of trouble while he's alive, and what do I end up with? I don't have the money for the pills, which burned up with the bomb, and I don't have the pills, which the police have confiscated."

"You got shit," Berto agreed.

Ricky's heartbeat had steadied over the last few days, as if the decision to pass the organization off to Berto had eliminated enough stress to let him live a few more good years. He couldn't leave without taking care of Tommy's killer, though—it was not only a matter of professional pride, but setting an example for Berto, who was committed to sending Ricky an envelope full of hundred-dollar bills every month for the next three years. Ricky needed Berto to know he could still take care of himself, if necessary.

"The best time to get him is before he goes into the prison system," Ricky said. "If he even does. Right now he's at Mass General."

"I can do that, boss. Just walk in and take him out? It's no problem."

Berto's eyes were colorless as spit and they got brighter when he talked about killing someone. Ricky sighed.

"You don't have to call me boss, Berto. Remember? You're the *capo* now."

Ricky had been unfamiliar with the Mob terminology until Berto had asked him to call him by the title. For the moment, Ricky was going to give Berto everything he wanted, until Ricky had avenged Tommy and headed off to Miami.

But the last thing he wanted was Berto walking into the hospital and shooting desRosiers five or six times between the eyes. A firefight in the hospital would attract too much attention, and he wanted to send desRosiers a more private message from himself and Tesar and Spengler and Tommy, his people. Regardless of the fact Tommy had betrayed Ricky, you always took care of your people. Regardless. It was a message he wanted Berto to comprehend.

"I'm not sure head-on is the best way to handle this," he said.

Berto jabbed a wart on his left hand with a paring knife.

Ricky knew the cops saw his organization as vaguely laughable and he'd always used that to his advantage. Berto wasn't experienced or cool-headed enough to see it, but Ricky could at least explain the possibilities and leave him the reputation. The money Berto was supposed to send wouldn't make or break Ricky's retirement, but it would make it a little more comfortable. Kind of a pension.

"Can you act like a doctor, Berto?"

He didn't like repeating the kid's name so much, but it was the most reliable way to keep his attention.

"No problem," Berto said. "I'll just act real arrogant, and if anybody asks what I'm doing there, I'll scream at them."

Dressed as a doctor, Berto could walk into desRosiers's hospital room easily and execute the specific revenge Ricky had in mind. He liked the irony there, too, a fake doctor treating a real one.

"One thing," Ricky said. "If there's a guard on duty, you can't hurt him. This whole thing is between us and desRosiers."

Berto shrugged noncommittally. Ricky hoped that meant he was learning.

"That's cool."

"And we're not going to kill the doc, either. Here's what I want."

Berto's eyes dulled when Ricky said it, but regained their shine as Ricky explained. He was so eager that Ricky wondered if it were smart for him to leave an address when he finally did leave Boston.

He pulled a small white paper bag out of his desk drawer. He and Vindalia had already discussed substances and dosages. They weren't going to kill desRosiers, but with any luck at all the combination of pills would scramble his brains for a while.

Berto looked at the bag and Ricky handed it over.

"I'm pretty sure the doc is going to try for an insanity plea," Ricky said. "Let's make sure he isn't lying."

Berto frowned, then flipped down the paring knife so it stuck in the floorboards.

"No problem, boss. I mean, Ricky."

His mouth formed a little-boy devil's grin and for the first time since this had started, Ricky could say he was happy.

CHAPTER 35

Costain called me down to headquarters the next morning, but he was polite when I got there and no one said anything to make me think they saw desRosiers's shooting as anything but self-defense. Manelli was conspicuously absent but Costain stayed through the whole interview, even offered me a cup of the battery acid they passed off as coffee. I shook my head.

"I'm glad to have Burton back on the job," he said. "I was pretty sure he'd gone off the reservation for a while."

I didn't know if he was telling me he knew that Burton had been at the scene, but he didn't push it.

"Friends are good," I said.

And the clerk returned before the conversation got deeper. He pointed at a line at the bottom of the third page and I signed.

I wasn't surprised they hadn't pushed any harder. The Boston papers, uncharacteristically, were pouring praise all over the BPD for cracking a prescription drug ring. The idea of pills that didn't alleviate your pain or disease was newsworthy enough to attract the TV people, who even managed a sidebar on Alison. I hoped her music would get more exposure. The FBI went unmentioned, another triumph for local journalism and police work.

On Sunday afternoon, I opened up the Esposito for a private party. The Boston Opera set manager had loved Mrs. Rinaldi's miniature and wanted her to start the sets for the fall season right away. And after everything else that happened, I thought we could use a party.

Though she'd told me she wasn't supposed to drink very much after her heart attack, Mrs. Rinaldi accepted a small glass of sherry. She sat with her back to the wall, her face pink and smiling under her freshly touched-up hair. Henri sat beside her, calmly enough, though once I saw him try to pick up her hand.

Dorothea slapped at him lightly and I wondered if Alzheimer's might have some benefit for him. At least he wouldn't remember his rejections.

Rejection was on my mind. Susan and I were dancing around the subject of whether she would take over Henri's apartment. Her house in the Fens sold more quickly than she'd thought and she would have to find a place by the first of the month, next Wednesday.

"It's not as if we'd be living together," I was saying. "It's your own apartment. If we don't work out, we don't."

"Elder," she said. "Believe me, I know what I want to do. I just don't know what the best thing for Henri is."

"You'll be able to spend more time with him."

The assisted-living facility opening was a false alarm. They were back to a three-month waiting period. Susan gave me a look that suggested I shut up before I rammed my foot deeper in my mouth.

"OK." I raised my hands and backed away behind the bar.

Burton bounced down the steel steps and walked right up to me.

"Thanks for covering my ass. Costain suspects, but that's all."

"Which he can do all he wants," I said. "He knows he got much better press than if the FBI made the bust."

"You hear what happened to desRosiers? Got a bad dose of something that fucked up his brain."

"Poetic justice." I poured him a ginger ale. He was temporarily dry. "And one more reason to stay out of the hospital, if they can mix your meds up that badly."

Burton carried his glass over to Marina, who sat with Carmen. They fell into a deep conversation. Marina looked determined about something, but I wasn't worried. They were good-hearted people, and whatever they worked out would be the right thing for them.

The street door opened again and a familiar face appeared. He must have been passing and tried the knob out of habit. Delford was clean-shaven and wearing pressed khaki pants and a short-sleeved sport shirt under a navy blue windbreaker. He looked so good I almost didn't recognize him.

"Elder." He shook my hand. "I never thanked you for getting me to the hospital that time."

"No big deal, Delford." My face felt warm, as if I were blushing.

"It was," he said. "I'd gotten myself a little too inner-directed, I guess. I needed that kick in the seat. I won't say I'm going to stay sober, but I plan to be a lot less drunk."

I let go of his hand. "Glad to help."

I walked back to the sound system and put on some Sinatra. Susan, sipping her Cape Codder at the bar, crooked a finger at me.

"You really want to know why I'm holding back?" she said. "It's Alison. I don't want to spend my time with you shadowboxing her memory."

I relaxed. This I had an answer for. Somewhere along the way, this had become less about Alison's promise to me and more about satisfying my own sense of order. However Alison had died, she was not going to sing again, and I'd wanted to help her finish her song.

"Alison isn't here anymore," I said.

"I just want us to do the right things."

"Can't tell until you do them. Even desRosiers thought he was doing the right thing, in a twisted kind of way."

"How's that?" She put her glass down. I'd heard the story second-hand, from Burton.

"His mother died when he was seven, overdose of painkillers. Somehow out of that, he got the notion he could cure the addicts of the world by withholding their fixes. Not that everyone who ever needed pills was an addict."

"Demented." Her eyes shone with tears. "I hope he fries."

"Attorney Markham says that juries are better than lawyers at sorting out the bullshit. He thinks they'll do the right thing, even if he's *non compos mentis* now."

The street door opened one last time that day, and Eric O'Hanian walked down the stairs, carrying a gold-wrapped bottle-box with a red bow on top. The pain of losing Lorelei had fined the boyishness from his features, though he still wore that damn fedora. The charge of causing Tommy's death, and incidentally Lorelei, had been dropped, the arrest a too-quick reaction on the part of a DA's office worried that bombs meant terrorism.

He set the box on the bar in front of me. I didn't think he knew about me and the booze but I smiled anyway.

"You back to playing?"

He flexed his hands. "A little stiff still. I'm practicing."

He nodded politely to Susan, as if she were too old to engage his interest. She cocked an eyebrow at me and smiled. I walked down the bar and muted the Chairman, as Eric climbed the three steps to the stage.

Conversation stopped momentarily but he sat and noodled at the keys until everyone started ignoring him again.

I picked up the box.

"And what the hell am I supposed to do with this?"

"Moron," Susan said. "Open it up, say 'Thank you very much.' You don't have to drink it to be polite."

I pulled the wrappings apart and withdrew a bottle of nonalcoholic sparkling grape juice, and for no reason I understood, I lost it completely. Tears spilled down my face and I finally realized what a lucky man I was.

As I set the bottle to one side, I saw the papers that had padded it inside the package, printed out Web pages for the *Anarchist's Cookbook:* instructions on making a bomb out of household substances.

I didn't know if Eric was trying to confess to me or it was inadvertent, but there was nothing I could do with the knowledge that would improve the world. The fact that Lorelei had been caught in the middle of it explained the deeper sadness he was carrying. I raised the bottle toward the stage and nodded. He waved minutely.

"What's wrong?" Susan said.

"Not a damn thing." I wiped my eyes.

"All right," she said. "I'll move into your damned building. Just quit your crying."

We both laughed, and something clicked into alignment between us.

In one important way, I'd lost Alison long before she died. But I understood now that it hadn't been my own neglect or selfishness that hurt her so much as the world's. Too many people wrap their hearts in a deep indifference to beauty, believing that will forever keep them from being hurt, but all that does is guarantee the pain.

I looked around the Esposito, which contained all the people I cared about in the world. I didn't know if Alison would have approved of everything I'd done, but I'd tried to be faithful to her song, her last solo act. Having done that, I could go forward.

All the people she'd left behind had their own lives and loves and songs to sing, too. And that was enough to keep us all alive, and thriving.

ABOUT THE AUTHOR

Richard Cass began writing as a poet but slowly became enamored of the possibilities of prose: first short stories, then novels. He graduated from Colby College in Maine and earned an MA in Writing from the University of New Hampshire. His short fiction has won prizes from magazines like *Redbook, Writers' Digest,* and *Playboy.* His first collection of stories is called *Gleam of Bone.*

A section of *Solo Act* won a Finalist's Award at the Pacific Northwest Writers' Conference. He has been an Individual Artist's Fellow for New Hampshire and a Fellow at the Fishtrap Writers' Conference in Oregon. He lives in Cape Elizabeth, Maine, with his wife Anne and a Maine Coon cat named Tinker, where he is writing another novel featuring Elder Darrow.